BATTLE FOR DRAGON ISLE

WAR OF STAFFS TRILOGY: BOOK THREE

STEVE STEPHENSON
& K.M. TEDRICK

Black Rose Writing | Texas

ISBN: 978-1-68433-369-1
PUBLISHED BY BLACK ROSE WRITING
www.blackrosewriting.com

Printed in the United States of America
Suggested Retail Price (SRP) $18.95

Battle for Dragon Isle is printed in Garamond Premier Pro

*As a planet-friendly publisher, Black Rose Writing does its best to eliminate unnecessary waste to reduce paper usage and energy costs, while never compromising the reading experience. As a result, the final word count vs. page count may not meet common expectations.

I'd like to dedicate this book to my husband, Dave.
His belief in me, and his support, especially with the household chores, makes it possible for me to spend hours writing each day, not only on this book but also the ones I ghost write. Thanks, honey.
—K.M. Tedrick

I'd like to thank my family and my mother.
—Steve Stephenson

Praise for the
War of the Staffs Series

Hard-core fantasy and sci-fi fans will become enraptured with this book from the opening chapter. The authorial duo's sequel to *War of the Staffs* delivers a fast punch in genre fiction and follows up with a stunning series of breathtaking events that will keep readers enthralled from start to finish.

In the magical world of Muiria, the vampire lord Taza continues to weave intense dark spells in a demonic attempt to obtain the Staff of Adois in order to bring the world under his exclusive control for evil purposes. Taza uses a dark warlock named Melgor to find and destroy Taza's nemesis, the great wizard Celedant, who accompanies Prince Tarquin, the prophesied savior of the world, on a dangerous quest to destroy both staffs, encountering horrific attacks by earthly and inhuman bands of assailants.

Freedom and existence itself is at stake for all Muiria dwellers, and the adventurers who are desperately seeking to destroy the staffs, successfully bring together supporters that include elves, dwarves, humans, and other races who join forces against Taza's dark magic to save their beloved world and peaceful way of life. Against the backdrop of the raging conflict that flares in unspeakably violent battles destroying life and limb, tender romance begins to blossom between pure-hearted souls who find each other in the midst of a war-torn landscape and mythical quest. Loyalties are tested and lives are lost in the classic battle between good and evil.

Admirable heroes, humorous sidekicks, knowledgeable healers, and powerful rulers vie for survival and ultimate control in this epic battle of good vs. evil. This is a book that readers will never forget. The authors have crafted a work of art that deserves a place of honor in contemporary fantasy / sci-fi fiction.

~ Roman A. Littlefield, author of *Say What You Really Mean*

Battle for Dragon Isle

CHAPTER ONE

Melgor the Red had been watching events unfold between the Wizard Celedant, his group of adventurers, and the army of undead led by the evil and deformed Emperor of Zeiglon. The warlock sat on his chimera from the safety of one of the few remaining walls still standing in the former palace of the kingdom of Zeiglon. To remain unseen, he had cast an invisibility spell on himself and his mount. Its three heads watched the battle below with intrigue. As the epic battle unfolded, Melgor saw Tarquin fall off the cliff before being jerked to a painful stop by a rope knotted around his waist – arresting his fall just a few feet shy of the crashing waves below.

The monstrosity that was Zackary climbed down the sheer cliff face, his spider-like claws finding purchase where there appeared to be none to attack the dangling boy. It was during this fight that Melgor saw Tarquin wrench the mithril Staff of Adaman from the monster and toss it up to Celedant. Out of nowhere, a huge golden dragon snatched Zachary from the cliffside and took the monster out to sea, where he was dropped hundreds of feet with dragon flame following to ensure his end.

Melgor remained unperturbed. The warlock had kept his eyes on the boy and witnessed his frantic movements in trying to climb the rope. He cast a simple spell that increased his powers of vision. Zooming in on the rope, he watched it fray under the boy's weight, just out of Tarquin's reach.

That was a deciding moment as Melgor urged his mount to leap from the wall and fly at breakneck speed towards the boy. The rope broke - and Tarquin plunged toward the jagged rocks and churning sea to certain death.

Melgor pressed his head to the chimera's neck, concentrating on the boy as he fell. At the last instant, he dropped the invisibility spell and grasped the boy's arm. Instead of swinging the body of what he thought of as a boy onto the Chimera, he found himself burdened with the weight of a fully-grown man. His muscles strained as he brought Tarquin to slap against his mount's side. Using all his strength, he jerked the captive across the saddle. His mount lifted so fast that the prince started to slide off. It took all of Melgor's strength to hold his burden steady.

As the chimera continued gaining altitude thousands of feet in the air, Tarquin slipped off the saddle. The warlock caught the prince by his belt. When Melgor felt the victim slam against the side of his mount, the chimera spouted flame in objection. The warlock quickly cast a binding spell that kept Tarquin pinned against the Chimera's side. A quick spell of invisibility and Melgor was speeding through the perpetual darkness that covered the city of Zeiglon into the deep blue sky.

Trapped against the Chimera, Tarquin struggled until Melgor called to him over the rushing wind.

"Stop, Tarquin. I just saved your life. Keep still before you kill us both!"

Tarquin grew quiet, watching the dark clouds disappear.

Melgor was worried about being tracked by the dragon he had seen, but whenever he looked back, the golden beast was nowhere in sight. Deep over the desert, Melgor pushed the steed faster. It did not try to resist the mental control the warlock had imposed.

Halfway across the vast desert, Melgor loosened his mental reins and steered the taxed chimera downward in a slow curve to land on a huge dune. The chimera sank to its haunches in fine sand. Night had fallen, and there was a chill in the air. The warlock summoned water and tossed each head of his mount a haunch of venison that he had kept fresh with magic. He saved the best food for the beast in case it grew jealous of Melgor's fare. He would rather not face the fires of the creature.

Only then did he turn to Tarquin still adhered to the Chimera and said, "I'll let you go, but don't try to run. We're in the desert, and you would never make it out alive. Besides, I'm headed for the mountains surrounding Southgard, the way you ultimately want to go."

With a snap of his fingers, Melgor released Tarquin from the binding spell. The prince fell to the sand and quickly untied what remained of the frayed rope around his waist. Slowly he massaged his midsection that still bore angry welts from the rope, and studied his captor - or was the stranger figure his savior? He had not figured that out yet.

"I guess I owe you a debt of gratitude for saving me, although I don't know your name."

The chimera's rider gave a mock bow.

"I am Melgor the Red of the Warlock Council." He saw Tarquin's muscles tighten, his hand twitching toward his sword hilt, and he quickly added, "I am not here on their business. I must speak privately with you. I could not reach Celedant. We probably would have fought anyway."

The chimera gave a snort, and a spout of flame shot into the night air from its middle head. Melgor motioned toward her, saying, "She voices her opinion of the meal. I don't know if that meant that she liked it or not. Come."

After speaking the words of a spell, a fire appeared that burned blue.

"Sit and eat. I fear my fare is tasteless. I must save the best for the beast."

Tarquin sat across from the warlock, chewing on preserved meat and a chunk of bread.

"I never imagined I would be this close to the man that has daunted my every step - without trying to kill him."

Melgor laughed. "These are strange times, and strange alliances must be formed. I offer help in defeating Taza. I despise this vampire business as you do. I will swear on my own life to stop dogging your steps and turn my attention to Taza, but only if you and Celedant will allow me peace to conduct my business. I assure you I'm expendable in Taza's undead eyes."

Tarquin nodded, chewing the tough food. "I'm listening."

Chapter Two

The vampire warlock Taza sat in his tower room and felt a slight vibration from the Staff of Adois at his side. It meant that one of his minions or his nemesis Celedant was using magic. It was someone connected to the quest conjuring a minute amount. Quickly he summoned a piece of chalk and drew something on the floor while chanting under his breath. Finished, he stepped back to examine the completed a pentagram inscribed with spells of protection along its edges.

He began a summoning. Inside the pentagram, colors swirled crazily until a deep anguished scream was heard. From the streaming colors, a demon appeared from the depths of the nine hells. It was altogether unimpressive. Man-sized, it looked docile until fully formed. Red beams shot from its eyes, stabbing against the barrier of protective spells. It roared in rage as fire formed in its clawed and bony hands. Several flaming balls were hurled at its captor. The barrier bowed outward but held.

Roaring in frustration, the creature quieted as it stared at Taza with malice and murder in its eyes. Taza had not heard about this sort of demon before, but he stood his ground and in a commanding voice said, "I have bound you to the Staff of Adois, and you shall do my bidding."

The demon snarled, tossing its head while scrapping claws on the protective barrier.

Laughing at its feeble efforts, the undead warlock raised his staff and with small power, thrust it at the creature. The demon shrieked and flew backward, slamming into the opposite wall of the protective field. Seeing that escape was useless, it settled into dejection.

Taza spoke in a normal voice, the staff translating for him.

"I have a simple duty for you to perform. Afterward, I will send you back to the hell you came from."

The creature nodded, wanting no more than to escape.

The warlock continued. "I will open a rift in space, allowing you to travel to where my enemies plot against me. Kill all who are there. Then you must loot the bodies and find a staff with a jeweled head like this staff I now hold. Are you intelligent enough to understand your mission?"

The demon nodded and in a gravelly voice snarled a half-defiant statement, "Will you send me back?"

Taza grinned. "Of course. Return first with the Staff of Adaman and hand it to me. But I warn you. Do not try to use the staff - for it is an instrument of good and will destroy you. There must be no tricks, or I will destroy you."

With the staff of Adois in hand, Taza walked to the middle of the room where he used a forgotten language to summon swirling circles of darkness. In a moment, a dark hole opened before him. With a single archaic word, Melgor brought down the protective barrier. The demon took two cautious steps, mindful of the warlock's threat, and bounded through the hole.

Almost instantly it landed, feet sinking into soft sand. Seeing two of its targets, the evil entity formed fireballs in its clawed hand.

Tarquin, facing the demon, saw it appear, and the flaming light it held; he jumped to his feet. Reacting instinctually, he dove across the campfire and slammed Melgor to the ground. Thinking the Borderer was attacking him, the wizard was about to cast a spell at Tarquin when two balls of fire shot through the camp to assault the places where they had just been sitting.

Acting quickly, Tarquin rolled off the warlock and drew his sword - Dragon Bolt - that glowed bright red, warning of evil in their presence. Having grown attached to its master, the chimera took flight and flew at the intruder, flames shooting from all three mouths.

Now that he understood their peril, Melgor scrambled to his knees and cast a spell that sent a fireball rolling in the direction of their attacker.

A dark shape sped past, knocking both humans aside. Tarquin's sword, which had a mind of its own when protecting its master, reacted automatically. It scored a hit that left the tip covered in a black substance. The chimera returned, breathing fire at the assailant, but their attacks did not faze this inhabitant of the infernal hells of the underworld.

Melgor called to Tarquin: "Be wary - it's not of this world."

The words had barely left his mouth when the monstrous creature appeared in front of Tarquin, claws slashing for the kill. Fortunately, the prince was marginally faster, owing to his training and his sword. He stabbed forward, the blade running completely through the monster. Focusing on its face, he was amazed that the sword had little effect on the demon. He witnessed power surging into the demon's eyes, and Tarquin instinctively ducked as two blue beams shot out and sizzled in the sand, turning it to glass.

"Look out!" Melgor shouted.

Instinctively, Tarquin dropped and rolled out of the way as Melgor attacked, calling a spell that shot a jet of pure energy from his fingers. It struck the demon in the chest, hurling it backward into a deep sand dune.

On cue, the chimera attacked again. Melgor's beast flew down and straddled the demon, raking it with all four claws. It screamed in pain as the creature struck back, its own claws sinking deep into her body. With a giant flap of wings, the chimera retreated into the darkness.

The demon stood up, and Melgor cast another spell. This time, a spear of ice shot from his extended finger, striking the monster in the side and spinning it around.

Tarquin charged sword held high in both hands. He reached the creature as it tried to stand up, and he aimed his weapon at the demon's head. But the evil thing was quicker and dodged the swing of the blade.

Reaching out, it grabbed Tarquin by the throat and hurled him backward to tumble over a sand dune, where he lost sight of the camp. He was stunned for a moment, gasping for air, before he could climb the dune and race back to the fight.

Melgor watched the Borderer tossed away like a rag doll, and attacked the beast again. He dared to take time for a more powerful spell and summoned several giants from thin air that immediately attacked the demon. While the giants kept it busy with massive axes, Melgor cast another incantation, sending a bright white light across the camp that slammed into the creature. This energy blast severely injured the beast as it howled, yet it managed to fend off the giants who were battering it with axe blows.

Wailing into the night air, the monster jumped onto a giant and ripped off its head. It did the same with the second and cast its own spell. The sand around Melgor soared into a funnel, grabbing the wizard off the ground and spinning him so that he slammed into the sides of the funnel. The final giant was dispatched by a clawed blow that tore open its throat.

But it had forgotten about Tarquin, who rushed over the dune to attack from the rear. The prince swung his sword like a madman - in great arcs, striking first the monster's sides, and its arms. Black blood flew into the air to land in the sand where it was sucked up by the porous granules.

Weakened by injuries, the demon's spell over Melgor ended, dropping the warlock thirty feet away in the sand. Although dazed, the warlock struggled up from the dune and cast a spell he had learned in Edain as a student before turning to the dark arts. The spell swept through an invisible tunnel across the camp and grasped the demon, clamping its body with force and pinning the creature's arms to its side, crushing it.

This gave Tarquin the opening he needed. Before the spell wore off, he struck the demon with Dragon Bolt, piercing the back of its head and exiting its forehead. The borderer withdrew his weapon, but the demon remained standing until Melgor's spell disintegrated. It crashed to the ground where its body twitched from the mortal wound.

Tarquin stared at it as Melgor approached from the opposite side.

The two men, once dire enemies, stood over the demon, staring at its corpse.

"Where did the thing come from?" Tarquin asked.

"The fires of hell. The Staff of Adois must have alerted Taza when I used magic to summon our fire. It would only do that if sensing magic used by one of the vampire's enemies. I believe he may know that I have changed sides, and the hatred is mutual between the two of us."

The chimera flew into the camp and landed, but it stumbled and fell to its knees.

Melgor rushed to his mount's aid. Dark blood flowed from the wounds the demon had inflicted. The warlock began pressing hard on the deepest cut to stem the flow.

His magic was useless, and he shouted. "In my bag are several bottles of elixir. Bring them here. Quickly."

Melgor had never tried healing draughts on a creature as a chimera. He wasn't sure they would work. When Tarquin rushed back with the draughts, he bit into the cork stopper of one and spit it to the ground. Cautiously he approached one of the chimera's heads, cooing softly. It was as if the beast knew what the human was trying to do. It opened its mouth, allowing Melgor to pour the liquid inside. He added two more small bottles of the precious fluid, pouring each into a different head. In a moment, he saw that the wound, though still evident, had stopped bleeding.

Relieved, he motioned toward the defeated demon.

"Taza will still send other warlocks and creatures from the void to track you."

Tarquin blew a long breath of air. "I have seen firsthand the truthfulness in your tale. It puzzles me, though. Why should I let you go on living after all the monsters and killers you have sent to hound my friends?"

Melgor shrugged. "I have no answer except assurances that I seek to put an end to Taza as well. I could kill you here and now. It would look like the demon did it. Still, the spells and my saving you in Zeiglon would raise questions. And if I caused your death, I would have all your companions searching for me relentlessly until they achieved their revenge. I don't want to rile Celedant any more than I already have."

"So, the enemy of my enemy is my friend, as the saying goes."

"You will have to trust what I say. We did fight well together tonight." The warlock continued, "I am a dark warlock. I admit that but here we face a greater evil, one I couldn't destroy on my own, but you and Celedant might. I would rather be conniving free and clear without your troupe troubling me. What say you, Tarquin?"

The young man nodded. "You were good at delaying us. Having you out of the way would help, but your actions caused the deaths of some of our company. I cannot forget that."

Melgor's expression was grave. "Once Taza is destroyed, I promise the next time we meet you can run me through with your sword – if you can." With a wicked smile, he added, "But you will forgive me if I defend myself. Just remember. I was only your enemy because of the compulsion of doing the vampire lord's bidding. Now that I am no longer bound to him, I have no desire to harm you or your friends."

Tarquin considered this and nodded. "I will honor what you put forth. Although I can't speak for the others, I will try to persuade them, but I cannot make any promises."

"I will do my best to stay out of their way. May our paths never cross again."

The warlock returned to the campfire, doused it, and lay back in the sand.

"Best not to leave a beacon of our presence. We must sleep before leaving this accused desert."

They slept lightly, each expecting the other to attack. Thus, a strange partnership began.

CHAPTER THREE

The next morning, flying lazily across the desert as the sun crested the eastern horizon, Tarquin's curiosity made him ask, "How will you escape Taza's eye?"

Melgor laughed. "I will get rid of everything the creature gave me. I'm taking a gamble that not using magic and disposing of the vampire's talismans will buy sufficient time to do what I need to do." He shrugged. "It's a small price when playing against Taza."

It took several days to make their way across the great desert before reaching the arid foothills of the southern Mordolwyn Mountains. Melgor cast an invisibility spell, and soon they were flying low toward Southgard, the southernmost dwarvan city. Finally, Tarquin spotted Melgor's small encampment on a rocky shelf that overlooked the valley. They landed, and both approached the edge of the cliff, thunderstruck by what had been done to the lush valley of Southgard. Even from that height, the massive damage wrought during the siege was devastating.

Melgor quietly said, "A great battle was fought here. I cannot tell who won or lost the blood fest. Come - let us prepare to leave."

The two returned from the cliff's edge and looked about the area. The warlock began collecting salvageable items from around the camp and placing them in the tent.

"What are you going to do?" Tarquin asked.

The mage smiled. "I'm taking a sabbatical from magic for the next few months, or at least until Taza is dead."

Melgor took several trinkets given him by the vampire warlock out of his cloak and patted himself down, finding one other before he tossed the magical devices into the tent. Using flint and steel, he sparked a small portion of the tent, as the burning coal started a fire that slowly spread. In moments all his belongings were soon engulfed in tongues of flame that lapped up the tent's sides.

He walked slowly over to his Chimera and rubbed its neck. An audible groaning sound could be heard.

Melgor went to the saddle and with a dagger first cut the restraining belts. Grimacing, he cut carefully into his forearm, letting the blood pool and drip down the sides of the saddle, even splattering some droplets onto the beast's necks and sides. Tying a bandage around his arm, he proceeded to the head of the beast where he whispered in its three sets of ears. In a moment, the Chimera took to the air and disappeared into the western sky.

"She will return slowly to Taza, and hopefully it will appear I died in battle or flight."

Melgor headed over to where he had tied the Illanni's horses and vaulted into the saddle. He shook his head as he remembered how he had barely escaped their attack.

Pointing to a narrow path, he said, "That will take you to the valley below. Send my regrets to Celedant. With that said, may we never meet again."

The warlock pulled on the reins, and the horse quickly turned, pounding down another path and leading the other Illanni horses, leaving one behind for Tarquin.

As the Borderer started out on his route, he watched a colorful flight of dragons fly into the valley and settle down on the outskirts of the ruined city of Southgard. His foremost thought was that his friends had survived the battle.

The vampire Taza sat in his dark tower, ruminating over thoughts far from the present. He listened to the screams of a human as the victim was flayed alive behind him, while with cold, distant eyes, he stared out into the night. Part of him deplored what was taking place behind, but the servant was a suspected traitor and had to be made an example. Two guards collected the human's blood in a golden chalice. He could smell the fresh fluid as it was drawn out and delivered to him.

The gruesome task of drinking blood eventually restored and rested his mind, giving him time to think more clearly. Somehow the Staff of Adaman was obscured from Taza. Celedant had found a means to hide its presence. Although he was using the Staff of Adois, which should have targeted it immediately, Taza failed to locate even the general location.

That was disturbing and was why he now drank the warm blood. His mind raced faster than any mortal could ever dream of as he searched into what the future might bring - a thousand different scenarios.

Most of these calculations were unfavorable to his position. However, he was comforted in that he was still protected by his vampire guards, ten of the most fearsome and powerful creatures he had ever created. He had hoped never to have to use them, but at present, that was still a question to be answered, and he was not about to take chances. Taza had been the aggressor throughout the search for the Staff of Adaman. Now that his enemies were in possession of it, they would be the aggressors. He would have to be on guard and anticipate their moves.

When the powerful crystal of the Staff of Adaman first had been uncovered and held by human hands, the ancient relic reconnected to its sister Staff. That had given Taza a feeling of the area where it was being kept. He had known that it lay somewhere in the orc-occupied city of Brackus, but throughout the years, his agents had never found it. Once the crystal was joined to the mithril staff, its presence had become even more powerful. When used in battle, the mental flash of the Staff of Adaman had nearly stunned him. At first, his visions were of the ruins that had been Zeiglon. High in the air over the valley of Southgard, he witnessed the weakening power of the Shadow Lords as they fell in defeat.

The Shadow Lords had been a powerful piece of the puzzle. If the plan had gone right, those arrogant fools would have won the day. Truly, they had performed their duty, the valley had fallen, but the warlock had not considered that the dragons would muster and fight. Only the dragons' interference had driven the Shadow Lords away, and the creatures were now his to command. The evil that confined them to the city of Zeiglon had fallen, but their minions had also fled without the Shadow Lords to control the city. Yet, Taza had openly offered them the safety of Dormin until the balance could be restored in Zeiglon.

As he contemplated these developments, Taza felt the power of his staff rise, striving for control. This was the most direct attack to date, and it openly announced the Staff of Adois' intentions to unite with the Staff of Adaman and destroy it. The vampire warlock had to use almost all his reserves of will and strength to wrest control from the artifact.

CHAPTER FOUR

The battle for Southgard had long since been over, but continuing skirmishes plagued the southern and northern hills. Wagons filled with seriously wounded dwarves, men, and elves were being sent back to the city for healing and recovery. The lightly injured were treated on the battlefields by clerics assigned to the troops because soldiers could not be spared. Southgard under the mountain stood undefeated, the outer works of the city, however, had been destroyed - along with the valley.

There had not been enough soldiers to keep the orcs and others from going north toward the dwarvan confederation and the city-states. Several times the defenders were forced to watch helplessly as large parties of orcs crossed the valley. Short on fighters and with the dragons returned to the north, there was nothing they could do to stop them. Some orcs had had enough and limped westward to return to their territories. The dwarvan army and its allies had fled to Southgard, seeking safety in the deep caverns below the city, along with the valley citizens.

The valley of Southgard was teeming with rotting corpses. Heavily guarded wagon trains drove out into the once-beautiful fields to recover the dead. The orc and their vile allies would be burned in funeral pyres to the east of the city. In the minds of the enemies, the valley had fallen, and there was little interest in securing it when easy riches lay further north. The death of the Giant King left the orcan companies once under the giants' control, free to roam at will.

Celedant, a powerful wizard of Dragon Isle, appeared younger than his age would indicate. The magical testing and trials had changed him not only magically but also mentally and physically. He wore simple clothing and a new cloak as the sun's bright light clearly showed the travails of the battle-strewn valley. He knew that time, sun, and rain would revitalize this once-serene valley. Yet, he inwardly mourned the tens of thousands that had lost their lives and the defilement of what once had been a bountiful land. Celedant was reminded of the trial of the Dragon Tear and that his choice of path had led through killing grounds like Southgard.

Now, a soft breeze blowing east to west carried the charnel smells of battle in the valley toward the city from where thousands of dead orcs, which had littered the valley, were slowly being burned to ashes. That had been a simple solution to keep disease to a minimum, as there was nowhere to properly bury so many dead. Indeed, the slight wind was kind to them this morning. He stood silently at the huge stone gates that led into the mountain where the dwarves of Southgard lived and worked. The wizard watched in silence as a wagon filled with dwarvan dead rambled by.

After a valiant dwarvan defense, the gates to the outer city had fallen, torn down by the invading orcs and their unearthly allies. It hadn't stopped there. When the orcs broke through, they ran roughshod throughout the city, looking for loot of all kinds. A single torch and the inner city were ablaze. The town within the walled area had been totally destroyed. All residents had been taken within the mountain to safety or died escaping the orcs.

The inner wall had withstood the continued onslaughts, but there were many scars left from the siege. The once-pristine walls were missing portions of their crenulations and revealed impact craters where siege stones and fire pots had struck.

Taza had not been to Illan, the dark elf city deep underground, in many months. He had come to visit Tibersu, the leader of the Illanni. The city was darker than usual. He worried about those on the street that looked fearful of vampires as they hurried about their duties. The warlock preferred safety for the slaves because without them, there would be no one to do the menial work. Taza would have to talk to Tibersu about this. A leader of one of the great houses, Tibersu had been turned into a vampire early in Taza's transformation of Illan.

Taza could feel the essence of the vampires throughout the city and was pleased. It was a sure sign that his transformations were coming along. He reached the Illanni Temple erected to honor him, and a sly smiled revealed his fangs. An infantile race, so easily deceived and ready to follow any new idea to save their people. Staring at the Temple, he almost laughed. The Temple was massive, with two stories. The top front story opened to the darkness of the city.

Illanni guards stood by the door as Taza scanned the marble stairs. He slammed the butt of the Staff of Adois on the stone floor, causing him to disappear from sight - only to reappear on the second floor of the building. Tibersu was pacing when suddenly Taza appeared before him. If Taza had surprised him, Tibersu hid it well.

The Illanni vampire executed a curt bow to his master. "What brings my Lord to our fair city?"

Taza motioned Tibersu to have a seat and sat down across from the Illanni. The warlock propped the Staff of Adois against the table.

"Tibersu, I have a quest for you and your people. As you may know, Southgard was seized, and the dwarves have suffered a major defeat. I need you to raise a force and attack from the underworld through the tunnels of Southgard."

Tibersu slammed his fist against the arm of the chair. "To be sure, it will be a pleasure to deal death to the long beards."

Taza steepled his hands and continued. "I also need your soldiers to draw Celedant and Tarquin out into open battle. You should find a way into Southgard and begin picking off lone individuals and small parties. The dwarves are sure to send search parties out. Celedant and Tarquin will accompany them. They are good to the point of idiocy. It is their courageous if foolish way," he added with a grimace.

Tibersu called to one of his servants.

"Bring me the generals." Turning back to Taza, he said, "We will do your bidding. I will send a large attack force to Southgard, and we shall ferret out the wizard and the boy. I'll send you their heads within a fortnight."

Taza smiled evilly. "I hope you do for your sake. Others have made the same claim, only to fail. Celedant is a powerful wizard. He won't be easily defeated."

"Powerful or not, we will defeat him," Tibersu assured him.

Chapter Five

As Tarquin began his descent down the mountain, he noticed the billowing smoke from the burning of dead orcs. It cast a slight fog over the entire eastern valley, polluting it with a sickening stench. He rounded a corner, surprising seven orcs tending a fire. Tarquin drew his sword that blazed red in the presence of enemies.

The orcs drew their weapons and sprang to their feet.

Tarquin jumped into the thick of it, swinging left and right, taking down his enemies like from his horse. When there were but two orcs left, they fell to their knees, pleading in their harsh guttural language for mercy. Tarquin nodded.

"Never return this way again!" He kept his sword pointed at them as they rushed off.

Looking at the fire, he noticed two cooked hares. It had been a long time since the meager meal of the previous night, and there was no reason to waste the food at hand. Dismounting, he bent down and removed the spit that held the meat. Even though the food was hot, he tore into the first rabbit, devouring it quickly but for a few bones, he tossed aside. He ate the second one more slowly as he headed down the trail.

The sun was high when he emerged on the outskirts of the valley of Southgard. It looked like a wildfire had swept through the area. Trees had been burned, their trunks resembling tall sticks of charcoal, and the land showed only charred undergrowth. Tarquin finally entered the valley proper, and before long he came across a dozen soldiers gathering the dead. Their wagon, pulled by sturdy mountain ponies, was half full of dead dwarves and several humans. Tarquin raised a hand in salute to the sergeant in command.

When he turned to go east to the city, tears came to his eyes as he witnessed the devastation. He passed several guard points and finally reached what had been the outer city. The buildings were skeletons. The sight brought back haunting memories of the ruins of Zeiglon.

Keeping his horse to a walk, he headed up the main street, constantly having to move aside for wagons and soldiers marching out of town. Several companies of Borderers were leaving, and he exchanged words with their lieutenants. He noticed that all had dark circles under their eyes, and many looked upward at the sky like they were scared and silently praying for relief – or fearing an airborne assault.

Surely, they aren't frightened of the dragons, he thought. The dragons had gone into open combat in Zeiglon, revealing themselves to the world.

Upon entering Southgard under the mountain, he saw the city was coming back to life. Merchants were selling their wares, and a few handed out free homespun blankets to those who needed them. Tarquin threaded his way through the mismatched crowd, astonished to see humans walking where once they would have been seized and thrown in jail for being inside the city proper. How could he find anyone he knew in this crowded place? Had any of his friends made it out of Zeiglon alive?

He would seek out the Borderer compound and ask for the wizard Celedant. He would start at the government bastion. Surely if Celedant were here, he would be closeted with the leaders of the city. Tarquin made it to the first Borderer hall and was saddened to see so many dwarves and men on makeshift cots being treated by the healers.

The hospital wards must be filled with wounded. He would later learn the Shadow Lord's attacks had made a lasting effect on some, causing great lingering fear that it could not be dispelled by a simple spell or potion.

The day drew on. Hungry again, Tarquin looked forward to a meal and a good night's sleep in a proper bed. He would have to be cautious about asking for Celedant and his friends.

"Tarquin!"

Strong hands gripped his arm, spinning him around. His old friend and fellow Borderer Botreg grinned from ear to ear. The dwarf wrapped Tarquin in a bear hug.

"We never thought to see ye again. I held out hope and thought ye would come here when able. Come, let's meet up with the others, and ye can tell us what happened when that giant beastie snatched ya out of thin air."

As he finished speaking and stepped back, Ress came running toward the pair.

"Tarquin!" She flew across the ground and slammed into him, nearly knocking them both over, tears spilling down her cheeks in surprise, anxiousness, and happiness. "Oh, Tarquin, I thought I would never see you again!"

The prince began to smile until Ress covered his lips with a kiss that brought whoops and hoots from onlookers. His arms came up and wrapped around her, holding her close, and when their lips parted, they looked into each other's eyes longingly.

"I'm okay."

"Truly?"

"Truly, but have I got a story to tell you and the others."

Releasing her, they held hands as Botreg led them to a tavern filled with soldiers trying to forget the horrors they had seen by swilling ale. The dwarf pulled Tarquin along and stopped at an old wooden table that had seen better days.

Most of his friends were there, and they cheered their missing comrade until Tarquin asked, "Where's Celedant, Hortus, and Hority?"

Botreg motioned to the table. "Celedant is with General Grimilzor. Hority slipped away somewhere. Abbot Hortus did not make it. He was killed under the colosseum."

Tarquin saw sadness pass through his friends' eyes.

"Come drink with us," Botreg urged. "Celedant will be along soon."

The group drank and dined the rest of the day away. Even though he had eaten the two rabbits much earlier, Tarquin put away two helpings of the fine fare.

<hr>

While he meditated on future attempts to gain mastery over the Staff of Adois, Taza sat on his black onyx throne. Once the staff was mastered, he would be almost completely in control of the known world. He had worked diligently toward this end for many years.

"All I need do is destroy the Staff of Adaman and declare my rule." He smiled, briefly exposing long, yellow fangs.

From the vibrations that beat a rhythm through his staff, Taza knew the tremble indicated that the Staff of Adaman was in play. In response, the Staff of Adois, which had been striving to control him since he first discovered it, was trying to distract its master. Taza exerted his vast mental control against centuries of dark power to fight off the attack. Yet, the warlock felt something else - a palpable eagerness of the staff to exact revenge upon its righteous counterpart.

"Patience," he urged, regaining control. "It is not the moment to attack your counterpart, but soon."

So far, most of his plans had been foiled. The vampire and his most trusted servants had unsuccessfully tried to learn the location of the Staff of Adaman. The many inept attempts at capturing or killing Celedant and the prophesized Prince

Tarquin were almost laughable if their elimination wasn't so important. As long as they lived, there was a chance his attempts to rule the world and turn it from light to darkness for his mistress, the goddess Adois would fail. At least he could pry its location from the captives. If he had the Staff of Adaman, he could oversee its destruction, guaranteeing his dominance of the whole world.

His plans had failed one way or another - by fate, yes, and from the ineptness of his lackeys. How powerful had his opponents grown? Melgor had won at Southgard, but he was missing. There was no need to blame him any longer, and Sellis the warlock had stolen from him and was still being punished for his foolishness and greed.

Taza had thrown the first dice. Now it was Celedant's turn. He would wait for the Staff of Adaman and its user - the wizard Celedant. Word would spread that Taza wanted the two. The southern hills and woods were crawling with orcs, bounty hunters, ex-soldiers, and disgruntled warriors that were leftovers from the army that had attacked Southgard. He would draw the Staff of Adaman to him like an insect to a spider's web, offering huge rewards.

Long ago, Taza had been sentenced by his home world and set to drift in the void between the fabrics of the universe for eternity. He would neither forgive nor forget it. Once he had control of the Staff of Adois and destroyed the Staff of Adaman, the world would be his. His rule would be absolute.

That meddlesome wizard, Celedant, should have died before reaching Dragon Isle. That runt of a boy had predicted Taza's downfall. It grated on his nerves, a mere boy, well - now a man full grown. He would not be undone by an old wizard and a worthless human prince.

The vampire smiled, teeth gleaming. Prophesy or not, they had lessened his burden by finding the Staff. Therefore, he had to prepare for its eventual appearance and prepare a strong defense to counter the accursed staff.

With Melgor, his right-hand man, dead or missing, Taza mulled over his replacement. It had to be a warlock, someone as intelligent as Melgor and as conniving as Sellis. One person that had just arrived from the western ocean might fit the description.

Taza's spies had reported that a female sorceress named Cyra had recently been seen in Dormin; he could feel her power through the Staff of Adois.

Although she had not yet turned to dark magic, she feared the dark warlord's growing undead army. When she spoke to the council a few days later, it did not seem to faze her that Taza was a vampire when members pointed it out.

The week passed since Taza had heard from his most talented henchman, Melgor. Then out of thin air, the chimera returned, and Taza examined the creature and the saddle in the early morning courtyard.

"Blood!" he exclaimed aloud to himself. Dried and rust-colored, the human fluid appeared to be several weeks old, and the beast's restraining harness was destroyed. There were fresh wounds on the creature's sides and belly.

"Melgor must be dead," he mused to the ignorant stable hand who came to take the chimera's reins.

Hurrying inside to the marble font, Taza poised his staff to locate the warlock. The water swirled blackly as the finely-crafted stick searched, shaking gently. If Melgor had any of the magical instruments Taza had given him, he should appear in the font. The magic font would also hone in on any magic the warlock had used recently. As the dark motion of the water calmed, it showed nothing except a smooth surface.

CHAPTER

SIX

Taza paced back and forth in his tower room, awaiting his guest Cyra from the western coast of Dormin. A member of his personal guard opened the door and announced:

"Cyra of the West."

The sorceress entered hood over her face, and advanced to the foot of the throne of Dormin. She waited silently as Taza was bombarded with tactile clues from his Staff.

Its motion conveyed: "She is the one. She carries great power."

Taza motioned to the woman. "Please, remove your hood if you don't mind. I like to see who I am dealing with."

Cyra carefully removed the hood, letting it drop against her back over a long braid of dark locks. Taza had to admit she was beautiful with ebony skin and a smooth countenance. Of course, she could have cast a beauty spell, but the Staff of Adois told him there was no magic being used. He examined her and thought many eons ago he would have found her attractive. However, the Staff would not allow a base desire to creep into its master.

"Please be seated." Taza pointed to an elegant seat that stood on a level lower than his. She took the designated place gracefully.

He motioned a guard that brought glasses of elven wine.

Cyra did not seem to care that the guards standing near the throne were vampires. Taza also believed that she did not fear him.

Smiling, he raised his glass toward the guest. "Please be at ease. You are safe here."

She responded in a condescending tone, "I have no fear. I lost that Muirian trait long ago."

"Good," Taza began. "I sense greatness in you. The Staff of Adois' acceptance of you reveals that. Tell me about yourself."

She shrugged. "There is little to tell. I was raised in a fishing village in the west. My talents appeared early. I was branded as a witch with demonic connections exiled from the nine levels of hell."

Taza raised his chin. "Were you dabbling in demonology?"

Cyra's laughter resonated throughout the chamber, almost penetrating the evil atmosphere of the tower room. Taza liked her. No one would have dared laugh in his presence. His guards stepped forward, but he waved them away.

"I was a child of seven and all alone. I prayed to each and every god I could think of for sustenance and safety. A trapper found me and took me in. My powers continued to grow, and the trapper thought it a blessing. I would enchant his traps, and he grew rich. All the while, I developed my arts. I had no teachers, and the trapper advised me. However, I soon learned he was an evil man. He never laid a hand on me, but encouraged my studies, though I refrained from the dark arts."

Taza smiled, his fangs clear to the young woman who did not blink. "I was fourteen when my benefactor went to a local town and never returned. After weeks of waiting, I made the trip to the village and found him hung and staked to the wall of the palisade."

"A shock, no doubt."

Cyra smiled as wicked a smile as Taza had seen for some time. "The town paid for their mistaken judgment. I magically locked the gates and searched out those responsible."

The vampire grinned with delight. "As I would have done."

She smiled in return. "I found the officials in charge. Their slow death was a joy to behold, so satisfying to my lust for revenge. To drive home my point, I set the town afire and stood in the city center, listening to everyone's screams."

Pausing, she glanced at Taza as if for approval in telling an entertaining tale – not describing the destruction of an entire town.

Taza stood, leaning on the staff of Adois. "Yet I sense you did so without delving into the dark arts. Amazing! I welcome you to Dormin. As you might have seen, this place is being changed for the better. I prefer the undead to humans. There is less opposition. A woman of your power could do well here. My most trustworthy warlock is missing, and I presume he is dead. I need allies in the South. There is a ruined Dwarvan city - Zigar-Shan. I would like you to take charge there and hold my southern border. What do you think of orcs and the assorted creatures that accompany them?"

She shrugged. "I have killed my fair share while traveling. I find that if you use magic to kill a few, the others will run. I will accept your offer - if there is a way you can bring me to my full potential."

The vampire smiled again. "A grasping sorceress. Come, kneel before me."

She did as he commanded.

Approaching her from the throne, he placed a pale boney hand on her head, and grasping the Staff of Adois he intoned, "Deific Adois, I beseech thee to bestow upon this worthy proponent of the cause, her full potency."

Cyra felt the warlock's power coursing through her veins as energy flowed from the staff through his body and into hers. There was great power that she could barely contain it. She had thought herself ready, but this was too much. With a scream, she bared her soul to the goddess Adois. Tears of pain flowed down her face as blood seeped from her ears and nose. In a moment, Cyra came to her senses, curled in a fetal position and moaning. Strong arms lifted her to stand. She wiped her ears and nose clear of bloody fluid and could barely hear.

Taza secretly thought, *Here is one weaker than I. The transfer almost killed her. I have to battle the Staff of Adois, but she has many demons to battle.*

The vampire leaned forward. Two of his guardsmen stood beside Cyra, holding her up. Her hair was in disarray, but Taza could easily make out the streak of white strands that flowed over her left shoulder and the gauntness of her once-beautiful face. Power did not come without a price.

"How do you feel?" he asked.

She straightened, shrugging off the vampires that had helped her stand. "The power in my body is trying to explode - I can barely keep it under control."

"That is the dark power of the Staff of Adois," he said firmly. "If you survive until tomorrow, you will adjust. The power of darkness has infused you. When you call upon your magic, it will be through darkness, not light. The Staff of Adois' enemies are approaching the ruins in Zigar-Shan, and I would have you capture them."

The vampire smiled wickedly. "Rest tonight. If you're alive in the morning, I will teleport you to the dwarvan ruins."

The Staff of Adois had almost killed Cyra. She had overcome life's arrows, and this was one more victory.

As she exited the tower, Taza reiterated, "If you survive the night, we will discuss my plans in the morning."

One of Taza's undead guards sneered at her, and Cyra became instantly alert. As she walked down the winding stairway approaching one of the landings, she saw a shadow flit across the floor. Pausing on the stairway, she cast a spell that allowed her to see into the other room. There were five of them waiting for her - dark elves she had noticed among the guards surrounding Taza. Another test!

Cyra reached the next to last stair and could see only an empty room, but she knew different. Diving to the hard stone floor was not what she wanted to do, but she must. Once in the room, she righted herself and faced the five Illanni. Three were male, and two female that she thought were possible sorceresses. She brought forth a curved blade ten inches long from her boot. It would be of little use in the coming battle.

The Illanni attacked as their sorceresses hurriedly cast spells. Cyra shoved the first Illanni to reach her in the chest with immense strength, flinging him into the sorceresses and breaking their spells. The other two male dark elves attacked. Though skilled with her long dagger, but against longswords, it was next to useless.

"Come forth, dark power, from within!" she whispered.

A dangerous lightning bolt spell was hurled at her. Cyra dropped to the floor, hugging it tightly as the bolt struck the closest Illanni, burning a hole through its torso and bouncing off the wall. As the bolt ricocheted around the room, it struck and killed the taller sorceress.

Taking a chance, Cyra ducked and rolled toward the remaining woman. As she raised up, she hurled her dagger through the air, striking the Illanni in the forehead. Then Cyra turned to face her two remaining adversaries. Without a weapon, her foes thought her easy prey as long as they could keep her from using any spells. Advancing, longswords at the ready, Cyra mulled her options. She tried to cast a simple spell, but a blade came within inches of her face, and she lost concentration.

On instinct, she stepped in close, bringing her face-to-face with the Illanni that had swung at her. With a vicious blow, she broke his arm, and the sword clattered to the floor. With tremendous strength, she slung her adversary into the other swordsman, knocking him to the floor. A solid twist of the wounded Illanni's neck brought a dull snap. Cyra punched the other in the throat, crushing and collapsing his esophagus. Unable to draw a breath, he lay on the cold stone floor, gasping for air and holding his neck.

Suddenly, she heard clapping from the corner of the room. Preparing a spell, she turned to find Taza with one of his Illanni guards.

"Well fought, Cyra," he congratulated her. "This guard will see you to your room. Sleep well. You are a stunning warrior. Survive this night, and one of my personal guards will escort you to breakfast."

CHAPTER SEVEN

Celedant had been too absorbed in the battles first at Zeiglon and then at Southgard to notice the odd flashes of imagery in the back of his mind. The visions were so quick, he could not grasp them to put the pictures together. His mind was too clouded on the after-effects of the battles to orchestrate an answer to what was occurring while they cleared the valley of orcs and others; the pull of the staff of Adaman became too much to ignore.

Flying on Azimuth, the wizard let the dragon unleash flames on a large pack of orcs crossing the battlefield. They were trying to escape west across the valley of Southgard to the hills and forests of their homeland. Suddenly Celedant's eyes rolled back into his head, and he fell from his dragon's back, plummeting toward the ground.

Azimuth felt the loss of consciousness when it hit his friend. The moment the wizard collapsed and fell, he nose-dived at breakneck speed to catch him, pinning his friend to his side with a few spoken words. He chose a clearing to land in that was a fair distance from prying eyes. Seeing this, Eldahir, Baldo, and Morganna spurred their horses to reach the spot as quickly as possible.

As he lay on the ground, watched over by the dragon, Celedant clearly saw the darkened tower of the Citadel of Dormin radiating pure malice and vile evil from its master.

Taza was in a rage. He screamed and struck out at everyone unfortunate enough to be near him. No one was safe from his fury – neither vampire nor slave, not even the city of Dormin. Several buildings exploded outward, killing everyone within and without.

As Celedant witnessed the scene, it was soon displaced by a vision of himself. He watched his own scene of destruction in horrified fascination, terrified. Until that moment, he had not truly realized what the staff's power was doing to him. He could not continue to use the staff. But what choice did he have?

By the time the others arrived, he was able to get to his feet with Azimuth's help. The dragon transformed into an elf and assisted the wizard to sit against the wide trunk of a nearby tree. The others dismounted, sitting on the ground around him: the dwarf Baldo, the most powerful cleric of the group. The elf Eldahir, son of one of his oldest friends and a now a close friend in his own right. The former dark elf turned wood elf, Morganna, a powerful sorceress who had become so important to their cause. Lastly was the dragon and trusted confidant, Azimuth. As they observed him, concern etching every feature of their faces, they realized that their leader looked old. His skin was yellowish, and his eyes were black rimmed.

He looked at them in return and confessed. "I don't know if I should continue using the staff."

"Does this have anything to do with your falling from me?" Azimuth.

"That and more," Celedant admitted. "I have had visions of Taza and the Staff of Adois. Both, as I suspected, are in Dormin."

"When did these visions occur?" Eldahir asked intently.

"Some moments ago, as I lay on the ground. I confess it was this last vision that brought me to my senses. After watching what Taza did to those around him and the city of Dormin. I was filled with terror."

The Staff of Adaman is too powerful of an artifact," Azimuth said.

"Yes, and its power has turned me so arrogant that I almost believed I had become a god myself." He shuddered. "I must not...cannot allow that feeling to possess me again."

"Would that be a bad thing?" Baldo asked.

"Yes," Eldahir replied for the wizard. "Not everything that is bad is necessarily evil, but to maintain the perfect balance on Muiria, both must be equally present."

Celedant nodded. "That is in accordance with the Dragon's Tear's teachings."

"Can't we use a protection spell to bind it?" Baldo asked.

"No, that wouldn't work."

Azimuth was deep in thought. After several moments, he asked, "What do you think of something magical that would allow you to carry the Staff of Adaman without tapping into its power? A magical bag, so to speak."

"Could it be carried safely that way?" Morganna asked.

"Yes, between the three of us – Baldo, Celedant, and myself, we could create a bag or satchel. Its purpose would be to both protect Celedant and hide the staff from

Taza," Azimuth stated.

Baldo nodded. "A simple carrying case would draw no attention."

"With your deity's aid, my dragon magic and Celedant's own magical abilities, we should be able to construct a case."

"That would be of great help. Otherwise, I fear we will never reach the end of the quest with my sanity intact. We must start with a simple hide so as not to attract attention and instill it with our separate magic," Celedant said with a sigh of relief.

"I have used my power before to make simple magical pieces, but never on a grand scale," Azimuth admitted.

"Or one of import," Baldo added. "It must be done, so we will try."

The next day after arriving back at Southgard, Celedant and his two friends went to the tanner's section of the city. They were almost overwhelmed by the smell of the area and the fumes that rose from the tanning solutions. The dwarves that worked in the tanneries seemed immune to the chemicals used to cure hides. Baldo had asked around and been told that Dagor the Tanner was the best in the business.

As they made their way down the narrow alley where the wares were sold, Baldo turned to the others. "See the store with the green banner? That's our dwarf."

He led his friends to a shop that had a huge selection of hides laid out on rough wooden tables. Other hides hung on dowels that jutted from the wall. A gentle dwarf in fashionable clothes greeted them at the door.

"I am Dagor. Welcome to my humble shop. Might I be of assistance?"

Dagor was the nicest dwarf Celedant had ever met. Most dwarves were very businesslike and uncaring to their customers. This dwarf would put the most jovial tavern owner to shame.

Baldo nodded, almost bowing. "I am Baldo of the Theirrian monastery at Nars, and these are my two companions, Celedant and Azimuth of Dragon Isle. We would look at your finest and most durable of hides."

Dagor bowed low. "Come in. I have a variety of hides. Also, I can make whatever finished item you require."

Dagor showed them a variety of hides in different colors and textures. Celedant chose a plain subtle-hued, tanned hide that was long enough for the staff to be carried in. They made a quick payment, and Dagor drew up the design needed on the spot, promising that it would be ready in two days' time.

The band of friends spent the interval days planning their next steps.

When the case was made, Baldo picked it up and delivered it to Celedant. Later that night the three conspirators gathered in Celedant's room.

"I have never done this, and don't know where to start," Baldo admitted.

"I don't think any of us have attempted a task. Each of us will add their magical power in our own way. I suggest that you get as close to Thierry as you can, Baldo. It will be his energy that will be transferred to this object. Azimuth has his particular power – the old magic that echoes from the beginning of the world of Muiria. Myself, I will draw upon the magic that I have learned during my long life and my studies at Edain."

The other two nodded solemnly.

"Let us begin," Celedant said softly.

CHAPTER

EIGHT

The following day, Cyra awoke with renewed energy. She had survived the transfer of power and looked forward to testing her new capabilities. There was a knock on the door. She opened it, finding one of Taza's personal guards standing outside.

"The Lord wishes me to find out if you had died and if not, to summon you to the tower."

She nodded and went to the mirror at the other end of the room to see the effects of the ordeal she had suffered. Cyra brushed out her hair, taking in the white streak that now contrasted with her raven locks. Her face was worse. She had come here a beautiful young woman. Now, a gaunt, haunted countenance looked back at her from the mirror, the smooth ebony skin gone forever. So, this was the trade-off? Harsh to be sure, she thought. Cyra, however, was practical. Her path was chosen.

She grabbed several pieces of fruit from her bedside table and followed the guard. Wolfing it down, she dropped the remains on the costly rug without a care. Someone could pick it up later. The guard led her to Taza's tower, and after climbing a steep, winding stair, she discovered that she wasn't even breathing hard. Was this part of her transformation?

She entered the antechamber where she found Taza seated at a table covered in delicacies of all kinds. He laughed when he saw her expression of surprise.

"I do miss the infrequency of a proper meal, Cyra. Come sit and share the bounty."

Starving, Cyra sat opposite the vampire and began busily filling her plate.

She looked across the table, saying, "I thought vampires did not eat?"

Taza shook his head. "A common misrepresentation. We do not need to eat at all, but some like me savor the flavor and consistency."

Taza looked into her eyes. "Since you are here, you made it through your ordeal. Admirable. After we eat, we shall get down to business."

The two ate for half a turn of the clock when finally, Taza broke the silence after pushing back his empty plate.

"Cyra, I need someone I can trust in the South. A group of adventurers will pass through on their way to kill me. I need constant patrols and any intelligence you might gather."

She nodded. "What is the number of my army?"

"I have been given an estimate that over 20,000 orcs and their followers have assembled in the ruins after the battle at Southgard. You will need to see that the ruins are refortified, and constant vigils kept in the South lands as well as around the great swamp. Can you do this?"

She stood, bowing before her warlock lord.

"It will be done as you wish."

Melgor guided his horse slowly along the southern portion of the foothills. His plan was dangerous. Zigar-Shan held his gold, and he needed that to survive. He had left the chest there as the army moved toward Southgard. His thinking had always been to keep the gold safely hidden until he came up with a good plan to escape. At present, it was stored in a secret chamber near his old quarters.

He thought he could simply get past the orc guards as a traveling warlock working for the Warlock Council. The orcs, for the most part, were dumb as stumps, and he would talk his way into the fortress. Once in the ruins of the city, he could make his way quickly to the fortress delved into the mountain.

Those were his plans until several rugged-looking men stepped on the trail. Melgor knew there were more located behind him and was torn about what to do. To use his magic might alert Taza, but he was trapped. Under his breath, he whispered a short incantation - and two electrical beams arched from the tip of his staff, striking both men.

The spell worked perfectly: the two men were blown backward, landing stunned on the path. Melgor lowered his head next to the horse's neck expecting arrows to follow him. He was right. Two whistled past, but a third struck him in the upper right arm. He almost lost his balance because that was the arm he was using to hold onto the horse's neck. By cutting the Illanni horses loose, he hoped the distraction would send the ambushers after valuable steeds and keep his attackers away. He managed to endure the pain until he was far enough away; then he sat up in the saddle normally.

The arrow had penetrated his bicep, but he managed to ignore the pain as he fled the area. He slowed his horse and looked down at his wound. The arrow had gone completely through his upper arm with the arrow tip sticking out five inches. There was nothing to do but clench his teeth as he grasped the bloody arrow point and snapped it off. The pain was intense, but Melgor wasn't finished. Taking hold of the fletching, he quickly pulled the remainder of the arrow out.

He sagged against the horse's head, in great pain. Melgor reached his left hand over to search through the satchel on his right side. After a maddening few tries, he found the vial he was looking for, berating himself for not retrieving it before pulling out the arrow. It did not matter at the moment. He pulled the plug out with his teeth, spitting it onto the trail, and drank the entire contents of the small vial.

Slowly the pain subsided, and he was able to sit comfortably in the saddle. Melgor could feel the healing effects taking place. His upper arm was warm as the potion cleansed the wound and magically healed it. Taking a strip of clean linen from his saddlebag, he wound it tightly around the wound. The warlock was glad that it had only been a small injury because he doubted that vial could have handled anything more serious. He only had a few more precious vials left.

Feeling normal again, he took a big swig of water and spurred his horse onward. Down the dusty trail, he set off for Zigar-Shan, hopeful that without his magical ties to Taza, the vampire had not picked up on his use of magic and there would be no more interruptions.

The companions grew bored with the pubs and hustle of the overcrowded city. They decided to roam around the outskirts to try and locate access to the underworld. Failing that, they wanted to see if there was any trouble they could get into.

On the fourth day of their wanderings, the company came to a section where the dwarvan Kel lights ended. The lights were made of chemicals that illuminated the area. But they had to be tended, or they would go dark. As a lark, Morganna and Eldahir raced each other to the dwarvan halls above to buy torches and lanterns. They ran back, returning at virtually the same moment.

"How much did ye pay for that?" Botreg asked.

They looked at each other. Morganna replied, "Less than five gold pieces."

Botreg shook his head. "Next time, let me go. Not only would they give a dwarf a better bargain, but I could have stolen them blind."

As the group grinned at the words being bandied about, Botreg soon had both the elves shaking their heads and grinning.

An excited Hority came out of the gloom, where he had hidden while the others talked. He stood before them like a child given a present.

"Me Lord, I pray ye aren't upset, but I went several corridors down into the dark."

Tarquin put his hand on the dwarvan monk's shoulder.

"Hority we must keep an eye on you so that your god does not lose one of his best ambassadors."

Hority grinned. "That I am glad for. Clor might have something to say in this matter later. However, down one passage, me nose caught an odd scent. It is a smell I have never encountered, and as ye know, I have experience with not only the types of odors but their textures as well."

CHAPTER NINE

Celedant gently laid the leather carrying case on a table. Baldo with Azimuth joining him gathered around it. Each concentrated on the case, memorizing every inch. They closed their eyes, the picture of the bag firmly etched in their minds. The three concentrated on it and let their spiritual energy flow over the leather.

Baldo experienced an odd sensation and at once knew that he was no longer in Celedant's room. He opened his eyes, and before him was the table with the case resting on it. That's where reality ended. Across from him was a dwarf dressed in full plate mail: Thierry.

His god smiled at Baldo. "I have followed ye during this quest. I was alerted by Dolgar and through the prayers of Abbot Hortus. He was a great loss for our presence on Muiria, but ye have carried on admirably, despite the lack of yer friends.

Nearly overcome by Thierry's presence, Baldo mustered his courage to speak. "This is a holy, righteous quest. I am honored to be a part of it."

"True," Thierry responded quickly. "But tell me, why do ye call upon me now?"

Baldo bent across the table and lifted up the leather case. "We must guard against the power of the Staff of Adaman. It calls for its sister Staff and consumes the magical energy of he who carries it."

"And who might that be?"

"Celedant, a wizard of Dragon Isle, but we do not know how long he can withstand the temptation of this power. He fears that should he be tempted again, he may lose his soul to it. Another - who does not fulfill the prophesy – might carry it and would be without the power and will of the wizard."

Thierry stared at Baldo without saying a word, causing the dwarf to become fearful.

Finally, he said, "Do not worry. I will do what is necessary to cloak the case. Yer mission is too important to run into trouble."

The benevolent deity smiled. "Once ye return to the reality of this room, ye will remember that I have placed my prayers upon the case. I wish ye well in the coming trying times, and know that I am with ye every step of the way."

While Baldo was swept up in his vision, Azimuth also focused on the case. He, too, had a vision of travelling back to the dawn of time. Muiria was like a lump of clay until the first dragons flew in from the void to mold the world into a form that could support life. The gods had created the sphere, but it had not yet been claimed by good or evil. The ancient dragons created the Dragon's Tear as a beacon for their kind when traveling through the void. They also wished for the Dragon Tear to sort out good and evil.

His mind drifted to the beginning of Edain and the power that the tower had brought to Muiria. He was in the void with ancient dragons slowly circling him.

An elderly red dragon spoke. "Why have you traveled back in time to seek the elders?"

Azimuth, having returned to his golden dragon form, replied, "A great evil hovers over Muiria. The Staff of Adois has thrown off balance between good and evil. We have recovered its opposite twin, the Staff of Adaman, which is the only icon capable of destroying Adois' Staff."

"The burden of the Staff of Adaman, however, is too much for any of us to carry. It enhances the magical power of the carrier and offers temptations no one can endure. We are attempting to dampen its power. This case that I am projecting to you will hold the Staff of Adaman in secret and protect those around it from its power. If you allow it to be so."

The red dragon conferred with the assembly for a moment.

"You may have our consent, and we will funnel energy through you into the carrying case. Know this. We find that you are a great leader of your aerie. Now return and place your hands on the item so that our power can pass into it."

Azimuth suddenly snapped out of his dream. Had the table not been there to grab hold of, he would have fallen.

Celedant's mind whirled, seeking the beginning of Edain and its first elders. Suddenly his mind cleared, and he stood on the beach before the tower that held the Dragon Tear. The Edain he knew as a wizarding community had yet to be built, and as he approached the tower, he saw a small hut leaning against the edifice.

Not wanting to approach uninvited, he called out. A bent old man pushed the wooden door open and stepped into the light. "Ah, Celedant, it is good to see you again."

"Have we met before?" the wizard asked. He could not recall having seen the man during his lifetime.

The old man smiled like a grandfather. "We have met twice in your short life. You will remember me as a different being."

Celedant looked puzzled, and the old man laughed.

"Come now," he said. "Do you not remember me as you went through your tests?"

Celedant released a breath of air and acknowledged the truth of the old man's words.

"You are the faceted man of the Dragon's Tear."

He smiled. "Good, your memory returns. I feared you were addled and would need more clues. However, I am much more than that. This body is a vessel. I have given over my life to be the protector of the Dragon Tear."

"You have proven yourself worthy in more ways than you know. Come, I have a pot of tea ready for us."

Celedant followed him into the cramped little cabin. "I never would have thought that Edain had started from this."

The old man laughed. "We had to start with something, and this is it."

He poured both of them a drink, and Celedant reveled in its flavor. "Are the dragons still here?"

"Oh, yes," he answered. "They are here and offer protection to their edifice, but you did not travel through the ages to see me and talk of the past. You may do that in Edain's library."

Celedant nodded. "I have come seeking aid in the handling of an artifact."

The old wizard nodded. "I had hoped that you would realize that you needed to come to me about the staff. It is a powerful object – one with a mind of its own, I fear," he said smiling.

"What do you need that I might be able to help with?"

Celedant took a sip of the fine brew and explained. "We have tailored a case for Adaman's staff, one that hopefully will protect me from gaining too much power and fail before the end of the quest. We must cloak it from being sought after by its sister staff. Without being cloaked, the enemy can follow our every move."

"A simple and cautionary work of magic is what you need," the wizard said. "I will allow you this request, and I am pleased that you realized the danger its power can create for you."

"I have no desire to be a god - or a powerless wisp of my former self."

"The staff, although it may seem to, cannot grant you that," the old man admonished.

"No, but using it enough could make one feel...even believe...that they are. I don't want that kind of temptation. Can you give me the strength to resist it?"

"I can strengthen you, but you must make that decision for yourself. It would be unwise to take away your will. That would leave you nothing more than a puppet. The staff needs strong followers who can stand up and take the bull by the horns, so to speak." Reaching into his pocket, he took out a small stone. "Take this and put it on the case. It will be absorbed by the leather and will increase its power. Hopefully, you will be able to move without injury and in secrecy."

He reached over to Celedant, simply touching his hand and suddenly the wizard was back in his room with the stone clutched in his fingers and the case before him. His companions' eyes open and eagerly awaiting his return.

The companions soon grew bored with the pubs and hustle of the overcrowded city. They decided to roam the outskirts and locate access to the underworld. Failing that, they wanted to see if there was any trouble they could get into. Tarquin, Ress, Morganna, and Eldahir took advantage of the lull to spend quality time together. The couples often wandered away from the others to talk about what their lives had been like before they met, and the dangers they still faced. In the evening, they kissed under the moonlight and talked about the future, separated from the rest of the company, yet remaining close enough in case of danger.

"What are your plans, once this is over?" Tarquin asked Ress one evening.

"That depends," she replied, searching his expression for clues as to what he had in mind.

"On what?"

"Before I answer that, what do you plan to do?" she asked.

"I would have to return home to Partha, I suppose. Since my brother, the crown prince, was killed in battle, my responsibilities will be greater."

Ress bowed her head in disappointment. "Does that mean you will inherit the throne?"

Tarquin smiled. "No. I have another brother ahead of me, but I would be expected to assume his duties as the second in line."

"You won't have to become an ambassador to the elves now, would you?" she asked.

"No, thank heavens," Tarquin said with a sigh. That position was filled once my family realized that I was part of the prophesy and needed elsewhere."

"That's good," she said, sighing with relief. She quickly looked up. "For you...I mean."

"Don't you like the elves?"

Her expression brightened. "I love Morganna and Eldahir, but I haven't met any other elves."

"I like them a lot. Of course, their way of life in the Elvan forests would take getting used to. I haven't met any high elves other than Azimuth...but he really isn't a high elf. He just looks like one when he is in that form. Whatever I do, it could become very lonely," Tarquin gently hinted.

She nodded. "I suppose so."

"But it wouldn't have to if I...."

Ress looked at him hopefully. "If you what?"

"Had someone special at my side."

"Yes, that would make a difference. Do you have anyone in mind? Are you betrothed to a princess from another kingdom?"

"Nope."

"A...a titled lady perhaps?"

Tarquin grinned. "Nothing has been prearranged." He turned serious. "I do know someone who I think would make me very happy."

"Really?" Her eyes sparkled.

"Uh huh."

Ress grew impatient. "Who? Tell me!"

"She's lovely, trustworthy, fun, outgoing, and I know I can always count on her to have my back."

"AND?" she urged impatiently.

"And I love her more than any woman I have ever known."

The couple had been standing, but now Tarquin dropped to one knee and took her hand.

"I won't have a ring to offer you until we return to Partha, but when this war is over, and things are back to normal, will you marry me?"

She smiled, eyes filled with all the love that she felt for him. "Yes, my love, I will, and love you for now and forever."

Tarquin rose to his feet, and they kissed. Grabbing her around the waist, he swung her around and let out a whoop of joy. The couple laughed until Ress put a hand on his arm.

"What of your parents?"

"What about them? They're already married," Tarquin teased.

"I'm serious, Tarquin. Won't they want you to marry someone important, maybe a princess from another kingdom to cement relations between your two nations?"

"That's my brother's problem. Since eventually, he will become king, it will be his responsibility to marry for the good of the kingdom. You are important. Once I tell my folks all about you, they will love and welcome you with open arms."

Tarquin looked at each of his friends, pulling his sword closer. They followed his cue.

"This scent might lead to something worse than a meaningful pile of filth. Let's make sure we map the area. If this leads to trouble, we want to be able to find our way out again."

The company lit a torch and a lantern, but feeling uncertain, Tarquin ordered the other lamp lit as well. Moving cautiously, they followed Hority's nose for about five hundred feet, all the time slightly angling downwards. They reached a four-way intersection of the tunnel, and Hority led them down the left corridor. At first, they were alarmed when a dark shape loomed up before them. As they drew closer, they discovered a section of the ceiling had fallen in. Hority was not the least bit confounded as he scampered up the rock pile to a crack that separated the ceiling from fallen debris.

"Morganna do you not see how the ceiling continues beyond the top stones?" Eldahir asked her.

"Yes," she answered. "These rocks have been piled here to give the appearance of a cave-in."

Botreg climbed up without disturbing the smallest stone, holding the torch to the roof. The torch burned brighter as air flowed from the rocks and ceiling. He turned and looked down at them. "Ye be right. This was placed here intentionally."

He joined the others, and Hority slid down the rocks.

"I smell what could be an offering to Clor," he declared, "but it has been befouled by some evil. I donna smell what the evil is. I just feel it in me bones."

In fact, when the dwarf brought it to their attention, the others noticed some type of aura leaking through the barricade. Tarquin motioned to the dark dwarf.

"Botreg, run as fast as you can to the Borderer's compound. Find an officer and fetch back at least four squads. Let them line up against the walls from here back to be safe. The last squad will act as our rear guard. Bring their captain to me."

Without a word, Botreg turned and silently ran up the passage as only a trained assassin could. Tarquin motioned the others to spread out and be watchful while they put out the torch and dimmed the lanterns. Hority, not at all disturbed by the situation, laid his head on a smooth rock and promptly fell asleep. Soft snores came from within his cowl. It did not take long for the borderers and Botreg to return. The trauma all the dwarves had faced the past weeks still had the entire population on edge, and he could see it etched in the troop's faces.

CHAPTER TEN

The trio knew what to do. Baldo knelt, and taking the leather case in both hands, he prayed over it. He passed it to Azimuth, who held it and whispered several sentences in the ancient dragon language. Finally, it was passed to Celedant, who, placing the small stone on the case, prayed to Adaman. As he did, the stone began to glow a brilliant gold, forcing all but Azimuth to shut their eyes and hold their arms over their eyes. Azimuth alone watched as it lost its form and flowed into the leather.

The glare faded, and the three friends looked at each other, wondering had they accomplished what they had set out to do?

Celedant was first to speak. "Let us see if we created a proper magical vessel."

He took the Staff of Adaman from where it rested in the corner of the room and slid it into the case, tying the end with the leather straps. Immediately Celedant blew out a breath of air.

"I can no longer feel the energy of the staff! I hope Taza discovers this."

Botreg came to Tarquin with a whipcord-thin Borderer. The dwarf saluted quietly, saying, "I'm Lieutenant Wynan Stonebreaker. I command the ready unit, since the siege, after our commanding officer was killed."

Tarquin shook Stonebreaker's hand, motioning to the tumble of rocks. He kicked Hority awake. "My Clorian monk has both a keen sense of smell and is a mite smelly himself."

The lieutenant grinned as Hority struggled to his feet. His habit was tangled about his filthy legs.

Tarquin continued, "Hority smelled something he believes is evil emanating from this barricade. We all have the same odd sense, which seems to manifest from there."

Stonebreaker closed his eyes and concentrated. "Yes, I too have a tingling that warns of danger. We should explore this immediately."

They began the slow removal of the barrier, rock by rock. Tarquin had long ago learned how slow and methodical dwarves could be. Because of the need for silence, the dwarves gathered in front of the wall, carefully choosing which rock should be moved without causing others to shift. The barrier was only ten feet tall, and little by little, the rocks were taken down and passed hand-to-hand down the lines of waiting soldiers.

Once they cleared the top rocks, they could see the passage continued into the darkness. The tedious work progressed as the dwarves disassembled the wall to one side, creating a two-foot clearing between the wall and stones for about ten feet. Lieutenant Stonebreaker agreed to let Tarquin's group go first. As they went forward, the dwarvan soldiers would follow.

The smooth tunnel continued for what seemed like forever, making few turns, and always with the fetid smell assaulting the company and borderers. Suddenly, a dark void opened at the edge of their eyesight.

Celedant sent a quick missive to Grimilzor's aide to see the chief cartographer with all the maps of the city. That very day a young dwarf showed up.

Feet propped on an elaborately carved stool in front of the blazing fireplace, Celedant felt quite at ease when a timid knock sounded at his door. Too comfortable to get up, he waved a hand, and with a simple spell, the door opened, revealing a dwarf in his mid-fifties. He was slight, having the pale skin that dwarves, who never saw much sunlight, often had. Still smoking his pipe, the wizard motioned him inside, closing the door with a slight wave of his hand. He gazed at his visitor, feeling puzzled.

"I thought Skally Moonseeker was cartographer of Southgard?"

The young dwarf answered quickly as if it was a difficult subject.

"He was me pa. He died on the walls defending Southgard, but he was a training me to take over the family occupation, if ye know what I mean."

The wizard shook his head reflectively, saying, "So many great souls lost these past months. Enough talk of sadness; we have work to be done. Please bring the maps over here to the table."

The wizard realized he had not introduced himself. "How rude of me. I was in deep thought and forgot myself. As you may know, my name is Celedant."

The dwarf responded quietly, "Me name is Padrig."

Celedant smiled. "Good, let's take a look at that rather large roll of maps with which you are burdened."

The parchment scrolls were smoothed out and weighted at the corners on the table by large crystal stones. The wizard examined the map showing the first level of Southgard.

"What are ye searching for, Celedant?" Padrig asked.

The wizard continued to study the map before looking up. "Humph, that is difficult to explain. I need a place of solitude where no sound can disturb me. I will be attempting a very powerful spell. Do you know of a place?"

The young dwarf paced to the small fire and back. "This might help. What if I run through what pops up in me mind, narrowing our search? Would the deepest crypts work, or would the interred offer interference?"

Surprised at the astuteness of the dwarf, the wizard nodded. "You are right, Padrig. What is left of their energy might distort my endeavor."

The dwarf arched an eyebrow. "How about an old mine where the vein has run out?" But then he answered himself. "No, that wouldna do. Echoes or a chance miner might disturb ya. We can also rule out the old watchtowers on the mountain."

The wizard asked, "Is there not a room with a sealable door far enough underground to ensure secrecy?"

Padrig snapped his fingers, and a big smile lit his face. "I have what ye need."

Padrig began thumbing through the index numbers at the top of the maps. When he reached a certain section he was looking for, he exclaimed, "Ah, here is where the passage starts. It was built to be as secret as a tomb could be. Me father told me once that Lord Tip the Axe commissioned the tomb. He had seen desecrated tombs in the past, and me father often said the Axe had desecrated a few himself, so Lord Axe devised the perfect tomb."

Padrig flipped through the maps that showed a dotted line.

"He created a law to stop miners from excavating around the steps of the tomb. Quite a feat when ye consider our race." He continued to flip the pages until he came to the correct map. Dust floated in the air as he moved it about. "It is still the deepest structure in Southgard," he said with a smile. "It avoids even the underworld. The dwarf that designed this was a genius. However, Tip the Axe died in a rockslide before it was finished. His body was never found, and the excavation stopped at the burial chamber."

He pointed to a room at the termination of the long stair where a notation in meticulous writing simply said, "End."

"Ah, yes indeed. I believe that will be perfect. Come, we must explore this hidden place."

Padrig looked ashamed as he took out three giant key rings. "As much as I know the maps, me father was in the process of learning me the keys," he said meekly. "I can narrow it down a bit. A small mark where stairs are located is marked on ring two. Eventually, I can find it through trying each one."

Not wanting to discourage the young dwarf, Celedant said, "We must start right away."

He called a page for food and water. Before they arrived, he continued.

"Along the way, we'll pick up a bundle of torches in the market. Padrig, you might want to arm yourself. However useful maps and keys are, they won't fend off anything that may have broken into the tomb."

The shocked look on Padrig's face caused Celedant to burst out laughing. "Don't worry lad; get your weapons and chainmail. With my magic, we'll be fine."

Padrig hurriedly rolled up his maps.

"No need to rush, lad. I won't leave without you."

Celedant gathered what he would need and brought forth a brown leather carrying case. He untied the string, wanting to be certain the Staff was still inside. The bejeweled head of the Staff of Adaman showed in the dark interior, as common sense had told him it would. Somewhat embarrassed, the wizard tied the opening securely, slinging the carrying strap over his head. He waited barely a turn of the clock before Padrig returned.

The dwarf had an iron peaked helmet with a nose guard, old, slightly rusted chainmail that hung to his knees and heavy leather boots. He bore a sharp, double-headed axe, and from his belt hung a huge pouch rattled.

Celedant pointed and asked, "The keys, I presume? We can stuff some cloth among them to muffle their clinking."

The wizard stood up and headed to the bed, where his gear was neatly packed and ready to go. When venturing through even recently searched passages, it was a good idea to take along packs in case they were detoured. They shouldered the packs, and Celedant unconsciously checked the staff case slung across his back.

They proceeded to the main hall. Despite the war, the market was filling. Crafty dwarves from the surrounding areas brought in produce, trying to charge extra for needed fare. By order of the Regent, however, armed guards strolled about, making sure no one was taking too much money. It was in this milling throng that they sought out stalls to make their purchases. They bought what was needed, securing the torches to their packs.

Padrig led them upwards through the crowd that was thinning to a trickle the further they ventured from the hall. Celedant saw another sign that they were in a section little used recently. There were only a few kel lights, which cast many shadows. Most had been allowed to fade. The lights in this far section were not being kept up.

Celedant called for a stop. "I'll need my magic when we reach the bottom of the tomb. Now's the time to light a torch, I think."

Chapter Eleven

Tarquin motioned for everyone to stop. They crouched down, tightly gripping their weapons - ready for any attack. Botreg and Morganna, both used to the ways of the underworld, joined Tarquin.

Morganna pointed to the debris beside the void. "Whatever we face they, or it, broke through into this tunnel."

Botreg nodded. "We need to send a scout or two ahead to the edge." He elbowed the once-dark elf. "Ye volunteering with me?"

Morganna looked on the grinning dwarf. "I guess I have no choice."

Botreg's smile left his face as he started crawling forward, followed by Morganna. It took only a few moments before they disappeared from sight in the inky darkness.

A quarter of an hour passed, then another before Botreg emerged from the darkness. He crawled to where Tarquin leaned against the tunnel wall. As silently as possible, the dwarf reported.

"There's a mighty big cavern up ahead. Morganna can sense dark elves. There's no way to tell how many. The cave is too big. To either side are rock formations and a cleared way to attack between them. It must be a hundred feet or more wide - the perfect place for an attacking host to muster forces and wait to advance on Nars."

Tarquin turned to Lieutenant Stonebreaker. "That's bad, right?"

The dwarf's grim visage nodded.

Tarquin whispered, "I don't want to walk into a hail of arrows and spells. Without knowing their numbers, I'm not venturing inside. To be safe, send five of your lads up for help. We need heavy infantry, a barbican, and as many clerics you can find that will fight."

The lieutenant nodded, crawling back until he was well enough away before he stood up and raced to the last squad.

Melgor had been in the saddle for over a week when he crested a hill and saw in the distance the mountain whose shadow hid the ruins of Zigar-Shan. He had known he was close when he had run into a patrol of orcs. They had allowed him to pass without question, but as he did, he heard them talk of someone called the sorceress.

As he looked across at the mountain, Melgor said out loud, "You must have put someone else in charge, Taza. That may complicate things, but I am still getting my gold."

Melgor trotted his horse down the main road to Zigar-Shan. Some sections still contained cobblestones from the original Dwarvan Roadway. As he neared the ruined city, he saw that the outer wall had been repaired where it had fallen in. Stones had been replaced. Other sections sported strong timber walls.

Someone has been busy, Melgor thought. This might endanger my mission. He slowed his mount as he approached the gate and the five orcs that guarded it.

One of the orcs called out in a harsh guttural voice, "Stop. State your business or die."

Melgor raised up in his seat to tower over the orc guard and in an authoritarian voice, answered, "Do you not recognize Melgor the Red, Lord Taza's lieutenant."

The dim-witted orc had to ponder these words' meaning and finally said, "You work for the master. Pass."

The warlock started to ride through. When he was among the guards, he nonchalantly asked, "Who commands? It is different since I was here last."

"The sorceress, Cyra," the orc stated firmly.

Melgor had no idea who this sorceress was, but he needed the guard's knowledge.

"The commander sent by Lord Taza," the orc added.

Melgor eyed the orc and said casually, "Thank you, master orc."

Melgor needed to hide his horse. Soon he found an old stone wall house with tall grass growing in the back courtyard. He dismounted, shutting the gate to allow the steed full range of the overgrown backyard. The warlock stopped before entering the building, reciting a long-forgotten prayer that he could navigate the ruins without encountering this Cyra.

He made good time on foot until he reached the old giant enclosure. Melgor had to follow the palisade to the gate that was guarded by a single orc of prodigious proportions. He was from the West where orc tribes appeared to grow larger than most. Melgor did not want to alert the guard who might hold him until this Cyra arrived. Even though he was supposed to be dead, he dared not risk his luck, so he cast an invisibility spell.

Inside the old giant compound, he lowered his spell only after he was a street further. Melgor watched from the shadows as a wagonload of stones rambled by, pulled by oxen straining at their yokes. He waited for them to pass and darted ahead to see that the giant's large wooden buildings had been destroyed.

Continuing on, he skirted the inner wall where the ruined buildings were still being torn down. This Cyra had some sense. She was clearing the area to give her archers a better field of fire. The more he saw, the less he wanted to meet this sorceress. She appeared to be a formidable foe, well, at least administratively. The warlock could teleport, but he only had cursory knowledge of the spell and could leap only a short distance. He made his way as far as the ruins could take him and looking at a distant balcony, he cast the transport spell. When he reappeared, he hadn't quite covered the distance, coming up a foot short. With flailing arms, he caught hold of the stone railing, locking onto it with his legs. He climbed over the obstacle.

Sitting with his back to the stone, heart pounding in his chest, he imagined missing the balcony altogether and falling to his death. Melgor glimpsed over the railing and saw nothing unusual in the courtyard below. He sighed, the air whooshing out of his mouth. He was safe - now to his treasure. He reckoned he could carry four bags of gold, and that would give him a good start to the East.

The hallways were empty of orcs. Twice, he came to overlooks of the great hall and saw this Cyra below the stairs. Tall and erect, she appeared to be a strong and confident leader. Obviously, Taza had increased her power by use of the Staff. That boded ill should he meet her face-to-face.

Melgor found the level he wanted and sprinted down the hallway to a long-abandoned complex of rooms. Here lay his treasure, and he found the wall. The simple spell he had placed on it was still intact. Pulling on the tail of a carved dragon adorning the far wall opened the secret portal.

Inside, he sought out a carved mural of a battle scene. Melgor pushed the button in the eye of one of the carved dwarves, and a small section of the wall slid open. There was his treasure! Gold he was supposed to bribe and pay operatives up and down the east coast. He tied two bags of golden coins together, and another, so he could carry them slung over his shoulders. Once he had two sets, as a last thought, he took a small bag of gems and pocketed it.

The gold was heavy, but this was his final payment from Taza, and he was soon striding down the hallways like he belonged in the city. When he reached the balcony, no one had questioned him. He was just about to cast the teleportation spell when he heard running footsteps behind him.

"Stop in the name of Taza!" A woman's voice called out.

The sorceress's image ran through his mind, but he never stopped and reached the balcony - throwing himself into the air. As the ground rushed to meet him, he used his staff to cast a slowing spell that allowed him to float to the ground. As soon as he landed, a lightning bolt exploded several feet from him. He staggered, and gravel rained down, but Melgor regained his balance. He used his staff to send a flash of energy that hit the underside of the balcony. It exploded, throwing stone shards into whoever stood in the archway.

Multiple explosions followed. The electricity of the lightning bolts caused his hair to stand on end. Reaching one of the carts hauling stone out of the giant courtyard, he vaulted over it with the help of his staff. He stopped momentarily to get his bearings. Soon he was bent over, running from the cart, when a huge explosion sounded behind him. Stones blew past him. His cloak and clothes deflected most, but a small pebble struck the back of his head, and he could feel a trickle of blood flowing down his neck.

Melgor ran like he had never run before. As he neared the large orc at the gate, he cast an invisibility spell in midstride and disappeared. This confused the orc, but he recovered and swung his spear in a wide arch, nearly the width of the gateway. Melgor hit the ground as the wickedly sharp spear point whizzed over his head.

Among the ruins, ducking down alleyways and crisscrossing streets, he realized that going for his horse would be suicide. He wasn't going to be riding out of Zigar-Shan, and he began to worry that this foray might have been a grave mistake.

Heavily-armored dwarves advanced down the passageway. Tarquin and Stonebreaker moved back to the end of the column, where they found a surly-looking dwarvan general wearing dented plate mail and a helmet with bull horns.

Lieutenant Stonebreaker saluted. "General Bull, ye might not have met Prince Tarquin?"

The dwarf looked Tarquin up and down. "Don't rightly live up to the stories told about ye, but pleased to meet ye. Now, I understand that we might have a nest of dark ones," he said eagerly.

About that time, Morganna appeared from the darkness, startling General Bull. Not knowing her past, he had not expected to see a Wood Elf here.

"They are Illanni," she told them. "I heard movement and felt the use of almost undetectable magic. Hopefully, there are no vampires with them."

"How do you want to approach this?" Tarquin asked the general.

The general pulled on his beard. "How far is the drop to the cavern floor?"

"I can't say for sure," Morganna replied, "but I think two, maybe three feet at deepest."

The general pointed to the barbican, a wood and metal wall angled slightly back with wooden beams attached to the bottom side, running backward to keep it from falling over.

"They know we're here. We move the barbican to the front, followed by two Borderer squads, one to go right, the other left. They are to take up defensive positions. A company of me heavy infantry follows the barbican and reacts accordingly. We will need some of the clerics. I wish we had a wizard."

Morganna interrupted. "Will a sorceress do? I am skilled in the magical arts."

Bull flashed a gap-toothed smile. "Do ye think they've trapped the entrance, and if so, how can we get around 'em?"

The auburn-haired elf smiled back. "They do not know a sorceress is facing them. I have a spell for this situation. I can disarm the traps twenty to thirty feet out into the cave. They will be busy watching and waiting for your attack, allowing us to pull one over on them."

General Bull slapped her good-naturedly on the upper arm, making her stagger backward. The general continued. "Yer other borderers and the rest of me troopers can attack. I'll keep a squad here in case."

He motioned for the barbican to move forward. There were four sweating dwarves grasping each leg to keep the wheels from making noise, while two held tightly to a rope attached to an eyebolt near the top to keep it from toppling forward when moved. Seven feet tall and five feet wide, it gave the dwarves a chance to charge around the sides, while offering protection to the ones taking cover behind it. When the barbican cleared the waiting soldiers, it was turned, facing the gaping cavern hole. The dwarves were industriously working on the barricade, while borderers removed the remaining blocking wall of stones so the engineers could move the barbican into place.

Chapter Twelve

Padrig used flint and steel to light a torch. The illumination showed what looked like dangerous creatures lurking along the inky dark passages, were nothing but shadows on the stone hallway, cast by the infrequent lighting. The young dwarf stared and looked up at Celedant.

"Ye can never be too careful. That's what me father said as we charted new additions to the city."

With the torches lighting their way, the two made better time.

"We may get a little wet, in case I forgot to mention," Padrig said.

The wizard patted his back. "You did, but that is a small hardship."

They could smell the dampness ahead before hearing the unmistakable sound of running water underground.

Padrig motioned ahead. "It's one of the cisterns that supplies the city. There is a natural stream that emerges above us that flows down the wall directly into the entrance of the cistern."

Before long, they came to the eroded rock wall down which the water flowed. The wall looked perfectly flat in the torchlight, but Padrig pointed out a ridge for their feet and a smaller ridge for their fingers.

"To those who know, there is a bit of a rim in the rock to hold onto as we cross the slippery surface. Halfway down there is a small hole under the rim that is all but invisible." The dwarf showed Celedant where the rim was. The rim was as slippery as the floor, but it did offer a firm hold to keep them going forward.

After moving a few dozen paces, Padrig motioned to the wizard. 'It's here." He pointed into the darkness, but Celedant saw nothing. Padrig disappeared from view. The wizard inched along until he felt a tug on his leg. He looked down to see the sodden dwarf smiling up at him.

The entrance was small, even for a dwarf. Celedant hung precariously to the hole as he crawled in backward with Padrig helpfully pulling on his legs. They sat in the dark, breathing heavily until the dwarf brought out a new torch and started it ablaze. What had appeared to be only a small, damp crawlspace opened up further inward. Eventually, the ceiling rose upward, forming a forty-by-forty-foot room. The room still bore the marks of the masons that had delved the tomb.

Padrig crossed the chamber to a door and took out the key rings. He gave the wizard a sorrowful look. "Sorry."

"Not a problem, my friend. We can dry out as you test them."

Padrig went to work, trying keys that appeared to fit the keyhole as he made his way around the second key ring. Celedant sat chewing on a bit of bread as he noticed the keyhole was a small slit in the stone a foot from the door. Even in daylight, a person would have a hard time finding a well-concealed lock. He mused in silence that dwarves used the best artisanship in tunneling, stonework, and now in making locks. One key slid completely in, and there was an audible click. They stood in front of the portal, expecting something to happen, but the door remained closed. A grating sound echoed through the chamber from long-unused levers that opened into the empty tomb of Tip the Axe.

The floor in front of the door agonizingly inched downward as the gears strained to work after so many years. At times it got stuck, stopping for a moment, but the sheer weight of the stone forced the gears to grind onward. Steps began to emerge, and the height of the stairwell grew as the opening opened larger. Celedant was delighted, for he'd had a brief thought of having to climb all the way down, stooped over. The opening looked to be tall enough for him to descend in an upright position.

Padrig looked back over his shoulder with apprehension. "It is over a mile of steps."

The wizard chuckled. "I'm still spry. I should not have any difficulties."

Downward the pair descended, using two torches to light the way. As they reached a flat passage, the torches began to sputter, the first warning signs emerged from the gloom. Thick, ropy webs impeded their advance.

Padrig was about to touch one until Celedant hissed a warning.

"The slightest touch might summon that which built the web."

Melgor found a place to hide as the day progressed. His plan was to wait until dark and make it over the wall when he would be on his own and in search of a horse. Had the stallion he had ridden been truly his, he could have called it to him. He missed his chimera. There was nothing better than soaring through the skies on his mount. Now he was going to have to settle on an orc horse, or worse.

As night fell, he sat on the second story of the building he was hiding in and watched the numerous patrols with torches searching throughout the city. All seemed quiet in his area, so he took off, moving slowly through the ruined buildings. He didn't spot a single patrol as he made his way to the wall.

A patrol of orcs appeared, torches lighting the darkness. Their leader sat astride a horse. Melgor waited in the shadows, a plan forming in his head. He stepped into the street and cast a spell, causing a great gust of wind to flow down the street. It blew out the torches and caused the horse to rear up, leaving the patrol leader fighting for control.

Using his staff, he struck out at the leader, hitting him in the temple and causing the orc to fall back into his panicked troops. Melgor vaulted into the saddle and kicked the horse into motion. He had trouble finding the stirrups and reins in the darkness. Once he did, a huge boulder appeared in front of him. Only his speedy reflexes enabled him to gallop around it. His sole purpose was getting to the gate.

He reached the main thoroughfare and pulled on the horse's reins, causing the horse's shoes to spark as they slid on the cobblestone. Coming to a stop halfway in the street, he could clearly see the gate. It was closed and guarded. Lowering his staff, he called upon its energy and with a word, sent a glowing red ball five feet in diameter streaking toward the gate. The orcs had no time to react as the spell struck. It incinerated the guards and blasted the gate to shreds. Then he was riding toward it, a quick jump by the horse, and he was free, at least for the moment.

Melgor looked back and saw no one following, but he knew there would be patrols in the lands surrounding the city. Once he had put a mile between himself and Zigar-Shan, he slowed and listened. There was no sound of pursuit, so he continued at a slower pace, looking for a trail that would lead him into the hills.

He came to a break in the trees and looked back at the ruined city. It had been his city for a very short time, and he was not about to cede control over it without a fight. The sorceress had stirred something in the warlock, and he was burning to exact revenge.

The dwarves moved out as Morganna whispered the words of a spell, causing several explosions and a number of arrow traps to trigger. One nasty trap was a lightning bolt that shot directly across the opening to electrify anyone in the first wave of the dwarvan attackers. Instead, it ricocheted through the cave, causing even the Illanni to duck for cover.

"Go! Go!" the general yelled.

The barbican was wheeled to the edge, eased into the cave before the wheels touched down, allowing it to be pushed into position. The borderer squads went right and left as the heavily-armed infantry followed.

A giant explosion went off amid Lieutenant Stonebreaker's borderers that had moved to the right. Several reeled about, wounded. Four lay dead on the floor. General Bull sent in more troops, while several dwarvan clerics began casting defensive and offensive spells. The offensive spells raised columns of fire that fell upon the far side of the cavern.

Tarquin and his company went left, where several dark elves were shooting arrows down at the attackers. When the Illanni saw they were being charged, they pivoted, and the arrows rained down among the assailants. A borderer next to Tarquin pitched backward. Tarquin glanced down briefly before placing his hand on the rock formation and jumping into the dark elves' position. As he entered, he lashed out with both booted feet and his sword. One Illanni fell dead. The other was knocked backward. As he swept another elf out of the way, he glanced down to a hidden portion of the cavern where even more Illanni waited to attack.

Ress, Morganna, and Eldahir shot their arrows nonstop into the masses. When arrows came their way, a borderer fell, and Morganna felt a sharp sting in her shoulder as she and Eldahir jumped back over the rock wall. Tarquin estimated the number of enemies at a hundred or more before he reached safety. Ress, her eyes unused to the darkness, was able to battle in the cave due to the campfires they used for cooking and the brightness of the dwarvan spells.

Tarquin grabbed a young dwarf. "Run to General Bull. There are up to a hundred Illanni hiding in front of my position."

The armed troops were moving steadily when a call to stop and take cover was blown on a horn. Hority looked at the massed troops, and beseeching his god Clor, he cast a spell that rained a gooey, foul-smelling substance into the crowded Illanni. Many were able to cast shield spells, but those not as quick were covered in the reeking detritus.

Lieutenant Stonebreaker lay in the tunnel, an arrow in his chest and blood frothing at his mouth. General Bull called to him but stopped when he saw the deadly wound. The general was about to call to another runner when Stonebreaker stood up. "I can take the message."

A call for reinforcements was sent, and with two borderers helping their commander, they ran stumbling for help. The lieutenant died soon after they reached the main passage, so a dwarf laid him on his back against the wall, and the two continued running.

General Bull's troops pushed forward on the right. In a lull between spell casting, Morganna and Eldahir turned to the mass of Illanni below them, each casting a shield spell to allow many dwarves to move forward. Even so, a number still lay dead, and the wounded were carried further down the tunnel past the general.

The dark elves were content to pick off their adversaries with arrows or spells. There was one section on the right that General Bull and Tarquin thought might offer more firing positions. Tarquin left Botreg in charge as fighting continued, running toward the ridge, fending off the dark elves as they charged at him.

Chapter Thirteen

Celedant stood pondering the situation. The ropy tendrils reminded him of a caterpillar's nest more than a spider's web. It was nothing he had experienced. He looked down at the armored Padrig.

"My magic should be able to burn through this web and destroy its maker or makers, but we had best be ready if an attack comes."

Padrig nodded, too frightened to say or do anything more.

"I will use my magic and sword to aid you. I think we should back up first," Celedant said, leading the dwarf back about twenty paces. With the Staff of Adaman secured to his back, the wizard was again using his old staff, Forestae. Raising it high in front of him, he spoke the words of a spell.

As the last syllable left his lips, a giant green fireball rushed down the passage. The instant it struck the silky ropes that blocked their way, and the fireball was deflected backward. Celedant had a mere second to cast a counterspell that formed a shield in front of Padrig and himself. When the fireball reached the protective shield, fingers of flame rushed around it and past them, causing Celedant and Padrig's clothes to smolder. Fortunately, the majority of the fire flowed around the edges of the spell, burning dirt and debris from the walls of the cave behind them as it flowed up the passage until it dissipated.

The wizard had never experienced a display. He turned and looked down at his companion. "Easy, Padrig. I think it best if we put more distance between us and whatever that barrier hides."

Before they could move any further away, they heard a chittering, and huge, worm-like creatures charged out of what Celedant would describe as a nest. Five glowing white beasts as thick as a man's thigh and four feet long rushed at them, moving on small legs with feet like suction cups. Each had a small round mouth filled with gleaming needle-like teeth.

Celedant drew his sword and gripped Padrig's shoulder tightly in reassurance. He cast a spell, sending a small flaming dart down the passage where it struck the first creature in the head, leaving a gaping hole and spraying yellow ichor everywhere. Its death spurred the creatures to move faster and, in a moment, the wizard and dwarf were surrounded.

Padrig blocked with his shield, striking with his axe to cleave huge chunks out of the monsters. Celedant's long sword hit swift and deadly, impaling the creatures as they advanced for the attack. One beast sunk its needle-like teeth into the dwarf's shield.

"Aiee! Let go, ye overgrown bug!" He pulled and tugged in vain. Had he been larger and stronger, Padrig could have raised the shield and shaken it off. His anger brought a burst of adrenaline, and with a quick flick of his wrist, his axe clove the fanged head from its body. Even in death, its teeth retained their grip like a steel trap. Padrig's booted foot tried vainly to kick it off.

Celedant's low chuckle snapped him out of his fervor, and Padrig looked around. The enemy had been vanquished, leaving them covered in the monsters' yellow blood. Turning to the wizard, he said.

"Will ye look at this?" He raised the shield and shook it, but the head remained attached. Lowering it again, he punctuated each word with a kick. "I...can't...get...the...cursed...thing...to...let...go!"

Celedant laughed again, now louder. "I can take care of that for you, my friend. Using the words of an ice spell, he targeted just the head, freezing it solid.

"Now try kicking it."

Padrig did so, and the insect's remains shattered into tiny shards of ice, freeing the shield, but leaving a distinctive bite mark on it.

"A trophy," Celedant said. "Just think of the stories you can tell the young ones."

Padrig grinned. "Aye."

Turning, Celedant approached the webbing and studied it.

"These creatures look like caterpillars, but the webbing is unique. We have to cut our way through."

"Should we not get help?" Padrig asked.

"How I wish my friend Azimuth could have come with us. His old magic might have worked."

"Old magic?" the dwarf asked.

Celedant nodded. "Dragon magic often accomplishes what other magic users can't."

"A dragon! Your friend's a dragon?" Padrig's eyes grew as large as saucers. "I have heard rumors they have revealed themselves to the rest of the world. I have yet to venture out of the city to see one. You know one?"

The wizard smiled. "I know a great many dragons. They don't call my place of residence Dragon Isle for naught. As a youngster developing my magic, I bonded with Azimuth, and we have remained life-long friends."

"Amazing! Still, a dragon wouldna be able to enter this passageway," the cartographer said, looking around. "Although I haven't seen one yet, I understand they are huge, even bigger than the fire drakes."

"That they are, but they can shapeshift. Azimuth would have no trouble traversing this tunnel. He would likely do it as a wolf or elf."

Padrig's mouth dropped open. "Truly, it is a shame he couldna come with us. Why not?"

"He was needed back on Dragon Isle. After receiving a message of dark magic swirling in the ether near the isle, as ruler of the dragons, he had to consult with the elders and the master wizards to decide what they needed to do to protect their home from this growing danger."

"That's not good."

"No, it isn't," the wizard said. "We'll handle this, and if we can't, we'll call for help. Come, let us ply our weapons."

Taking a step back, Celedant struck the ropy strands with his blade. The substance offered some resistance before succumbing to the sharp sword. Padrig moved next to him and started hacking at it with his gleaming axe. Every few seconds, they heard a chittering sound of warning and backed away from the webbing as the giant caterpillars attacked.

Their arms began to tire from the constant use of weapons, either on the webs or the agitated creatures. Celedant tried spell after spell as they rested, hoping for something that would work faster, but the webbing stood firm.

Pausing, Padrig said, "If only we could use this webbing in our armor."

Celedant patted the dwarf's back. "An excellent idea. Talk to General Grimilzor."

Padrig grinned. Emboldened, he said, "We canna have these creatures here. Let's go."

"Easy, young warrior; first, we must survive before you count gold for this discovery."

As they hacked at destroying the web, Celedant swung his blade waist-high. Out tumbled enough creatures to cover the breadth of the hallway – two and three feet on top of each other.

"Back! Back!" Padrig yelled.

While they ran from the horde, Celedant urged Forestae to send burning bolts of energy into the creatures at their heels. As they struck the monsters exploded, but there was no time to kill all, and the giant worms were soon upon them. Padrig used his shield to force them away, giving space enough to swing his axe.

Celedant waded among the creatures using both sword and staff to cut and beat them away. Although his cloak and leggings protected him from most bites, Padrig was not so lucky. One took hold of his boot, biting through the leather and into his ankle. The dwarf chopped the creature in half as he went to one knee.

Celedant was nearly overcome as the creatures swarmed his body. Suddenly, something strange happened. He had an urgent desire to open the end fastening of the case holding the Staff of Adaman. The wizard paused, resisting the lure of godlike power. A vicious bite to his leg gave him the strength of will needed. Pulling open the top end of the leather case, magic energy slithered through the opening like the tendrils of an octopus.

Celedant concentrated intently, directing the energy coils to wrap around the creatures on and surrounding him. They rapidly snaked round and round each giant worm until it was fully wrapped. Then the coils tightened, disintegrating the thing inside.

After the energy had killed all, Celedant turned to Padrig, who was almost covered with the biting monsters. The little cartographer felt blood running from several wounds, but he fought on until he realized that he was no longer being bitten. Weak from blood loss, he staggered backward and dropped to a sitting position on the floor. All around him, the caterpillars that had attacked him were engulfed within those same tendrils of magic that Celedant had used on the others.

Soon the creatures were all dead, and the wizard quickly summoned the energy and fastened the end of the case that held the Staff of Adaman. The magic disappeared in an instant, freeing Celedant of its influence. He looked down at Padrig, and seeing the numerous bite wounds and blood loss, fished through his cloak and brought forth a flask. Crouching down, he popped the lid.

"Drink this," he urged softly. Raising it to the injured dwarf's lips, he watched as Padrig gulped several swallows.

As he recapped the bottle and put it back in his cloak, the blood eased to a stop, and the wounds began to close, leaving small circular scars where the bite marks had been.

"Your wounds are healed, but we must wash them, and they will remain sore until the scars disappear in a few days." The dwarf took some time carefully bandaging the wounds.

Padrig nodded thanks. He had never needed magical healing before. It left him filled with wonder at its speed and power.

The two companions rested as long as they dared amid the bodies of the dead that had been killed by conventional means.

"I could make the rest of this disintegrate, but I'm tired, and the additional energy could cost us later."

To restore some of their strength, they gulped water and chewed on a small amount of dried beef. The ichor that covered everything and its odor was enough to churn their stomachs, and as soon as they could, Celedant led the intrepid dwarf back to the webbing. Several skirmishes with the creatures followed, as the webbing eventually gave way to the darkness of the tunnel. Padrig lit another torch for a better view as the first one began sputtering out.

They discovered a three to four-foot crack leading into darkness that must have occurred during a sudden shift in the rock formation long ago. Celedant illuminated Forestae and looked through the hole to find the gritty underworld staring back at him.

They came to an ending of smooth stone and moments later found the lichen-covered lock. Padrig scrubbed the rock with water and a stiff brush from his backpack until it was cleaned. Once the lock was exposed, he pulled out his key rings and began searching for the right one. Quickly he found it and inserted the slim key into the slot.

General Bull was about to call his troops forward when a battalion of new soldiers arrived. A corpulent dwarvan general named Minebeam, whose armor could barely contain his rotund body, waddled over. He jumped down to the floor with ease, despite his bulk, and looked around the barbican as arrows clinked and splintered against it.

He smiled at his counterpart. "Ye seem to have things well in hand, Bull. I've got 500 troops chomping at the bit to get in on this fight, and more are on the way."

Bull nodded. "I was about to attack that section." He pointed at a depression. "To tell the truth, me lads are bone tired. If ye have five hundred, me clerics can cast spells to keep the dark ones' heads down while yer lads attack there and what ye can of the central cavern. The Illanni don't seem to be going anywhere. They're holding ground."

"That's not good," Minebeam said with a worried head shake. "They're hiding something."

He called his troops forward, and when the clerical spells, along with Morganna and Eldahir's incantations, were released, the dwarves charged. Several dark elves hidden in niches offered excellent firing positions. They fought to the death with their backs to the wall.

A quarter of Minebeam's troops had gone nearly half the distance when the Illanni countered with assault spells, using energy flashes, electric beams, and fire bolts. Many troops fell, but their dwarvan armor made of mythril fended off most damage. While more troops flowed from behind the barbican, the first wave reached the cavern's ridge. Dark elves popped up from behind, and a melee ensued.

Elsewhere, Tarquin's blood was up, but the situation meant he was unable to fight his way to his friends, so he charged with the infantry. He and ten dwarves reached a depression, finding it occupied by twenty Illanni. The dwarves charged straight at them while the prince dove to the side, coming up with sword and dagger in his hands. The first two dark elves did not realize his presence until it was too late. Tarquin slit one's throat with his dagger and ran the other through with his sword. The dark elves were pushed back, but the dwarves paid a heavy price. Of the ten, only six remained after the battle, all bearing wounds.

The second wave of General Minebeam's reserve troops charged, taking out the Illanni while the dwarves held the depression. They now shot arrows into the flanks of their enemy, and the fight for the ridge raged on.

Seeing a dwarf stagger backward, Tarquin ran to him, and as the wounded fighter dropped to the ground, he faced a grinning dark elf. Quick and supple, the Illanni's sword danced in front of the prince, but for all his eloquence as a fighter, Tarquin managed to step inside the sword strokes and crush the dark elf's face with a blow from his sword hilt.

The enemy elves finally retreated, leaving the dwarves slumped just below the crest, tired and wounded. A new company of dwarves came to relieve the wounded. Tarquin was grateful for the break until his sword, Dragon Bolt, lit fiery red and began to vibrate, warning him that evil was nearby. A tingle of fear crept through his body, and he knew there was at least one vampire in the Illanni ranks – maybe more.

He wasn't the only one to notice. It was almost a clarion call from the clerics that rang through the dwarvan ranks.

"Vampires!"

Many fighters had never faced a vampire before, but they had heard stories from other battles. Those memories flashed into their minds, creating waves of fear in the dwarvan ranks. The clerics readied themselves.

"Remember, the only way to kill a vampire is by fire or beheading," they warned.

Moments later, the hidden dark elves attacked, quickly regaining the ridge.

Chapter Fourteen

Melgor had escaped from the Zigar-Shan orcs and their patrols, but as he rode further, the air unexpectedly rippled and churned, bringing him to a halt. A shiver of fear ran through him, and he thought that Taza had arrived. Two men and a woman stepped out of the void, members of the Dormin Warlock Council.

The sorceress, old and stately-looking, said, "This is a gift from Lord Taza. You should not have been using magic."

Melgor held up his hands, staff in his left. "Taza has no time for an ant like me. Let me go about on my business, and everyone will be pleased."

He was biding time for his staff to draw energy from the surrounding elements.

The sorceress, head held high, replied, "Taza wants to rid himself of your troublesomeness."

"I have done all he has asked. There is no reason for this," he replied vehemently.

The self-assured lady was about to reply when Melgor released power from his staff. An energy beam red as blood streaked across the short distance, burning through the sorceress's protection spell and throwing her ten paces backward to land stunned against a tree.

Melgor rolled off the horse to his left, casting dart-like magical arrows in hopes of disrupting the spells about to be cast at him. That stopped one warlock, who struggled to remain upright, but the other dodged the missiles and cast a force spell that brought down the tree Melgor hid behind.

Jumping clear, he cast a devastating spell that drew lightning from the sky. He ducked behind the splintered stump of the tree, which was all that remained. Bolts of lightning struck amid the council members, tossing them around like ragdolls. In the chaos, his horse screamed in terror and galloped away. The sorceress remained on the ground. Melgor concentrated on the remaining two warlocks, presuming the sorceress was dead. One cast a similar spell, striking the stump of the tree with a power that sent Melgor head over heels from his hiding place to land in a heap on the leaf-covered forest floor.

He had to act fast, as the other warlock's lips spoke the words of a complex incantation that could have ruinous effects. Reaching out with his staff, he swept it over the ground, forcefully launching a whirling disk of power that propelled the man back into the trunk of a tree. His body tingling with warning, Melgor rolled aside and to his feet, narrowly avoiding a bolt of lightning cast by the other warlock. As he sprang upward, a fireball appeared in his right hand, and he threw it toward his attacker, hitting him squarely in the chest. The man screamed, and he dropped, rib bones protruding through the devastated flesh.

Knowing he was no longer a threat, Melgor raced toward the warlock he had knocked aside. Rising to his knees, the warlock pointed his staff at the onrushing enemy and jerked it upward. Melgor felt the force grip and flip him backward, knocking the wind out of him. He was fortunate that his opponent took time to rise to his feet and shake off the remaining effects of his collision with the tree before summoning another spell.

Melgor had just enough time to regain his breath and start rolling again, narrowly avoiding the brunt of a raw lightning bolt that struck where he had just been. As the bolt blasted the ground, it caused a minor earthquake that lifted him and slammed him back into the foliage- covered rocky soil. He cried out while still in midair and sent an electrical charge at his attacker, striking him to the ground.

Melgor could not rest. He must be sure he had taken out the warlock. Up and running in an instant, he covered the distance to the fallen warlock in the flicker of an eye. As the man lay moaning on the ground, Melgor used the butt of his staff to strike a mighty blow to the side of his enemy's head. As the man lay moaning, blood streaming from his mouth, Melgor struck again, collapsing the man's skull.

He was about to turn when a red plume of energy hit the ground to his right, sending him careening into the same tree the man beneath his feet had crashed into. The blow numbed his mind, and he could not hear anything. As his eyes focused, Melgor saw the sorceress he had believed dead, standing where she had fallen. Nearly out of magical energy, Melgor pointed his staff and intoned one last spell, sending iron spikes speeding her way. Still woozy, the highbrow sorceress saw the inbound spikes too slowly as twelve spikes pierced her body and emerged from her back to stick in a distant tree.

She stared, eyes wide and open-mouthed. No sound escaped; she collapsed and died.

Melgor tried to rise to his feet, but when he attempted to push off from the ground, he felt an ache in this right arm. Puzzled, he looked down in shock to discover that it was missing from just above the elbow. Blood pumped out of the wound. If he didn't do something quick, he would be dead in moments. He turned his head and vomited. Wiping his mouth with his left sleeve, he dove into his bag and withdrew a healing potion. He gagged as his teeth grasped the cork and pulled it out. Instantly he downed the contents, dropped the bottle, and grabbed two more draughts. The blood slowly coagulated, reducing his dizziness and nausea.

Using his staff, Melgor struggled to his feet, his body feeling the worse for wear, even after using the healing potions. There was too much damage. He still was bruised and scratched from head to foot. With difficulty, he hobbled over to the bodies and quickly rifled their pockets for anything useful. When he reached the sorceress, a beautiful woman with long raven hair and lavender eyes, he tore a strip from her dress and wrapped the stump of his arm before spitting on her corpse.

"That's for my arm."

The wall in front of Celedant and Padrig creaked open. The grating of stone on stone made them wince as the bottom of the doors ground over loose pebbles. The pair lent their weight, pushing against the stone doors until they opened enough to let them inside the unfinished chamber. It contained nothing. The only sign that anyone had been there were stone chips that the stone wrights had left on the floor when the work was abandoned.

"Let's test it again before we go inside," Celedant advised.

The door had to be pushed hard to close, but when Padrig tested it, it opened much easier.

Inside, Celedant placed his Staff, the leather case, sword, and pack against the wall. Padrig did the same and began working on a small fire with the burned-out torches.

Soon the smoke from a cheerful blaze fire drifted up the tunnel toward the surface, helped by a breeze exiting from the hole to the underworld. This meant they had to keep the outer door ajar for the smoke to disappear up the passage. Celedant added a few chips of fragrant wood to dispel the odor from the battle site and make the air bearable.

Sitting down, Celedant warmed his hands by the flames. "After we finish, you might want to have that hole plugged, or more deadly creatures might venture into these passages."

Padrig agreed. "Yes. I'll report this incursion to the Regent's advisors. They will have it blocked." With trepidation, the dwarf asked, "Celedant, should I leave ye alone now?"

The wizard smiled. "We have a jolly fire, and I have placed a blocking spell on the doors to keep them stationary. That small crack serving as our flue cannot be opened. If a force powerful enough should manage to open or close it, we will be prepared. This is a haven for the time being. If you don't mind, I would like to rest now."

"I am feelin' a bit tired me self," Padrig agreed.

"We can rest in peace. But we need to save fuel for the fire for when we awaken."

They doused the blaze and lay down in darkness, falling asleep instantly. Celedant and Padrig awoke at about the same time, each hearing the rustling of the other in the darkness.

The wizard broke the silence. "Here, Padrig, I took the liberty of tearing my blanket to start the fire. We can go ahead and use up the torches. Once my duty is performed, I'll be able to light the way with my staff, Forestae."

The dwarf set about with steel and flint, and soon a small fire cast shadows about the room.

Celedant instructed the dwarf. "I would have preferred to accomplish this alone, but considering those creatures we faced, I am glad you were along. You must keep what I am about to do a secret. You will not understand the language, but keep to the corner and be quiet."

"Yes, Celedant, not a word," Padrig replied as he shuffled to a corner.

Hority and Morganna desperately searched for the vampire, but Tarquin saw him first, standing next to the cave opening the dark elves were passing through. Looking for a way to reach him, Tarquin located a narrow path that led up the cavern wall to another tunnel and past the Illanni's attack position. Jumping upward, he grasped the edge of the path. It was narrow, but a borderer was trained to make use of the smallest trails. The darkness and his forest green uniform blended into the shadows. In moments he was above the vampire, twenty feet below. Tarquin wondered if he could survive the jump.

Mentally preparing, he stepped off the path, feet aimed at the vampire's shoulders. When his weight hit, both of the vampire's shoulders were crushed, sending the creature crumpling to the floor. Tarquin saw another dark creature as he toppled forward, slamming into it, which broke his fall. As he lay stunned, it reached down and hauled Tarquin into the air. The prince could smell fetid breath and see long fangs glistening in the torchlight.

"It's not often that a meal is dropped right into my lap," the vampire snickered.

Shaking his head to clear it, Tarquin managed to whisper, "You forgot one thing." He quickly raised his sword and with a strong forehand, sliced the monster's head off. The vampire dropped him as it exploded into ash, giving Tarquin barely enough time to catch his breath before two Illanni attacked. If it hadn't been for his magical sword, Dragon's Bolt, all would have been lost. The prince spun it into the air and easily beat them off, wounding both.

Tarquin regained his feet and glanced at the vampire he had crushed, watching in astonishment as its body began healing itself. He waited no longer and with a quick swipe of his sword, it, too, became little more than dark ash that littered the cave.

"Well, that is that." Tarquin sighed aloud, nearly missing the horde of dark elves that now descended on him in fury. He dispatched one with ease before he saw a stalactite that offered cover. Making a dash for it, he realized that his right foot and ankle ached. Fire was running through them. Had he broken them in his fall? Peeking around the corner, he watched the Illanni fall back as the dwarves kept charging the retreating enemy.

An Illanni ran past and jumped into his hiding place. They looked at each other in surprise until daggers were drawn to commence a life-or-death struggle. Both had the other's wrist holding the daggers. One would gain the edge, then the other. Then, Tarquin brought his hurt leg up, knee crushing into the dark elf's small ribs. Air whooshed out of the elf, which was enough for Tarquin to drive his dagger into the dark elf's heart before collapsing as his bad leg gave out.

Moments later his friends ran through the advancing dwarves to gather near Tarquin, whose right leg was propped on top of the dead Illanni. Hority rushed to examine the ankle while the others assumed defensive positions.

"What happened?" Botreg asked.

After Tarquin explained his attack against the vampire, Botreg admonished him.

"What in the world were ye thinking? Jumping on a vampire. I taught ye better than that."

Tarquin was about to defend himself when Hority's prodding brought a deep grunt of pain. The Clorian tsked and muttered casting a few minor spells that eased the discomfort.

"Well, me fine prince, being a hero has fractured yer lower leg and ankle, and some foot bones might be broken as well. Eldahir, find two splints to bind his leg because I know it will take twenty dwarves to keep him out of this fight." He waved his hand, shooing the elf away.

A short time later with his leg in a splint, Tarquin hobbled up to Generals Bull and Minebeam, who were closely examining a map with their officers.

"Stupid thing to do, but also brave. How did ye fare?" the brutish dwarf grumbled.

Tarquin pointed at his leg. "Fractured, the cleric thinks. He spoke magic words, and the splints help. I'm a little less nimble, that's all."

"Good," Bull replied. "We have permission to follow them attacking Illanni, if possible."

"I'll gather the Borderers," Tarquin said. "They fled up those three passages. We'll take the lead while you organize your troops."

The other Borderer leaders gathered two companies, taking the outer tunnels while Tarquin and the depleted Borderers, who had fought under Lieutenant Stonebreaker, approached the middle tunnel. The young prince had seen many Illanni escaping this way. He was sure that the enemy was leading the dwarves into a hasty trap.

After traveling some distance, the company stopped, stooping behind boulders and tumbled stone piles. The tunnel ahead was pitch black, and even with the dwarves' excellent underground eyesight, there was almost an unnatural darkness. Behind them, the cavern filled quickly with dwarves. Torches had been lit so that order could be restored. Tarquin motioned to Botreg and pointed at the torch, miming throwing it into the tunnel. The torch flew through the air and bounced, with sparks shooting off it before disappearing into the darkness.

A spell had been cast to hide the far end of the tunnel, just as suspected. Eldahir called forth a counterspell, sending a barely visible lance of power that exploded against the wall and dissipated in the darkness, revealing a huge force of Illanni before they charged.

Leading the way were several vampires, who had settled on brute force rather than wait for the dwarves to attack the smaller cavern behind them. The two Illanni vampires took leaping strides, landing among the Borderers gathered at the tunnel opening.

The dwarves fought back, but the powerful undead creatures tossed many about as if they weighed nothing. Tarquin's sword gleamed red as he thrust its blade into the nearest foe. The sword pierced the monster's right side, and as it howled in pain, Morganna cut the head from the beast. As it exploded into ash, Tarquin turned to see Ralav on the back of the other vampire, slicing through its neck until the head fell off. There was no time for triumph. The Illanni soldiers charged from the tunnel, and the tumult that ensued was titanic as hundreds of Illanni swarmed each of the three tunnels, led by vampires.

They attacked ferociously, overwhelming some of the dwarves' closer units. Instinct made Tarquin turn and strike at an Illanni that jumped at him. Hority was beside himself, wielding his branch to strike down as many dark elves as possible. Morganna and Ronli stood back-to-back, driving away any that dared attack. In no time, a pile of dead accumulated around them. Ress used her spear efficiently to stab here and there, alternately using the spiked butt.

There was no order to this battle fought deep beneath the mountain in tunnels where flickering torches cast undulating shadows along the rock walls. A never-ending stream of Illanni advanced up the tunnels, while dwarvan reserves pushed back at the dark elves. A short time later, Tarquin and his friends, along with a handful of borderers and regular dwarvan troops, fought their way out from the mouth of the tunnel to a small incline in the new cavern.

There, they formed a semi-circle, fighting desperately to keep the Illanni at bay. Tarquin kept an eye on the other vampires, knowing that he alone might have to confront them one by one. Morganna could help as well as Botreg, but he knew in his mind that his sword, Dragon Bolt, could be used to better effect. As he watched, he saw the other vampires hauled down by sheer numbers never to rise again except as exploding ash.

Soon the battle began to turn as more dwarves funneled into the cavern. Tarquin and his band of mixed friends, borderers, and heavy infantry followed the dark elves foot by bloody foot through another tunnel. The Illanni formed a defensive line following the contours of the next cavern. Still, Tarquin led hundreds of dwarves, who crashed into their ancient foe.

Knowing that these same dark elves had willingly spread a vile, despicable disease like vampirism urged the dwarvan forces onward. The Illanni did not have the numbers to hold their attackers. They had lost too many in the fighting, so they started falling back. Foot by foot they gave way, retreating backward toward a small tunnel.

Between attacks, the wounded were carried away, while singularly and in pairs, the dark elves disappeared into the small tunnel.

Tarquin raised his voice above the din of battle.

"Hold, let them run. Bowmen - see how many you can bring down." Those dwarves that still had arrows began shooting at the enemy as they fled for their lives. Morganna and Eldahir knelt ahead of Tarquin, sending arrow after arrow into the pack until their quivers were empty.

The dwarves fell on the Illanni still living as Tarquin ran to the smaller tunnel.

"Use boulders, rocks, bodies, anything to stop up this tunnel."

When it was done, the commanders left fifty dwarves to guard the smaller cavern. Tarquin's friends escaped the battle with just a few scrapes. It was a glorious triumph!

CHAPTER FIFTEEN

Tibersu was beside himself. Because of their incompetence, his generals were discovered and had failed, unable to even start the campaign. He had learned that it was Prince Tarquin who had led the assault on his forces. Three of his generals had died in the battle. The fourth brought him the wretched news and recounted to him what was left of the Illanni forces.

The short, bearded ones had bested his forces. Tibersu was furious. Taza was sure to be enraged. The Illanni leader sat motionless in his chair. There was nothing to be done. His generals had let him down, and the dwarves had routed his finest warriors. There was the distinct possibility that Tarquin might have died in the battle, but he was unsure. He would report his uncertainty to Taza. The vampire valued his life, so he would not lie to his Lord.

Tibersu took off the medallion he wore around his neck and placed it on the marble tabletop next to him. Concentrating on the medallion, he called out to Taza.

After a few moments, Taza's voice echoed in his mind. "What is it, Tibersu?"

"The forces we sent against the dwarves were discovered, and a great battle was fought. Prince Tarquin was among the dwarves, who had overwhelming numbers and drove our forces from the caverns. There was much loss of life on both sides. I cannot be sure, but Tarquin may have survived the battle, or he could have been killed. There is no solid evidence either way."

Sitting in his tower, Taza pounded on the arm of the throne in an effort to calm himself. "What went wrong?" he asked venomously.

"The dwarves discovered our soldiers as we were mustering for the attack," the

Illanni vampire said. "We were never able to enter Southgard. Our undead kindred suffered greatly as they tried to hold their lines."

Taza sighed, and Tibersu could hear frustration in his cold voice.

"A mistake like this should not have happened. Kill your generals. Replace them with more eager and imaginative vampires. If there are things in Illan."

"Yes, my Lord. It will be done. You should know, however, that three of my generals were killed in battle. The fourth will pay for his ineptitude in a painful and prolonged way."

"I will not punish you this time. However, if you fail again, you will feel my wrath."

Celedant untied the leather case that contained the Staff of Adaman while he walked to the center of the room. The wizard was aware that Taza would know he was using the staff, but what he was about to do was important to the quest. Standing silently, he held it aloft in both hands. He heard Padrig gasp. Celedant began speaking in a strange language that had not been uttered since the dawn of time. With each word, the bejeweled staff glowed brighter, forcing Padrig to cover his eyes.

Using the power of his mind, Celedant called out, "Adaman, this world needs your advice. The balance of good and evil rests on a knife's edge. The slightest miscue could send it sliding in either direction. I, Celedant, a wizard of Dragon Isle, humbly beseech your aid."

In his mind, the image of the haggard old man sitting cross-legged in a field came to mind. Ancient oaks dotted a beautiful meadow covered with a multitude of unfamiliar wildflowers in full bloom. The old man appeared to be meditating, although why a deity would need to meditate was beyond the wizard's knowing. Adaman opened his eyes and made contact with Celedant. Those fathomless depths contained so much hidden misery and elation that in the deep chamber under Southgard, Celedant fell to his knees.

A strong voice resonated in his mind. It was unlike the voice he had heard previously.

"Until you had approached me earlier about the case for my staff, I had forgotten that small world for a time. For many eons, I had hoped the seeds of goodness would flourish without interference."

"No matter how many seeds are sown in a field, my lord, sickness, weeds, and briars still appear. Your sister's staff was revealed to a vampire warlock - evil beyond description. I do not believe he is of this world." Celedant bowed his head. "I hope I did not overstep my bounds by calling upon you once more."

Adaman laughed. "Not at all; that which upsets my sister brings me joy and laughter."

A moment of silence followed, and suddenly, the old man appeared inside the cave. Seeing this, Padrig fell prostrate on the floor. Although this was not a dwarvan god, he instinctively knew that this was indeed a deity, possibly more powerful than the others.

"Come, sit at my feet, Celedant, so that we may converse in comfort."

The wizard was grateful. Kneeling on the hard, stone surface of the floor was uncomfortable. "What of Padrig?"

Adaman smiled knowingly. "The young dwarf has fallen into a state of animated suspension and will be released once I have gone from here. Our words are not for his ears."

"I understand."

"How do the dragons fare?"

Celedant smiled. "They prosper, and in times of need, offer transport and aid. I have bonded with their leader."

Adaman laughed. "Ha. That is good. I always liked those ancient winged beasts. Your bond adds credence to what you say. Now tell me. Does the case for my staff give you the protection you need?"

"Yes, my lord, and I discovered that by loosening the ties a bit, I was able to use its power to help in desperate need, without it overwhelming me."

Adaman nodded, pleased with the wizard's discovery. "Good. Now what evil is my sister's staff perpetuating?"

"The Staff of Adois is being used in an attempt to dominate Muiria. Taza, the warlock I mentioned earlier, is using it to bring forth creatures from beyond the void. These creatures have wreaked havoc on our world. My companions and I wish to secure the Staff of Adois in hopes of destroying both staffs. Yet as you know, the staffs are linked so that each staff knows the location of its twin. While the case hides your staff quite well, when I am forced to use it, its location is broadcast like a beacon."

Adaman had tears in his eyes and a quaver in his voice when he spoke. "I was naive, still young in my godhood. I thought the staff would be a beacon of light and purity, offering creatures of goodness a peaceful existence. Unfortunately, it turned out to be a fantasy. How could I be so foolish as to think that I could simply turn a world to peace and prosperity with just an artifact? Nevertheless, I have gained wisdom over the eons."

He paused to reflect. "At the time, I did not foresee that my sister, in her jealousy, would create her own staff – one of immense evil." He shook his head sadly. "How it is that twins can be complete opposites? The staffs have already decimated this world once before. I hoped they had destroyed each other. Sadly, that did not happen."

"Now the world is once more plagued by their destructive powers," Celedant said. "I cannot...if you will forgive my forthrightness, WE cannot allow that to happen again. I believe that the destruction of not only certain territories but also a way of life set the stage for what is now happening, driving a dark spike into the crust of Muiria. Had the Illanni not been forced underground, becoming dark elves in their misery and plight, maybe Taza would not have found a ready and willing audience to turn into vampires and expound the evil."

"This must stop. It is not a magical staff that will determine a world's destiny, but the inhabitants themselves. Do you have the means to destroy them?"

"We think we do," the wizard replied.

"There is one way I can help. Secreted on Muiria are magical nexus points. They are situated over portions of the land where magic comes closest to the surface of the world. One nexus is at Edain on Dragon Isle. This is one of the reasons the dragons built the Dragon's Tear there and how the magical community has flourished."

Celedant was deep in concentration, absorbing all that Adaman had to say. One rarely conversed with a god, and the wizard was not going to waste a moment of it.

Adaman pointed to the staff. It shook so violently that it jerked free of the wizard's hand and zoomed into the god's, although that had not been his intent. It came of its own volition.

"Yes, my beauty. It has been a long time since the two of us were together." His words stroked the staff, like a hand caressing a well-loved pet.

If he didn't know better, the wizard would have sworn that it actually shivered in ecstasy. Maybe it did since it had been created by a god with a life and a will of its own.

Adaman sent the staff back to Celedant. "Gather both staffs to destroy them."

"We must travel half the continent to obtain the staff of Adois. We have been dogged by the evil of Adois' staff constantly - since the beginning."

The god smiled. "Perhaps I can help and anger my sister as well. There is a nexus point near your present location. I will place the position in your mind. The staff and you will be drawn to the nexus. Once there, the staff's power and your own magic will be exponentially increased. It is from there that you can travel to another nexus."

"That would be greatly appreciated," Celedant said.

Where do you need to go?" Adaman asked.

The wizard pictured a map of the West in his mind, showing Dormin and its environs.

"The Staff of Adois is located somewhere within the city."

"Hmm," Adaman thought out loud. "There is a nexus in that area, but it is not near the city. I will implant its location in your mind. I'm assuming you can teleport. Any wizard worth his while should be able to."

"Yes, my lord," Celedant answered, "but not that far."

Adaman waved him to silence. "The nexus will have more than enough power to transport you and your companions. It opens a rift that you will step through and exit at the other nexus."

Celedant stood and bowed. "I will heed your words of wisdom and take the nexus to the termination of our quest at Dragon Isle."

Adaman laughed. "Flattering a god comes with consequences. Nevertheless, I tend to favor you. At Dragon Isle, the staffs can be destroyed. If you complete the task, I will be able to hold this one over my sister's head for eons." As he began to fade, he added, "Oh, and by the way, I would duck if I were you."

Chapter

Sixteen

Melgor used a beckoning spell to retrieve his horse. He gathered up his gold and dragged himself onto its back. He had to get out of here. Taza would have picked up on his use of magic and would be sending more assassins. He needed a place to recover from the fight and let the healing draughts take full effect on his arm. The southern hills were pock marked with caves, and it was into one of these that he directed his horse.

He got as comfortable as he could in his bedroll that he placed on the dirt floor, and fell into a deep sleep. He dreamed of nothing other than getting revenge on Taza, but the sorceress at Zigar-Shan stood in his way. He would need an army to draw forth Taza and there, nearby within the ruined city, was an army. He would kill the sorceress. She had not seen his face, and now with a missing arm, he was certain that she would not recognize him. A quick shave and shorter hair would throw off any guards he might come across.

Melgor awoke with a plan, in pain. The warlock tightly bound his arm while downing a vial of potion for comfort. He let the horse go so that no one would recognize it and buried three of the bags of gold. He kept the gems and one bag of gold to grease the palms of the orcs, should it come to that. He needed a retinue to show his high standing, so he set off in search of an orc village close to his present location.

After crisscrossing the hills for several days, he came across a rutted path and the telltale sign of a colony, judging by the amount of smoke that filtered through the trees into the air. He approached carefully and stopped when he saw the guards at a convergence of paths.

"Hoy, can I approach," he called in orcish.

The guards grabbed their weapons and faced the direction from which he called.

Melgor tried again. "I seek to speak to your clan leader."

One of the orcs stepped forward to get a better view of the interloper. "Come slowly, or you die."

"Typical orc," Melgor thought disdainfully. He stepped forward, his lone arm held out to the side.

"What do you have in your other hand?" the orc demanded.

"I have but one arm. Now escort me to your leader before I get angry. I am from the Warlock Council in Dormin."

He stepped into the firelight, and the orcs saw that he was carrying only a staff and a long sword attached to his belt.

"Come, follow me," the orc in charge told him.

The orc wore an assortment of armor, some even dwarvan made, telling Melgor that he had been at the siege of Southgard. Melgor could use that knowledge to good effect when conversing with the leader of these orcs. As they entered the village, the warlock saw several females but only a few males as he was taken up to a house made of saplings for walls and evergreen branches woven together for the roof.

They entered the chief's home, and Melgor bowed.

"I am Melgor of the Warlock Council."

The orc waved him to a seat across from him. Melgor, still not used to having one arm, relied on his staff, making it difficult to sit down.

"Why does a warlock visit my camp?"

"Before I answer that, what is the esteemed leader's name?"

The orc laughed. "I am not esteemed. You look surprised that I know that word. I learned a great many things from the giants and their human mercenaries. My name is Oligog."

The warlock smiled. "It is a pleasure to meet an educated orc here in the wild."

"Tell me why you are here," the chieftain asked warily.

"I am here," began Melgor, "looking for allies that might go with me to Zigar-Shan. I am not liked by the new commander, a sorceress, named Cyra. I need soldiers I can trust and will pay well for their services."

Oligog smiled evilly. "Why don't I take the gold from you now, one-armed human?"

Melgor stared him down. "Because the moment one of your soldiers moves, I will kill every living being within twenty paces."

The orc shook his head. He had hoped to fatten his coffers without having to work for it.

"I tire of warlocks and their meddling. I lost half my people when I went east, and it wasn't even from the war. Disease took most of them. We never fought so hard to gather so little loot."

Melgor smiled wryly. "The Warlock Council was the cause. I was in the West when the invasion started," he lied, "but I have gold enough to pay for the services of your soldiers for a month."

Taking out a gold piece from his satchel, he tossed it to Oligog, who caught it one-handed. His other hand remained on the dagger attached to his belt. The orc stared at the coin.

Grinning, he nodded. "It's real. What can we do for you?"

Melgor joined in the smile and said, "Ten of your best soldiers to act as my guards. Five pieces of gold per guard and ten for you. Fair?"

Oligog took his hand from his dagger, and making a fist in the air, said, "Done."

As Celedant became aware of the stone-cold room once more, he heeded Adaman's instructions, hitting the floor as the swish of an axe parted the air above his body. The wizard rolled to the wall and stood up to find Padrig, with a crazed look on his face, armed and advancing.

The dwarf said, "Lord Taza sends his greetings."

Then - in a mad rush, he charged.

Celedant sidestepped, grabbing the dwarf by the nape of his neck and slamming Padrig's head into the wall. He tried to step back, knees buckling, but Celedant gave him two more bone-crushing blows into the stone. Padrig slid to the floor dead, with a bloody mark on the stone wall.

After gathering the dwarf's maps and the rest of what he would need, he secured Adaman's Staff in its leather case. Celedant used Padrig's keys to open the massive tomb door. As the stone door began to wind shut, he took one last look at the dwarf. He was shocked by the betrayal. Adaman must have known. That's why he made sure Padrig couldn't hear what we were talking about. He shook his head. Tis a fitting grave for a traitor.

Melgor bought a horse from the chieftain. He and ten orc warriors rode toward Zigar-Shan. The orcs that followed were festooned with weapons and kept constant vigil for enemies. After a few hours, they came in sight of the city, and a warlock called Halic, the leader of this small troop of orcs stepped forward.

"As far as your company is concerned, you are mercenaries," he told him. "You are to address me as Talchic. It's an old family name in the eastern city-states to fool the new master."

Halic barked the orders to the rest of the soldiers and asked, "What do we do?"

Melgor breathed deeply; at least Oligog had sent him a bright enough orc.

"Watch my back. They should not recognize me. I have shaved and cut my hair short, and no one knows yet what has happened to my arm. You should do all the talking. I want them to think I don't understand orcish, so I can judge their temperament."

The orc grunted and spurred ahead of Melgor as they reached the gate. In response to the call to halt, Halic replied, "Me have warlock to see the commander of the city."

A cruel-looking orc with filed teeth looked over the company and waved them in, saying, "At the next gate, they decide to let you in or not."

Melgor's group rode through the gate, hardly breaking a sweat. They made good time up the cleared main pathway and were soon facing a large guard. He stood in their way, the spear's butt grounded, daring them to advance.

Halic called from his horse. "Great one, I bring warlock to see your commander."

The giant orc, easily taller than Melgor sitting on the horse, approached, spear ready.

"You half man. No reason to fear you. Go to gate that leads under mountain and ask for meeting with lady Cyra. She commands here."

Prior to a couple days ago, Melgor had never heard of her, which meant she was new to the Council. That had benefits. She would not recognize a false name of a traveling warlock. In daylight, the huge courtyard separating the inner wall and the main gates had nearly been cleared. His foe was meticulous and careful. An attacking force would be under constant arrow fire as they advanced toward the gate. Melgor saw great wagon loads of stone being hauled by mules from the main gate.

Melgor readied himself mentally. He needed to believe that Talchic was his name to avoid slip-ups. He was still astounded by the massive gates, probably made of mythril. Although they looked dull, they would shine silver in moonlight. A company of human guards at the gate lazed around but were dressed in well-used plate mail.

A stern-looking fellow stepped up. "Your business in Zigar-Shan?"

Halic explained why they were there, and the captain of the guards called out to an orc without armor, a message runner. Melgor prepared for the worst and gripped his staff till his fingers turned white. He noticed that Halic sat easily on his horse, but with one hand on his sword. Treachery among these sorts was a well-known fact.

The runner returned, panting. "The lady will see them tomorrow. They may follow me to their rooms."

The captain nodded and waved them through the gate, where they took up positions behind the messenger. He led them upwards through the paths of the city to the habitable regions. There were surprisingly few orcs here, but they all looked like warriors. There was also a mixture of human mercenaries. This both surprised and worried Melgor. Men would be more cautious than mere orcs, who only wanted gold and an easy job.

The messenger led them up two floors from the main hall and stopped at an open doorway. He motioned them inside. "You may keep your horses tethered outside and sleep in the three rooms."

Melgor tossed the young orc a silver coin and nodded thanks.

They disappeared inside. In the morning, he would face his biggest test. Was Cyra really an ally of Taza?

CHAPTER SEVENTEEN

Taza needed allies, and there were no reliable ones to be had. Everything and everyone he had tried, had failed. He could feel the staff continuously exerting power over him. Just holding the ebony staff was becoming a strain. Dare he venture into the void one more time to recruit an army? It was his last resort. Most of the servants had fled the Citadel. The only ones remaining were Taza's guards and the undead he had called forth. There was Rodel the King, whom Taza ignored. He was bedded down with the latest slave girls. For some reason, his personal guards and the commanders of the army had remained loyal and stayed behind.

The warlock paced the marble floor of his tower. After tirelessly going over everything he had learned and done, he knew where he needed to strike to end this. However, to assault Dragon Isle, he needed allies, lots of them, to use as fodder. They would become a simple distraction while he accomplished the final act for world dominance. He used the power of the staff to reach out, penetrating the void in search of creatures. Floating through the endless void, the Staff of Adois found a world, a world dominated by one species separated into clans and at perpetual war.

Usually brash and fearless, Taza was amazed that he felt a pinch of fear as he remembered his banishment to this blighted space, floating for eons. He shook the feeling away and headed toward his intended world. The journey was eventless, and on arrival, he stopped, hovering in the void to examine the best place for his approach.

The world was a dusty tan color, broken by high, wispy clouds. Continents of varying terrain covered its surface. The living race he sought inhabited a small portion of the largest land mass. It was one of savannah, rolling hills, and flatlands covered in lush grass and intersected by meandering riverways. As beautiful as it was, he knew it was not serene. Living there were numerous warring clans of the type he came to seek. Here lay the fodder for the final battle.

All this information was fed to him by the Staff of Adois. It also helped him choose which clan to approach. He did not and never would realize that while in the void, the staff regained its foothold in parts of his brain. Instead of attempting to seize control outright, the staff now calmly infiltrated the undead warlock's psyche.

Taza used the staff to open a rift high above the world and began to slowly circle, descending toward the clan he intended to contact. The sun was bright, but it affected only his eyesight as it was a blue dwarf, an underdeveloped star that, unlike the yellow sun over Muiria, would not kill him if he remained outdoors.

He headed for the clan's largest city, which he knew housed the leaders. The staff had informed him that this clan was on the verge of being wiped from the face of the world by several aligned clans. The city was made entirely of mud bricks. The roofs were formed from the long grasses of the plains and woven thickly to keep out the rain. It was surrounded by a twenty-foot wall of adobe, and great mounds of dirt behind the walls provided a walkway along the top. The dirt had been excavated from a deep trench all around the city.

Taza approached the city cautiously, and he cast a spell to increase the volume of his voice. He did not want to appear unannounced and be set upon by the locals. There needn't be any violence. Using the staff, he drew on its power to speak the local language, a language that was made from the clicks of their beaks, gurgles from their long throats, and the coloration of their plumage to indicate the creature's mood. Taza's magnified voice called forth, assuring them that he was here only to talk.

"I am an emissary from another world, seeking to speak with the city's chieftain."

His plan was to land near the end of the adobe bridge that spanned the moat - a goodly distance that would allow him to disappear if necessary. He would hate to kill a large number of future allies. His eyes were drawn to places along the bridge ingeniously devised so that the defenders could collapse it.

He could feel the magic that emanated from the city, the presence of mages within the walls. The city appeared as if it could hold several thousand creatures when viewed from above. Yet on the ground, he was surprised to discover the multistoried buildings. This was excellent. Surely it contained more than the two thousand troops he needed.

While Taza waited, the walls filled with soldiers, their helmet and long neck armor shining in the sun. Across the bridge at the opening of the city, he could detect no gatehouse, only covered adobe walls with a small entrance that zigzagged into the interior interspaced with arrow slits. Since his arrival, a line of soldiers stood at the end of the bridge. They, too, wore neck armor and helms as well as wide breastplates, and many had leg protection.

They were descendants of bird-like creatures: Long, hairless necks encased in armor with short, feathered heads covered with ornate helms. Similar to the ostrich that lived on the Muirian plains, large chests encased in armor, with muscular hindquarters and birdlike heads adorned with deadly sharp beaks. That was where the likeness ended. Instead of wings, they had muscular arms covered in an abundance of fine feathers that acted as lightweight armor. The Staff informed him that they were called Zartarians.

The muscled arms of the clan members held a variety of weapons, including spears, staffs, and lances, their butts braced against the ground next to each warrior. Most carried shields covered in the rough black hide of a Daskar bull. Behind them were even more soldiers – a square of creatures armed with spears ready to throw in an instant. Taza pondered the wooden implements. He had not seen any forests and then realized the weapons appeared whitened. Instead of wood, these creatures had shaped the bones of the dead into weapons, along with probably most of the implements in their culture.

Taza had to give them credit. Glancing at the moat, he saw that it was filled with many sharpened bones protruding from the ground. Soon the crowd parted, and a huge warrior appeared, followed by a smaller, unarmed Zartarian.

The warrior stood in the center of the bridge with the smaller one slightly behind its bulk. The warrior's feathers gleamed blood red, telling Taza he was ready for battle. The meek one's feathers were grey, a sign that it was frightened.

It cleared its long throat and asked, "What are you? Why are you here on our doorstep?"

Taza bowed just his head, keeping his mouth closed; teeth would have shown he had less than good intentions toward this particular species. He straightened, speaking perfectly in their tongue.

"I bring peace to your land. I request an audience with your King and Council."

The creature's feathers began to lose its dark red coloring as it became less anxious.

"We cannot allow that without knowing of your intentions."

Taza bowed his head. It was galling to humble himself. He was used to projecting an image of power, but the Staff had warned him not to do so.

"I am not of this world. I have traveled through the void in search of allies. As you find yourself encircled with enemies, I, too, witness my clan and its lands in danger. On my world, I am known as a warlock. I believe that in your lands, I am considered a shaman."

"If you are not of this world, how can you speak our language?" the bird-like creature asked.

The warlock answered politely, "I hold deep knowledge. With my staff's innate ability, I am able to discern these facts."

The warrior bowed his neck in affirmation. "I will submit this to the Council. They will weigh the matter. It could take a few days."

Taza bowed. "Thank you for your patience and generosity. I will await the esteemed Council's ruling away from the entrance to your city and off the road in the meadow, so as not to raise suspicions of traders or your town folk."

All the creatures watched as Taza strolled into the waist-high grass and sat down. He had brought enough blood-infused wine in hide flasks for a week, carefully preserved with herbs to avoid decay. After that, he might have to sample the local nectar.

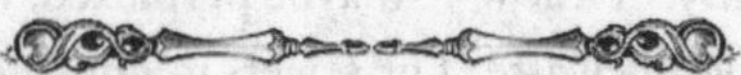

The company sat at a large round table in one of the numerous pubs in Southgard. Tarquin had to convince the owner with extra gold to allow Hority into his establishment. He had promised the dwarf would sit in the corner as far from the paying customers as possible.

Although everyone was well fed, Tarquin was quickly running out of money, due to bribes paid to the pub owners.

Baldo understood Tarquin's dilemma and intervened, approaching the foul-smelling dwarf.

"Hority, I had a dream last night. I was sitting in front of me god, Thierry, explaining what had happened at Southgard. Clor entered in greatly used and smelly garments. Ye should be proud because it was ye that Clor had a question about."

Hority hung on every word, eyes wide. "Ye saw Clor? Ye are blessed."

Baldo told Hority that he had heard Clor changing the codicil of his religion, striking the collection of sewage. "It concerned, as ye would guess, filth, which is the source of yer god's energy and power. Clor was worried, and Thierry motioned me to wait until he was finished. Yer god took out a grimy piece of paper."

This made Hority happy, knowing that his dead Abbot in the far hills had followed the correct codes of writing on well-used parchment.

Baldo continued. "I will tell ye what I heard while in the presence of the two gods. Clor asked Thierry for help in the matter concerning a certain type of filth."

"At what point in yer tenets are ye having this conundrum?" Thierry had asked.

Clor looked concerned while he pointed to the stained parchment, saying, "This will be a radical revision, but it concerns bodily waste."

Thierry looked at the ceiling before replying.

"Clor, old friend, me thoughts are this. The tenets of yer flock are sound. Nevertheless, ye bring up a well-thought-out point; bodily waste appears not to be righteous filth. That kind of waste over a long term might even kill one of yer followers."

Clor nodded. "That is me general feeling. Ye know that me flock is small enough."

Thierry answered solemnly. "Ah, a vast number of followers need not empower a certain god. It's the number of strict and devoted followers that speaks of a god's ultimate power."

"I shall strike this from our tenets, Clor stated emphatically. "Tonight, I shall visit the new abbot to advise him of this matter. It will have to be in his dreams since he followed his predecessor and walled himself up in a very small cell."

Baldo looked at Hority. "I know ye maybe perplexed. However, ye must follow Clor's tenet concerning bodily waste. The sewers might be off limits."

Hority jumped from his seat, calling out to his friends, "I need a bath. I need a bath. Where can I find one?"

Tarquin shook his head, turning to Baldo. "Where did you come up with that idea?"

The dwarf continued eating, saying between bites, "Even devout and solemn clerics can have a sense of humor. In addition, I have at least cleaned up little Hority for the present."

"Thank the gods for that," Tarquin replied gratefully.

Chapter

Eighteen

Lord Grimilzor sent a message in response to one from Celedant. The wizard and the others were to meet with him early that evening.

The day passed quickly, and soon, the company passed through the entrance hall to the palace complex. Large, beautiful murals and tapestries of the finest workmanship covered the walls, while guards dressed in plate mail stood in their appointed places.

The band of friends were met by a courier and led to the regent's private, oak-paneled dining room. He bade them wait there while wine and ale were poured. They sat at a huge oaken table, drinking from silver mugs. Hority was downcast as the company filed in and took their seats, for these areas were kept sparkling clean. He surmised that an evil god had placed a cleanliness curse in this area. He would be sure to ask Baldo to pray with him over it tonight.

The table could have easily seated double their number. The head of the table was wide, while the length and width narrowed as it progressed down the room, much like an arrow point. Long ago, it had been carved thus so the regent could speak to all his guests.

Grimilzor entered alone as Celedant had requested, leaving his royal guards at their stations at each entrance, faces etched like worn stone. His tankard was filled, and several of the others enjoyed ample refills, kept cold by ice that filled a long tub spanning a sideboard. The ice had been brought from the peaks of the surrounding mountains.

The larders had been running short during the siege, but dwarvan hunters had bravely combed the hills to the east for animals not soiled by the orcs, who had camped in the surrounding valley. It would be some time before the river was dammed properly and cleansed for fishing.

The meal began with venison soup, followed by tender cuts of venison and boar swimming in luscious gravy. Normally, an array of vegetables would also have been served, but the shortage made that impossible. When the dinner was finished, Grimilzor called to the sentries.

"Make sure no one disturbs us, lads." Receiving a nod, he turned to Celedant. "Why did ye ask for a secret meeting. Although I must admit, this was the grandest gathering I've had in many a week."

Celedant spoke in a deep, resounding voice.

"I'm reluctant to ruin your mood, but I have dire news. Taza has planted spies throughout the eastern kingdoms. Eldahir thinks these spies caused the deaths of the Wood Elves' King and Queen."

Grimilzor sighed and turned to the elf. "Me condolences, Eldahir. I had the pleasure of meeting them both. It was a sad day when they were cruelly murdered."

The solemn elf nodded thanks.

"I just completed a journey in the depths of Southgard with a dwarf who tried to kill me. He told me that Taza would triumph. I am sorry to inform you that the dwarf was young Padrig, your new cartographer since his father's death in the siege. You are new to the city and may have spent time alone with Taza spies. However, I was able to take care of one worry, young Padrig."

Grimilzor took a long pull from his tankard. "Dire news, dire news indeed. That means I canna trust anyone. Even dwarves I have served with for years."

Baldo spoke up. "My lord. In the absence of Abbot Hortus, may I speak?"

The dwarf lord waved a tankard of ale in his direction.

"Any ideas at this crucial time are welcome."

He continued. "I believe Aegir and Hority will agree with me. There is an old spell rarely used except by some of the novices in training. These spies will be well hidden and possibly have an enchantment to help them integrate into yer society. This simple spell will detect one that is masked or has evil intentions."

"Ho, Ho!" Celedant laughed. "I had forgotten about that spell. Often when searching for a solution, one tends to seek out a more complicated means, overlooking a simple one that would do."

"I, too, can see the true nature of a being," Azimuth added. He turned to Celedant. "If I had been with you on that journey, I could have helped you avoid that near-fatal attack."

Grimilzor thought a moment, scratching his beard and downing his drink. The new Regent asked, "Brother Baldo, are there enough of yer fellow clerics here to begin the process of identifying potential enemies? I think we should start by testing the staff, servants, and soldiers here in the palace complex."

Baldo nodded.

Grimilzor beckoned a nearby soldier. "The Palace is to be sealed immediately by me order. Baldo, Azimuth, what think ye of this fellow?"

Azimuth magically examined the soldier and gave a nod of approval. The cleric answered. "He is brave, me Lord. I will send word to the hospital wards, asking for volunteers. Once they arrive, the process can begin in earnest. Ye should first have yer immediate guards and advisors within the complex checked. I will gladly help, and I am certain that Aegir and Hority will lend a hand."

Grimilzor looked back at Celedant. "One significant problem solved. What other problems do ye lay at me door step?"

"I just wanted you to know we will be leaving soon, old friend," he said with a grandfatherly smile. "There is much to be accomplished and very little time."

Grimilzor nodded. "I wish ye all well in yer endeavors. A toast to our combined success."

All in the room raised glasses or tankards and drank in unison. As the others left, Baldo, Aegir, and Hority stayed behind.

"There will be only a single doorway located by the main entrance to this area, Aegir," Grimilzor told him. "Would ye go and begin the monitoring there?"

"Of course, me lord."

Grimilzor turned to Baldo. "I would like ye to remain with me until the clerics clear the present palace staff."

"It would be an honor," Baldo replied. Catching the Regent's meaningful look, he turned to Hority. This would be a way to keep the dwarf busy and out of trouble. "We need someone to check the drainage ways for overflow of rain and many streams in the mountain to keep the city dry and to see if the gates are intact and solid."

Hority was so excited, he jumped about like a puppy ready to play, eyes practically bulging out with excitement and pride.

"Clor be praised! I'll be off right away. Me nose will lead me." He ran out the door his nose sniffing the air before anyone could stop him.

Taza waited two days before the warrior with light red feathers, and the smaller emissary returned.

"The council has agreed to hear you. Please follow me," the nervous emissary said.

He and the warrior led Taza across the bridge into the Dorman through the zigzagging, covered defensive entrance. When they exited, the avenue was crowded with curious onlookers. The three marched through the streets until it opened up onto a circular adobe building, much smaller than the rest.

"It is dark within, and only members and their guests may enter," the emissary informed the vampire.

He pulled back the hide that acted as a door, and Taza stepped into the council house. The darkened interior bothered him not at all. The room was circular and ringed by creatures sitting in oddly-shaped chairs with tables adapted for their long, feathered legs. Taza recognized the Clan Chief sitting on a decorated seat. As he walked the short distance to the center of the room, he felt their thoughts and feelings surrounding him. Out of the corner of his eye, he saw that the council consisted of elders, marked by the loss of feathers and scars from ancient battles that left puckered flesh where feathers would not regrow. He turned to their leader, bowing at the neck for an extended time, a custom to those of power.

"The full council and our most glorious chief would hear your words," an aide to the chief proclaimed.

Taza retold his story, mindful of the need to remain calm and not overwhelm them. When he finished, he waited for the chief to speak.

"What exactly do you want of my clan?" he asked.

Taza bowed to the question. As he spoke, the council hung on every word.

"The other clans have joined to destroy your city and everyone in it. Riddled with jealousy, these clans seek to end your bloodline. The option I offer is another world where you can be free of adversity. I have the power to open 'tunnels', if you will, between the worlds. The one I will open for this clan must be over water, near the shore of an island. The wizards or shaman of this island have warded it, preventing the opening of a rift on its grounds."

One of the council members spoke up. "I am concerned about this sea of which you speak. Most of our clan cannot swim."

"Do you know about boats here on the great plains?"

"Yes," the council member replied. "Many of our brethren have traded with boats from the east. We know how to build them, but we lack a vital source of wood."

Taza closed his eyes, and after a single word to his staff, they heard a great thump outside shaking the ground. A warrior stuck his head in through the doorway.

"The sentries report a massive supply of wood has appeared out of thin air."

His report caused the council members to exclaim loudly.

"We will discuss this among ourselves," the chief declared.

Taza placed a small amulet on the ground in front of him. "You may contact me through this magical talisman. If you accept my offer, start building the boats immediately. Time is short."

There were many open grunts and clacking of beaks, but this was silenced by a deep rumble from the chief. "Please continue."

"I need aid. My enemies are many, and to unify this world, I need warriors like you. There will be fighting on this island for a powerful magical artifact to take peaceful control of the races. In return, I will give you land where you can live free of threat from others with little danger to your clan. Once finished, I will have no more need of you. You can live as you see fit. I leave the council this proposition to debate."

One gangly member spoke up. "What exactly will we be fighting?"

Taza smiled, showing teeth without realizing it.

"Creatures like myself. When you land on the island, the fortress walls will have already been breached in several places. You just need to attack what is left of the defenders. When finished, I will send you to the land that will become your home." Once more, his teeth gleamed yellow in the fires.

This unwitting clan had no idea what type of beasts and magical beings they would face. If they had, they would never agree. Either way, the outcome meant only one thing for them. Extinction!

Chapter Nineteen

Hority finally had something to do. A monk of Clor seldom had many comrades, but now he was traveling the world with close allies. Oh, what a chance to spread Clor's wisdom! He followed his nose to several privies but did not find what he needed. Finally, he had to ask where to find access to one of the many water drains that lay beneath the city.

Following a passerby's directions, Hority soon found one of the iron covers to the waterways of Southgard. He grabbed the handle and lifted, but it did not budge. The iron rim had rusted around the edges, keeping it tightly sealed.

"This will never do." Hority waved his pumice-laced branch over the erosion, and the rust vanished.

He spoke aloud in the empty room. "Clor, may ye find that rust useful."

The second time he grabbed the handle, the cover opened as if well oiled. Beneath it was an iron ladder secured to the tunnel wall leading downward. He descended several steps before easing the lid shut. He did not want to ruin the serene silence of the tunnel with its gurgling water echoing up from the depths. Surrounded by darkness, Hority's dwarvan eyes had no trouble adjusting to the darkness, his eyes quickly adapted to the dim waterways.

Hority paused with tears in his eyes as the water rushed below.

"Clor, I thank ye for sending me on this quest with Tarquin and Celedant," he whispered. "I've witnessed sights never before known. There is much waste and filth in the outside world. I feel the order could grow." He looked around almost guiltily and added, "I hope that was not too presumptuous. In Clor's name."

He began his climb downward. As his foot left the final rung, he turned and looked around in total awe. The tunnel, made from carefully cut stone, was twice his height and at least six feet wide. A stone walkway ran alongside the flowing water, offering safety from the deep waterway. He placed his boots by the ladder so that his feet could better feel the walkway. It was slippery from the water's old overflow. He took his time, turned, and walked deeper into the darkness.

Hority was upset when he came to a tunnel gate after traveling only a hundred paces. The gate was rusted but sound on top. He disrobed and jumped into the cold water, feeling about the bottom. Several iron rods were weak, which he would report to Tarquin. Dripping wet, he climbed out of the waterway, drying himself with the dirty clothes he called a habit. A bit dry and gloriously smelly still, he turned in the other direction.

After a thorough search, Hority found the tunnels to be secured with only minor wear to some of the gates. The search took a long time because he was constantly stopping to examine debris. He would smell the spot and sift through the trash, hardly finding anything worthwhile. Whenever he came across something of interest, he slipped it into his pocket and continued onward. He was many turns of the clock into his search when he came to the set of iron rungs that took him back up into the city, but he wasn't ready to leave just yet, happy that the tunnel continued well past the ladder.

Hority walked along several more paces and halted when an eerie feeling ran up his spine. Something about the area ahead did not feel right.

Blessed Clor must be sending me a warning.

He was glad he had rid himself of his boots earlier. Walking barefoot allowed him to slide his feet silently through the detritus that had formed on the walkway. Suddenly, Hority saw movement ahead in the dark tunnel. He eased forward and dropped into a crouch, flattening his back against the wall to appear as a mere lump in the grey light.

He watched as something moved up the tunnel until he realized that the two dark shapes must have come through another drainage gate.

These trespassers are here to seek treasure under the regent's palace. Contaminators of purity! I have to stop them before they taint the righteousness of a holy place.

Stealthily, the men advanced, a hand ready to draw their swords at a moment's notice while they held torches in their other. Hority noted they both wore black clothing, and their faces were covered. A seething rage built within the dwarf. These two trespassers had come to defile this tunnel, and they were not even brave enough to uncover their faces. By Clor, that smacked of pure heresy, and he could stand it no more.

As the first black-clad man stepped over him, Hority lashed out with his twisted branch and its oddly tied rock. He struck the intruder's right temple, and the human fell unmoving into the water. Seeing the first man fall, the second drew his sword. Before him stood a dripping wet dwarf. Hority used his branch to counter several slashes of the man's sword. Then he dove into the waterway, astonishing his attacker. A moment later, he reemerged several feet down the stream of water, striking out with the butt of his branch. He caught the intruder behind a knee, causing it to buckle. Hority vaulted from the water and smashed his pumice stone against the dead man's head with a bone-breaking swing.

After years of protecting the valley, he knew that if these two had made it this far, the gate had to have been sabotaged. He was still seething that mere sewer rats would dare come into the regent's tunnels.

Aloud he asked, "Is nothing sacred?"

He pushed the men into the water, using his branch to direct the bodies until the branch hit upon several planks. Gathering them, he continued until he reached the breached gate. He would use the bodies and planks to secure it until they could be repaired.

At the gate, Hority discovered that two of the iron poles had been bent to the side, allowing the muckers easy access to the walkway. The dwarf examined the gate underwater, finding a large rusted hole. Straining with effort, Hority retrieved the dead men and maneuvered the two bodies to plug the hole. Using the boards, he did his best to strengthen the side of the gate at the walkway.

He studied his work before returning to report to Tarquin. Looking at his soiled clothes, he knew the worst part was they would surely make him take a bath. Hority had begun to wonder if that had been a specific test placed by Clor to see if he would be a devout enough follower. He was adamant that a mere cleansing would not stop him from representing his god in this quest.

When he returned to report, the palace servants ushered him to a vat of strong-smelling soap and hot water.

As two servants dunked him and scrubbed him from head to foot, Hority could hardly stand it.

He called out, "Me Lord, this bathing is driving me mad."

The words had no sooner left his mouth when Tarquin and Azimuth entered. They exchanged grins, even though they felt sorry for the poor servants having to scrub the wiggling, cursing dwarf. There was more water on the floor than in the vat as Hority flopped and splashed.

Tarquin shouted above the curses. "Hority, what did you find?"

That settled the dwarf for the moment as he answered.

"Several gates need repair. In addition, I ran into some unsavory men defiling the drains. Muckers they be, some of the foulest creatures in the world. They travel the waterways tainting its holiness as they steal Clor's rightful belongings. Then they clean and sell those holy relics. Blasphemy."

Tarquin's and Azimuth's smiles disappeared.

"What did the muckers look like?" Tarquin asked.

Hority described them exactly and gave the location of where their corpses were. When he finished, Tarquin looked at Azimuth, who turned and sprinted out of the room to find the regent.

Tarquin patted the dwarf's bony back.

"You did well, my friend. I will see that Clor's holy place is secured. Now get a meal and rest. We will be leaving soon."

The council on the far world within the void was hardly impressed by a warlock blinking from view. Their own shaman could do the same. The clan chief spoke first.

"The offer is rife with danger. I cannot trust this shaman. He offers salvation, yet showed his teeth at several important points. If he was not lying, he was bending the truth. He did not make it clear, but the land he is offering might be that island. What does the council say?"

The head of the council, a shaman of great power, telepathically gathered what the others felt. He stood leaning on a cane for support. His feathers had long since gone white with age. Even so, he spoke clear and strong.

"Great chief, we share your misgivings. Yet it is only a matter of time before our enemies overpower us, should we stay here. Our neighbors grow stronger by the day. What he asks is a major undertaking. The ships can be built with the aid of our magic. Now that we have significant quantities of wood, we might, and I stress *might*, be able to duplicate the material. It would take every shaman, but it may be possible."

The clan chief listened intently. His decision could save or eliminate the entire clan.

The Shaman continued. "Besides his facial expressions, which could be attributed to his lack of information of our customs, I know the shaman in the room have reason for worry. This Taza and his staff reek of evil. Such vileness I have never encountered. He needs our support to win domination. However, it would be an evil domination, subject to his rule. If we accept the offer, and we will or die, we must be ready for serious complications."

He limped closer the Chief. "We have never supported nor allowed evil to gain an upper hand among us. Yet, now we are pinned between two evils: one, the clan alliances who want to wipe us from existence. The other offers a rotted rope, dangled by evil, to another world."

Many bowed their heads in agreement.

"As I said before, I think it wise to take this rope, but we must be ever so careful. Our supposed fleet will arrive at a distant unknown place completely unfamiliar to us. To do this, we must put aside many of our beliefs. Appearing with our warriors ready for battle, as is this clan's credo, we must be cautious and not rush into an agreement until we witness the situation. I urge caution."

He continued to the nodding agreement of the council. "I would not follow evil to achieve its goals. This offer of land sounds a generous trade for our people, but it is not his land to give. Those who occupy it now will not welcome us. We have looked into his mind, and there is no passion for our tribe. I felt utter disdain deep within his speech. Build the ships - but build them strong. They should not be made to just land on this island. These foes are no doubt powerful since he cannot deal with them himself. It may be better to side with them against him. In any case, our ships must be strong for the civilians. Should there be foul play, we may need to escape this evil."

Thunderous banging on the table from council members filled the air, and the clan chief declared, "So be it."

Chapter

Twenty

Taza returned to his tower room and drank red elven wine with a dash of blood as he reclined on his throne. He wasn't alone for long. A knock sounded on the door.

"Enter."

One of his vampire guards approached the throne and went down on one knee.

"My lord Taza, our spies around Zigar-Shan report a large gathering of troops in the city."

Taza arched an eyebrow. "Do our spies suspect anything else?"

"There is word that Cyra's orcs work on the dwarvan way to the west, clearing the passages so an army may use the route," he declared. "It is done in great secrecy, but we have well-placed spies, and they confirm these events."

Taza took a sip of the soothing wine. "This upstart, Cyra, is making a power play," he seethed. "Go and take this news to the imbecilic king. Tell him I have ordered the army and five warlocks to move south to the mouth of the dwarvan way. Remind him that if he does not act, I will pay him a visit, one that he will regret."

After the guard left, Taza spoke out loud. "All I want is peace! Can't they see that?"

The peace he wanted, however, was not the type of peace that people of light could live with. His peace offered domination, intolerance, and slavery. Even those of the darker arts were beginning to realize that life under Taza would not be easy, but the vampire warlock was powerful. Could anything overcome him?

While Hority was kept occupied, Tarquin and the others, including Lord Grimilzor's closest advisors, met in the regent's smaller dining room, often used for private meetings.

"Is the description correct?" Grimilzor asked.

"Yes," Tarquin replied. "Hority felt he had descended into a holy place and was still fuming about the intruders."

"Me lord, he describes assassins," Botreg added. "Ye might not know, but I was one once."

Grimilzor thought a moment. "We must honor his god. What's his name? Have the engineers work up a small temple that will smell bad. Maybe it can be next to a sewer grate."

That brought laughs from the assembly, and Lord Grimilzor let it die down before continuing. "I am assured the gates in the waterway are being repaired or replaced as we speak. We will adjourn for now."

Taza was in a black mood, certain that King Rodel was frolicking with his bevy of slave girls instead of tending to the duties of the realm. That idiot, he thought. He thinks of nothing but pleasure.

The undead warlock sat on his massive onyx throne, eyes closed as he silently sent messages summoning all that was evil within the city. Moments later, his tower room was filled with every imaginable ilk of foul creatures that lurked within and under the city. Taza took up the staff of Adois and stood among his new allies.

"The King is weak." He raised the staff. "By this ancient artifact, we will prevail. I command you to purify the city in the following nights. The army has marched out the gate, leaving few guards to command the walls of this city. They will be easily overpowered. Soon only the foolhardy will remain, and our strength will grow."

He basked in their roars of delight. Sweat glistened on his forehead, and he screamed, "From this day forward, Taza and the Staff of Adois will rule Dormin!"

Loud cheers poured from the evil throng. The horrid creatures began shuffling down the stairs to commence their reign of terror. The city of Dormin was about to undergo a cleansing so evil, it would go down in the annals of the world as one of the most horrific events to blacken the face of Muiria.

Taza contemplated his next move. Then he got an idea and knew what to do. Once more, he traveled the void, looking for allies. Since the monsters he had brought from there previously had failed to kill the wizard and prince, he needed a force of soldiers to track down and eliminate them once and for all. Feeling the familiar tug of the Staff of Adois, he turned his flight over to it, allowing it to direct. The staff informed the vampire that there was a world that contained a powerful yet evil empire that could provide the soldiers needed.

Before long, he floated downward on the air currents. The sky was a golden yellow, a reflection of a setting sun that did not bother the vampire.

Once he passed through the cloud cover, he noticed a city, the enormity of which reminded him of his own long-lost homeworld. The city stretched for miles in all directions. He wondered how he should approach the denizens of this empire. Below was the city center and a plaza of gigantic proportions. He would land there and await the arrival of the city guardians. If all went well, he would request a meeting with whoever ruled. He floated down to land beside a fountain, where he saw the inhabitants for the first time.

Hideous, he thought. Their body skin was pulled tightly to the right, leaving their faces with a permanent sneer and eyes that were so off-center, it left them blind on the left side. Disgusting, Taza thought. Looking around, he saw mostly females with only a few males. The next moment the soldiers arrived, running in perfect time from every direction. They were covered in plate mail armor either painted or made of solid gold. Even on this cloudy day, the armor gleamed. The soldiers, quickly and in unison, formed a square surrounding Taza.

The vampire waited as the soldiers lowered their spears horizontally to point at him. Orders were shouted in offensive voices, distorted by their twisted visages. The soldiers wore face plates engraved with individualized images from the nine hells and its myriad of demons. The soldiers facing Taza separated as an officer and emerged, wearing red plate mail. Taza surmised the color would make him stand out on the battlefield, daring the enemy to kill him.

Bravery, Taza thought, is a self-centered trait, more akin to arrogance than leadership.

The alien approached Taza, his sword sheaved, stopping within a few feet. In a harsh voice translated by the Staff of Adois, the alien asked, "Who are you, and why do you come uninvited into our city?"

Taza's grin exposed his fangs. "I have come with a proposition for your leader."

The warrior cocked his head to one side. "Why should I allow that?"

"I can offer him anything he desires, including immortality."

"I will convey your request immediately."

Chapter Twenty-One

General Grimilzor lost the battle of Southgard. It had been a rout, yet he retained control of the city under the mountain and a small fortress to the west of the city near the fallen dam. He had never faced defeat before. The battle, however, was one-sided. They had fought countless orcs and encountered never-before-seen creatures. His main aide, Dargan, who had fought alongside him for a century and a half, had recently been promoted to general after the siege. While Grimilzor saw to the rebuilding of the city and all the minutia that it entailed, Dargan was given the task of assembling soldiers to keep the valley and surrounding hills safe.

It was a nearly impossible task. He was determined to amass enough militia to get the job done, but there just weren't many left. He had watched Lord Grimilzor throughout his career, dealing with intricate details like how many extra furriers would be needed, but Dargan did not have the knack for it. Unfortunately, neither did his advisors or commanders. Thus far, everyone he had picked to be on his staff either could not read or could not write well enough to help.

Dargan had just set his mug of ale down on the table when a royal courier arrived. The young dwarf must have run the whole way by how hard he was breathing. He gave a small bow and handed Dargan a note before saying, "Lord Grimilzor asked that I bring this immediately."

"Go outside and refresh yerself before heading back," Dargan told him. "And for the gods' sakes, donna run the whole way."

The courier dipped his head in thanks as Dargan slit-opened the letter, quickly scanning it. "Come to the palace as soon as possible." It was signed with the prominent letter G that Grimilzor used as his signature.

The newly-promoted general called for his horse and was soon trotting back to the city. At least this interruption gave him a break from planning a defense for Southgard's valley. As he rode along at an easy pace, he noticed that many of the burned-down farmhouses were being reconstructed by either their old owners or in cases, where the previous owners had been killed, new families that had received the titles from the Regent's advisor.

That's a good sign, Dargan thought, hoping it would encourage volunteers to round out the small army he was commanding. Revenge was a difficult emotion to control, but he had seen many join up for that very reason.

The gates to the outer wall were manned by grim-eyed veterans of the siege, checking everyone and everything wishing to enter the city. He noticed that along the top of the wall, vigilant dwarves stared into the valley, determined never to have another surprise attack occur like the last one.

Just about every soldier knew Dargan from the stories of his deeds at the dam. He quickly made his way to the stables, where a young dwarf in the old lord's livery took the reins and led his horse away. Dargan took the shortest route to the regent's section of the city, coming up short when he found it closed and two soldiers standing guard.

"What's this all about?" Dargan asked in astonishment.

"Tis the lord's orders," one of the sentries replied. "All ways into the regent's area are blocked. Ye'll have to go through the main entrance."

The general found that odd but traversed the streets until he reached the main entrance. The main door, a huge stone slab, had been lowered, leaving only a single door to its side open as an entrance. It had been a sally port but was now the main access to this part of the city. A throng of dwarves and humans waited to enter. Seeing how long the line was, he walked directly up to the gate. There was no complaining from the crowd as one of the heroes of the battle passed them. The guards immediately allowed him inside. Oddly enough, he noticed groups of clerics gathered about the entryway. This struck him as unusual, but he paid little attention as he continued toward Grimilzor's chambers.

A soldier tapped the shoulder of a young dwarf and sent him hurrying to the regent's chamber with the news of Dargan's impending arrival. The door to the larger meeting chambers was closed, and a squad of soldiers was deployed, facing the gates.

"Why are the doors shut?" the general demanded.

"We don't rightly know," the captain in command replied. "I was ordered to guard this junction of corridors. I am ordered to lead important arrivals to a door down the hall." His expression showed exasperation. "I don't know how to tell who's important or who isn't."

Dargan, who had risen through the ranks, assured him. "Donna worry, captain. Ye'll be able to tell."

He knew which door the captain meant. It was an exit from Grimilzor's dining room.

"Ye must obey yer orders, so follow me to the door. I know where it is."

When they arrived, Dargan found that it, too, was guarded.

"Is Lord Grimilzor all right? Has there been an attempt on his life?"

The guards shrugged. "Sorry, general. They donna tell us anything."

Dargan understood the orders. He, himself, had been in that position too many times and had hated the tedium and boredom. He entered a small hallway to the room where a single guard stood at the far door. Dargan was getting used to this by now and wondered what had Grimilzor so worried. The sentry opened the door, and as Dargan passed him, he gave the general a powerful thrust that made him stumble. His face hit a table with force that he was sure his nose was broken. He fell to the stone floor on his left side, and two guards roughly grabbed his arms, holding him upright at the foot of the table.

"Why, old friend?" Grimilzor asked with tears in his eyes.

Dargan hung his head. He should have sensed his charade was ending.

"All these years I have fought beside ye and come to love ye. Nevertheless, the creature within me guided me hands for the warlock, Taza. I am sorry, me lord."

As he finished speaking, Baldo stepped forward, intoning a spell to Thierry.

Dargan was not going down without a fight. He threw the two guards away from him with tremendous strength; they may as well have been rag dolls. Baldo's spell struck, reveling the monster within. There before the assembly of dwarves and humans stood an Illanni.

The dark elf snarled. "I have no qualms about killing ye, dwarvan scum."

The dark elf dove, sliding across the table, his sword pointed toward the regent's midsection. Grimilzor sidestepped the attack, so that the sword slammed into the back of the chair, toppling it. Grimilzor brought down his axe on the dark elf, severing his spine. In anger, the strength of his blow split through both the body and the table with the steel edge sticking an inch out the bottom of the table. The guards rushed to the Illanni, but the elf was dead. At that moment, the realization hit the regent that his mentor and teacher had been an unknown spy and enemy all these years. Anger and sadness warred within him.

The guards began to pull on the axe handle, but Grimilzor stopped them.

"Leave it. Take the body and let that rat Hority find a suitable place to dispose of it. We are loyal to our king, and this episode will never leave this room. If rumors begin, I will know who leaked it, and ye all will die. From this moment, ye will become me personal guards."

"As ye will, me lord. We will protect ye or die trying," the soldiers answered stoically.

Grimilzor chuckled even in this sad moment and added, "Let's not go too far, lads."

The guards extracted the dark elf, and a servant cleaned the blood off the table. Grimilzor motioned to the axe and told Baldo, "That will forever remind me that no one is completely safe, even a regent of a fortress city. Come, Baldo."

Something warned Taza, whether it was the staff or his intuition, and he quickly cast a protection spell about himself. The front line of troops knelt, and the second line stepped forward, each wielding a strange weapon. Broad beams of energy shot forth, striking Taza's protective spell, but caused no damage.

If it's a fight they want, I'll give them one they won't forget, he thought. He swept the staff in a wide arc, first right and then left. The lines of the aliens were thrown back ten feet to land in heaps. Turning and pointing behind him, Taza called forth the power of the Staff of Adois. A wall of flame appeared before him and rolled away, striking the massed soldiers. Screams filled the air as fire engulfed the soldiers, roasting them in their suits of armor.

Taza called forth in a loud voice.

"Go, underling. Report this to your commander. I will not attack again unless forced to. I came to offer gifts and a proposal to your lord."

Melgor called a meeting of orc mercenaries. "You could earn loot from this place."

"What kind of loot with a city full of guards?" Halic asked cynically.

"Let me take care of that. Once Cyra is gone, the city will be ours."

The orcs made a comfortable place on the cold stones of the of an underground building in the former dwarvan city. They could not tell that the sun had risen outside, but instinctively they got up, lit the candles, and fed themselves and the horses.

Soon thereafter, a messenger arrived, informing Melgor that he should follow him. Melgor took Halic and two of his most valiant soldiers as an escort in case they were heading into a trap. They made good time, climbing two sets of stairs and were soon standing outside a door guarded by two men in plate mail.

Assuming his Talchic personality, Melgor declared, "I have come to meet with Cyra, commander of the city."

A guard silently opened the door. Leaving his two orc companions but taking Halic with him, Melgor entered a sitting room where a harried-looking man sat behind a desk.

"Her ladyship will be with you in a moment," the clerk told him. "Don't upset her. It could lead to dire consequences."

After a short wait, the door opened, and a slick-appearing man with greased back hair met them. "Please enter. Lady Cyra welcomes a warlock of Taza. She tires of orcs."

Talchic nodded.

The valet led them down a narrow corridor and opened a door for them into a conference room. He disappeared. They walked inside to find a woman with an arrogant stance and a white streak running through her raven black hair. Melgor had seen this before on warlocks and sorceresses. It was the Staff of Adois' branding.

"Be seated," the lady said. "My servant says your name is Talchic."

He leaned his staff against the table and used his left arm to pull the chair back.

Seeing his handicap, she asked, "How did you lose your arm?"

He smiled and raised what remained of his right limb. "I lost it in a duel with several wizards."

She mused, "Your name is unfamiliar to me."

"I am from the city-states, where a small portion of my relatives still reside," he replied. "I check in with them from time to time. In fact, I was just there. I was too late for the battle of Southgard and thought I would head to Dormin. It's been an age since I made the journey."

"It is a dark place," she warned. "The undead roam the streets at night, and citizens are abandoning the city."

"I had heard our master preferred the undead to the living, but isn't the council still in control?" Melgor asked.

She snorted. "Those who are left have no power. Most slipped out of town with the citizens." She stated vehemently. "Lord Taza controls the city now."

There was a fervor in her eyes that made Melgor choke. She needed to be removed from the playing board.

"Come. I will show you, my children," she said, getting to her feet.

She led him out the door with Halic following behind Melgor, along with his two guards. A full squad of human soldiers marched alongside her.

She is a megalomaniac and paranoid, he thought. This makes for a difficult situation.

When they finally came to an overlook, she spread her hands.

"See, Talchic? This is my army - twenty thousand strong."

Melgor had seen the siege of Southgard, but he acted surprised at the campfires that spread out before him.

"By Taza's Staff, I have never seen so many soldiers. What will you do with them?"

She smiled wickedly. "This is where you choose to live or die. I march on Dormin. What say you?"

Melgor considered this. It was a trap, testing his loyalty to Taza or her. Either choice, he could end up dead.

He said with trepidation. "I have no love of the undead. I prefer my allies to be of the living sort."

CHAPTER TWENTY-TWO

The alien in the red armor stared in disbelief at what a single man could do and sprinted off in search of his king.

Taza waited. He had played these games before with an underling who implied that the king was too busy to see him. This king, however, did not know he was dealing with a vampire who could outwait anyone before seeking him out with the Staff of Adois.

From around a corner came a sedan buggy, drawn by yellowish camel-looking creatures. He could only guess what they were. The buggy pulled to a stop in front of him. Seeing no one inside, he climbed into the sedan, balancing himself as it rocked on its springs. He was no sooner settled onto his seat when the driver snapped a whip, and the carriage took off at a terrific pace.

When they entered the city proper, Taza studied the buildings as they sped past. All were made from yellowish bricks, and he figured most were living quarters for the populous of the city's occupants. Taza mentally asked the Staff of Adois what the people were called, but the staff remained silent.

Thinking about the upcoming meeting, the vampire decided to take the upper hand. He had demonstrated what he was capable of doing. If they did not treat him well, the undead warlock was ready to respond accordingly. The sedan moved into an empty space some three hundred paces in circumference that encircled a massive structure, the central citadel. He was driven across an open range used to fire at anyone assaulting the building, through an opening with what looked like a solid metal gate and into the inner courtyard. He estimated five thousand soldiers were being paraded in front of the colorful building – a show of force? Up a long flight of stairs in the center of the building was an overstuffed throne that held a male he suspected was the king.

The soldiers opened an aisle through their ranks, and as Taza descended from the carriage and walked between them, the rear rank closed, leaving him completely surrounded. He could only move forward as the lines of soldiers allowed him. There was nothing nefarious about this, and the vampire soon found himself at the foot of the stairs. The word Eirolings passed through Taza's brain. The Staff of Adois had finally given the name of the people. Apparently, it was not only trying to take him over but now it toyed with him.

He looked up at the king and decided to posture. Setting the butt end of the Staff on the ground, he called out a spell and began to levitate, moving up the stairs, as if floating was ordinary.

The king was dressed in regal finery in contrasting shades of gold and yellow, but he was as ugly as the pedestrians the vampire had seen at the town center.

The proud ruler of a distant world bowed his head to the king. "I am called Taza, and it is a pleasure to meet the ruler of the Eirolings."

The alien ruler looked hard at him. Friend or foe, he was unsure.

"How did you kill so many of my soldiers and fling them about as if they were nothing more than blades of grass in the wind?"

The vampire smiled, baring his fangs. "I used magic, aided by the Staff of Adois."

The regent looked curious. "What is this magic you speak of?"

Surprised, Taza mentally reached out and realized there was no magic on this world. That explained the things that shot out beams. They had crafted mundane materials as weapons. He would like to take one with him to produce for the Illanni. Meanwhile, he had to explain his power, something he had never done before because he had lived on two worlds where magical people were born every day. He found the task distasteful.

"In my world, magic is an ability that a person is born with. Either you have the ability, or you don't. It would appear that this world does not have magic intertwined with the inhabitants." He changed the subject, needing soldiers. "Should I address you as King? Lord?"

Baldo followed Grimilzor into the next room, which was the study. To a warrior like Grimilzor, the place had little value, but a scholar could spend a lifetime amid its dusty tomes. The cleric discreetly closed the door behind them. When Grimilzor reached the desk, he crumpled to his knees, hitting the stone floor as sobs overwhelmed him. The regent pounded on the desk, his shoulders heaving in grief.

Baldo approached the new regent, raising his shoulders until he could see the grief-ridden face.

"May Thierry and all the dwarvan gods walk with ye in the coming times. This was unforeseen and having it be yer closest confidant is crushing to yer soul. Dargan will live on in yer memories as the soldier and common folks' hero. We'll bury him in the Tombs of the Kings with full honors. The people will mourn."

Grimilzor, tears slowing asked, "Me mind is addled. What must I do?"

Baldo squeezed his friend's shoulders. "I will take care of everything. Ye must put on a good face and remember yer friend as he was – a stout warrior who would have died for ye. One of me brothers can help ye forget some of what happened."

Baldo offered a glass full of brandy. "This will help ye sleep."

Grimilzor never saw the fizzing sleeping powder the cleric had dropped into the glass.

Baldo called the guards. "Yer lord needs ye."

They entered and saw him, exhausted and half-asleep. Baldo grabbed an arm, and the guards helped him carry the regent to his quarters, where they gently placed him on his bed.

"I have given our lord a pill that will make him sleep for a day," Baldo explained. "A cleric bearing this will come." He showed them an intricately carved bone, sacred to Thierry. "Do not be alarmed, no matter how Regent Grimilzor cries out. The cleric will erase the worst of what we witnessed today, so let him do his work."

"Could the cleric do that for me?" one soldier asked.

Baldo shook his head. "All of ye and that cleric are now the regent's protectors. Ye must remember what happened and be ever vigilant. I fear Dargan was not the only spy in this city."

Chapter Twenty-Three

The day came when the company had to leave the valley. They rode on horses, leading several pack mules with their food and gear. Lord Grimilzor had provided them with everything needed. They were in good health, and despite the fact that they were heading toward danger and possible death, the members of Tarquin's group were quite jovial.

Hority had acquired mud from the river. His habit was covered, and he wore a contented smile. "I have anointed me self before me god, so Clor will watch over our journey," he declared.

At one of the many fords they crossed, Eldahir leaned over a group of tracks and examined them. "Orc. These were made but a day ago. They head into the hills, not toward the west."

Celedant addressed them all as he turned his horse in a circle.

"Keep your eyes open. From this night on, we must be extremely vigilant. We may not use fires or cook meals. I'm afraid we will have to survive on hard tack and parched corn."

Melgor and Halic sat in the furthest room of their apartment from the doorway.

"We have been invited.... No, Cyra insists that we follow her to Dormin."

"Our mission was to get you here," Halic replied. "Nothing was said about traveling to Dormin." He waved his arm. "Wherever that may be."

"I can offer you no more gold, except for what may be found in that city," Melgor said, nodding in agreement. "Unfortunately, I can't give you any reassurance that we'll find anything. Apparently, the undead patrol the streets, and people are leaving in droves."

"I will follow you," the orc captain informed him. "I have no family and find this offer interesting. I will put it to the others."

Melgor wrapped up to sleep, but it was a troubled rest. He dreamed all night of Taza torturing him until he begged for death.

They awoke as the sun rose in the east. As Melgor broke his fast, Halic approached him.

"I told the others, and three want to continue on to see if there is gold to be had. The rest will travel back to the village."

"The others must keep our secret, or I will roast them over a fire."

"They will listen to me," Halic reassured him. "The chieftain has ordered us to care for you, and they dare not go against his word."

Later that day, a messenger arrived and gave Melgor a letter bearing his false name.

He cut through the wax seal and read the short note.

Talchic,

My forces leave tomorrow, using the dwarvan tunnels through to the other side of the mountains to march on Dormin. If you would join me, come to my chambers as soon as possible.

Cyra

Finishing his ale first, Melgor went to Cyra's chambers and found several high-ranking men and orcs in attendance. They would meet in the lower hall tonight, ready to march in the morning.

Returning to his rooms, Halic said goodbye to the orcs returning to the village. Melgor also penned a note to allow them to exit the city and not be enlisted into the attacking forces.

"Good luck to ye," his note concluded. "I've not dealt with better orcs."

That night, the four remaining members of Melgor's group worked their way through the halls to a position near the front of the army. No one was certain what they would face on this journey, but whatever it was, they wanted to be ready for it.

Chapter Twenty-Four

In the Palace of the Eirolings, the hideous creature answered Taza.

"You may call me King. How did you come here from another world?"

Taza held out the Staff of Adois. "This ancient artifact made by my patron, the Goddess Adois, led me here. It has many powers, and I command it."

"Why have you come?" the Eiroling King asked dubiously.

"I seek soldiers for a mission on my world."

The King looked hard at Taza. "Why our soldiers? Why not your own?"

Taza laughed. "I grow tired of my minions. They have failed to achieve their goals, so I am forced to search elsewhere for better."

The alien motioned to his soldiers. "I have many who serve. This is but a few household guards. What can you offer that would entice me to become involved in your cause? I already control this entire world."

"I, too, know great power, but where there is power, there are others who crave it. Why else would you have an army? I can supply you with what you need most. Whatever is valuable or scarce on this world, I can create more than you will ever desire."

"Our mountains produce little in the way of gems. That is what I wish," the greedy Eiroling king answered immediately.

Taza smiled, teeth gleaming in the golden sunlight. Tapping the Staff of Adois on the ground, he pointed to an area behind the king. "Will that do?"

The King turned around. What he saw took his breath away. He stood up and walked over to examine trunk after trunk filled with costly gems. Lifting a large, unblemished ruby, he fondled it and smiled. He had never seen a ruby nor many of the other gems before. These he could proudly display in the castle.

Taza knew he had the King in the palm of his hand, so he added a warning.

"Remember, to cross me is death. That treasure will disappear in a moment, and I can kill you just as easily."

"I don't renege on my bargains," the king responded angrily. In his position of power, he was unused to threats. "How many soldiers do you want? Will they be returned to me after you are through with them?"

Taza grinned. "I need only five hundred. Once they have completed the task, they can return here." In the back of his mind, he laughed at the king's puny effort to get his troops back. He had the gems. What were the lives of five hundred soldiers to a ruler with so many? Besides, with his help, they would be unable to travel through the void to return home.

A mere wave of the Staff of Adois brought twenty silver staffs out of thin air.

"Give these to your wisest soldiers with my instructions. When they encounter my foes, tap these on any object, and it will come to life and attack their enemies."

Five hundred soldiers drew up in a square and waited for Taza. The warlock vampire tapped into the Staff of Adois and pictured a glen on Muiria. Without a word to the King, they blinked from existence.

Celedant and the others had been riding for several miles when an arrow whistled past, burying itself in the bark of a tree. Eldahir's elven bow was instantly ready, and he shot an arrow back in the direction from which the arrow had come. A scream of pain was followed by the sound of many feet pounding the ground. War cries issued from the trees.

"That's more than a foraging party! Follow me and be quick about it!" Celedant ordered.

They turned their horses to gallop down the slope, riding as fast as they dared on the wooded hill. Battle cries chased them. A final spear was thrown, but it landed well behind the party. Tarquin signaled for them to slow as they left the slope and headed into level woodland.

Once they reached level ground, they found more tracks. When darkness descended, they spent a sleepless night, while Eldahir and Morganna paced around the camp, ever alert for intruders. Their elven heritage allowed them to go for days, even weeks without sleep.

In the morning as they packed up to leave, Eldahir raised his head and listened a moment before darting off into the ever-thinning pine trees. His lengthy departure brought a sense of urgency to the others, making them pack quicker. Most were still tying gear to their horses when they heard the call.

"Mount up and ride! We're being attacked," Eldahir shouted as he ran back into camp.

Just as he burst through the brush, an arrowhead tore through his leather armor, piercing his thigh. He mounted his horse in pain, while several companions nocked arrows and sent them speeding toward the oncoming attackers before mounting up and racing for their lives.

A few moments later, when Tarquin thought they had lost their pursuers, a dozen orcs sprang from behind a large tree trunk that lay across their path and sent a round of arrows sailing toward them. A mule took an arrow to its heart. It stumbled and fell forward; the company charged toward the archers, their horses leaping over the fallen tree. Those orcs that did not scatter were ridden over. Others fell from well-aimed arrows that pierced their thick orcan hides.

A tree trunk hung by massive ropes was swung straight at the galloping riders. Most of the group was glancing back at their enemies when it was released. It swung through the trees and struck the first horses, crushing their legs upon impact. Their riders were thrown roughly to the ground. Azimuth and Celedant skillfully jumped their horses over the obstacle, careful to avoid its pendulum swing.

As Botreg and the others struggled to get to their fallen comrades, a giant came at them from the bushes, brandishing a huge axe. Two ogres lumbered beside the creature, bearing large wooden clubs wrapped with spiked iron strips.

Precious time was slipping by, and if Celedant did not unleash a devastating spell, all would be lost. He drew upon the energy pulsing in the forest and with the addition of his own power, he cast a spell. A pillar of flames descended from the sky, engulfing the giant. He screamed in agonizing pain and ran until he dropped dead, the fire consuming his remains.

Tarquin on horseback rode straight toward the ogres to go between them. At the last second, however, the ogres struck out. The prince pulled hard on the reins but could not stop his forward movement. He was thrown over the horse's head to land on his shoulder and rolled to a stop.

Tarquin drew his red-hued sword Dragon Bolt from its scabbard and stabbed out to his left, right through one of the monster's ribs. He quickly withdrew his blade, ducking instinctively to avoid the oncoming blow from the remaining ogre. As the club whipped past his head, Tarquin continued his turn, hamstringing it. The behemoth stumbled forward, reeling in pain as Ress ran up and thrust her spear deep into the other monster's brain. With that one out of the picture, Tarquin returned his attention to the other wounded ogre. The creature grabbed its side while it tried to swing a club at him. He jumped over the slow-moving club and with a powerful swing of Dragon Bolt's fiery blade, struck the ogre's throat, nearly beheading it.

Taking a moment to catch their breath, everyone checked their horses. Many neighed in pain from deep arrow wounds or broken bones. Since they did not have enough healing potions with them, these injured horses were quickly put out of their misery, a merciful act considering how the orcs would treat them before slaughtering the hapless animals for food.

"I can still hear our pursuers," Eldahir warned them. "They will catch up soon."

"What can we do without our mounts?" Ress asked. "We can't outrun them on foot."

"I have fought many battles in the great swamp in the north. We have a better chance there than if we are caught out in the open by the orcs."

"I agree," Tarquin told the others. "Our remaining horses won't last much longer. They're stand a better chance if we send them north as a decoy, while we enter the swamp."

Hority was about to speak, but Baldo gave him a menacing look.

"I have heard there are numerous trails into the swamp," Baldo said. "Many lead to nowhere. Others will take you through it. Is that not so, Eldahir?"

The elf agreed. "What he says is true, but I stand as good a chance as any of finding the path that will lead us to safety."

Celedant made a quick decision. "Our pursuers draw closer. We must go!"

CHAPTER TWENTY-FIVE

Cyra leaned against one of the battlements, taking in the fresh air. The gentle breeze that blew through her hair felt comforting, allowing her to let down her guard until she felt the evil tendrils of Taza reach out to her.

Cyra opened her mind. "Yes, my lord."

Taza's voice rang in her head. "Any word of the staff and those who carry it?"

"Nay, Lord Taza," the sorceress responded. "It is rumored a band of orcs drove them into the great swamp. Our forces are waiting at the known exits and patrolling its borders. Those who carry the staff will be caught and killed."

Madness filled Taza's response. "Remember - your life depends on the completion of this task. I sent five hundred troops into the area to bring me the enemies' heads."

The evil feeling blinked away, and Cyra once more enjoyed the sunshine.

Smiling, she muttered aloud. "I won't die as easy as Melgor. If it's a fight you want, I am ready to offer it."

Melgor, in his guise as Talchic, and guards waited in the cold underground passageway for Cyra to sound the advance. The stench of unwashed orcs and other creatures surrounding him was atrocious. He had attached himself to a column of well-armed mercenaries. In the torchlight, he could see their armor was well maintained and highly polished.

After what seemed like hours, he heard a commotion, and the soldiers made way for Cyra. As she reached the head of the column, the army began a snaking journey through the dwarvan passage. In most parts, they could only march two abreast, creating a great backup as the column moved forward.

Unknown to the head of the army, bloody fights had broken out at these bottlenecks as orcs of differing tribes fought to be first through the narrow passages. Melgor inwardly sighed, knowing he was on an endless march through what he considered to be a level of the nine hells.

The columns, marching through tunnels and caverns, came to a clumsy halt for a cold meal and whatever rest they could get while sitting up. Melgor shared a small space of floor between a mercenary and Halic. After a period of time, they were up and moving. This went on for days. Late one afternoon, he saw a distant light in the cavern they were marching through, and a shout was raised by the soldiers in front of him. They had reached the end of the passage.

As Melgor breathed in the fresh air as they exited, he believed it had never felt so good. Days of marching with the orcs had unsettled him. Glorious sunlight now buoyed his spirits. He noticed that Halic and the others were happy as well. Melgor had always thought of all orcs as living in caverns and being used to the fetid smells, but not his companions. They had lived above ground and hated this march as much as he did.

Before setting the horses free, Celedant leaned close to his steed and spoke in a whisper. It nickered and nodded its head up and down, then sprang forward into a gallop going north, the few remaining horses following closely behind.

Eldahir took the lead into the swamp, moving swiftly with the others following. The elven warrior led them to a washed-out hollow where the flow of a swampy stream had undercut the topsoil. They slipped into the murky water, their boots sinking ankle-deep.

In the hollow, Eldahir broke off the arrow shaft that protruded from his thigh. He left the companions to wait, telling them to duck down in the wet soil while he scouted ahead. The ground was soggy, and everyone was soon soaked and uncomfortable.

Meanwhile, Hority was delighted about the brown goo through which the water flowed. He slipped into the mud, covering his body with the wet soil, but Baldo reached out and pulled him back into their hiding place.

"Ye should all blanket yerselves in Clor's cloak," Hority whispered. "Clor has been favorable. This will mask our scent."

Tarquin looked oddly at Hority before nodding in agreement. "That seems soundly logical."

The others watched as he slid into the mud. He stopped at his face, and as he climbed out, the others did the same. When Eldahir returned and saw them, he smiled, for he, too, had smeared mud on his body. He pointed to Hority.

"It seems that Clor has provided you with insight to swamp travel," he said quietly.

Hority bowed his head. "Me lord, Clor, watches over all the faithful and their companions."

"Might I ask the mighty Clorian monk, Hority, to see to my wound?" Eldahir asked.

Hority jumped up, dripping mud as he crawled over his friends to sit next to the elf. He began to examine the wound. Baldo of Thierry kept his eyes following what the monk was doing. He was ready to help if needed.

Eldahir looked around at everyone and keeping his voice low said, "I doubled back. The woods are crawling with orcs. Strangely, they avoid the swampy areas, which could be for many reasons. There are monsters known and unknown in the deep swamps. I fought for many years in the northern swamps, but this portion is denser, and I detect more evil radiating from it than any I experienced in the north."

He stopped as Hority finished ministering to his wound, wrapping it tightly to keep the swamp water from causing infection.

Giving the company a devilish smile, Eldahir told them, "Do not worry. I know the swamps as well as any. I whetted my first blade while standing knee-deep in mud. We will make it through."

After the healing, Hority looked up at the elf with religious fervor in his eyes.

"I knew ye to be favored by Clor. Yes, killing yer first enemy in the swamp's mud. Ye may not know it yet, but I would reason that on that day ye were destined to fight by a Clorian in the future. Me god's eyes would have been drawn to that fight. The provider and protector...."

"Hority, we will speak of this later," Baldo interrupted. "We must move on."

"Yes, we must go," Hority agreed as some of the feverish gleam left his eyes.

"I scouted the path we are on," Eldahir went on. "It continues northward but slowly bends to the west. It may take us out of the swamp, but there are many paths we will cross."

As Eldahir and Ralav rose to their feet, the others did, too. They followed along the path, treading softly on the sodden ground, ferns, moss, and fallen leaves that made it more dangerous. They spread out in a long column with Botreg and Azimuth dropping back as rear guards. The path wove through magnificent scenery. The trees had never been forested, and Celedant reckoned it would take more than thirty people to link hands around a few.

The wizard was delighted as he took in the wonders of the swamp until his friend Azimuth tapped him on the arm.

"If the trees are this large and untouched, think of the danger the swamp's occupants might have in store for us."

Celedant agreed. "I was enchanted by something I had not seen in a lifetime. I'm afraid that I allowed old memories to disrupt my concentration. Thank you for reminding me of the danger we face, Azimuth."

"Have your spells detected anything Aegir?" Tarquin asked the cleric.

The dwarf snorted. "It registers danger all about us."

Baldo concurred. "Me own spells are of no practical use. It will be best to rely on only the wards we place about our camps."

They had been following the track for several miles when small runnels of trickling water cut through the path. Most of these hazards were small and could easily be jumped.

Eldahir called a halt to set up camp. Tarquin tired of slogging through the swamp and turned his back to look down the path where Botreg and Azimuth were in the far rear of the column. This would be a wet, miserable camp, but likely no worse than other parts of the swamp.

Baldo and Aegir stood by the bank, discussing the best way to clean the water and make it drinkable. Celedant listened to the debate, interested in its finer points. Much to his surprise, he found their little quibbles often relaxed him. He thought about what lay in store for their group. Tarquin's troops followed him because they loved their leader and trusted his abilities. Aware of potential dangers, they kept their morale up. Hority was one of the oddest dwarfs he had ever met. He could not help smiling as he thought, *On a Holy Crusade against the defilers of filth.*

Chapter Twenty-Six

Melgor, along with Halic and the other three orcs, followed the mercenaries to their place in the wider columns being formed as they waited for other troops to emerge. As the orcs and other creatures got organized into units, the sound of trumpets split the air from behind the hills surrounding them. The banner of Dormin appeared on the crest. Taza's army attacked.

From one side came a loud cry as thousands of soldiers rushed down the hill to attack Cyra and her army. From another hill, a thousand horsemen appeared and charged. The riders came directly at Melgor and the mercenaries. The warlock pointed his staff about ten paces away from where they stood. As the words left his mouth, a long trench opened between them and the horsemen, who tried to halt, but their companions behind pushed onwards. The first rows of horsemen fell into the pit as the mercenaries cheered.

To Melgor's back, he heard the crash as two walls of infantry came together in a cacophony of shields and swords. Those horsemen that had avoided the trench sounded their horns as they charged around it and sliced into the orc battalions. Mercenaries formed a square, making sure that Melgor was at its center. The warlock sent spell after spell into the melee. Lightning struck through them, and columns of fire fell from the sky, raining death on Dormin's forces and unfortunately, the orcs as well. That didn't bother him in the least.

The infantry charge slowed, and the two armies intermingled as fighting continued. Cyra cast spells for devastating effect, and her orcs fought like demons. Dormin's soldiers could not keep up man-to-man with the orc army as more and more poured from the mountain to surround the enemy. Melgor felt safer in the square the mercenaries had formed than with Cyra. The horsemen had trouble getting their horses to jump the mercenaries' shields, and the bowmen in the center of the square kept up a blistering rate of fire.

The horsemen's charge had taken them deep into the orc army. They were now surrounded, and very few could fight their way through. In places, they formed large groups and tried to fight to safety, but riders on the outside of the formation were dragged off their horses and killed.

Realizing the battle was hopeless, the infantry began to retreat, backing out of the valley. They were organized and more compact than the Dormin horsemen and made better headway. Seeing this, the defenders became the attackers, and Cyra sent fireballs and lightning into the crowded formations, while the orcs continued to mount charge after charge. Melgor was surprised by how many spells the sorceress used. His own power was already weakening from the myriad of magic he had expended.

Another horn blast was heard over the din of battle. It was a signal for the archers to appear at the top of the hill in front of the orcan army. They fired directly into the orcan forces.

With the attack centering on the front of the orc army, Melgor avoided the occasional horsemen, making a final run at the mercenaries. He switched from casting magical balls of energy that frightened the horses to casting giant illusions that caused the Dormin forces to swerve away from the mercenaries. His spectrum of offensive spells was depleted.

The Dormin bowmen shot true that day, bringing down orcs with every shot as Cyra's forward troops charged their position. The orcs took heavy casualties, but they were soon among the lightly armored bowmen. It became a rout as the bowmen sought a way to escape.

At the head of the column, Cyra fired off spell after spell as the Dormin infantry gained ground. At the head of the column, more infantry appeared and attacked, but they had expected to charge a routed army. Instead, the orcan army was more or less in good order. After a brief, bloody encounter with the orcs, the infantry retreated up the hill, fighting for every foothold.

Many had nearly reached the sorceress's position when a portion of the orc army exited the tunnels to quickly organize into battle formation and attack.

Atop the hill sat five figures on horseback. Melgor cast a spell that enhanced his eyesight and focused on them. He recognized the five as members of the warlock's council. He watched as the commander urged them forward to use their magic, but they would not. Instead, they turned their horses around and rode down the back of the hill.

Melgor was hopeful Cyra would be killed and save him the trouble of doing it. Yet the warlocks had retreated, and his wish was not answered. She would be spared on this bloody day as the Dormin forces withdrew. Many orcs chased them, but Cyra called them back. Their foe was beaten and scampering back toward the west or to their city.

Ralav, the group's lead tracker, stood and ran for the others.

Tarquin whispered loud enough for all to hear. "Ralav is coming fast."

The old tracker was breathing hard when he arrived at their resting place and motioned everyone to gather around. He made sure they were all there before reporting.

"While I was out there, I heard a series of clicks. The strange thing was that they were circling about me. The clicks sounded like some kind of language, but I could not judge how many were there. I hurried back. When I came to that little rise, I saw a troop of orcs strung out behind us."

Everyone turned to Eldahir for an explanation. "I told you there were strange beings in the southern swamps. I have never heard noises the like of Ralav's description."

"We must defend ourselves against these enemies as well as the orcs."

Eldahir was the first to launch an arrow into the oncoming orcs. The lead one in line dropped dead in the muddy swamp. The others joined in, launching arrow after arrow and picking off the enemy in the now-bloody swamp water.

Eldahir raised the alarm when he heard the loud clicks circling and closing in on the area.

"Hold," he called. "Something is happening."

Out on the trail, the orcs ran toward their prey when something green flashed across the trail, taking an orc with it. Soon it was happening all along the orcs' path. Some fought back, spearing and slinging small attackers away, but this new threat overwhelmed them within moments. Only a few made it to where Eldahir and the others waited. The orcs barely looked at them. Instead, they stared out at the swamp. An orc disappeared as it was pulled down into the swamp grass. The orcs cautiously retreated, swinging their weapons through the foliage.

Tarquin spoke quickly. "Gather all the equipment and pile it so that it makes a small wall where the path continues into the swamp."

While the others packed up and formed their wall, Eldahir stood tall, eyes scanning the area where the noises were coming from. He fired an arrow and heard a gurgling sound as it dealt its target a deathblow. Afterward, an intense keening erupted from the swamp. Eldahir ran, taking his place behind the others where Ress prepared her bow.

The orcs formed a circle as they engaged the creatures. One by one, the sleek attackers slaughtered the orcs. The speed with which they attacked made it nearly impossible to see what was exploding out of the swamp grass.

Dwarves and humans grew quiet as the last orc went down. Oddly, there were no more clicks. They grew restless waiting for the inevitable. Suddenly, four odd creatures charged from the underbrush: reptiles, dark in color but smaller than a dwarf. The reptiles ran on hind legs with tails stuck straight out.

The shock at seeing these odd creatures slowed the group and cost them precious clicks of the clock. Eldahir's bow sang, bringing down another of the creatures. Tarquin managed to wound one through the leg. It limped back to the underbrush. Two others continued their charge.

Being small with strong hind legs, the two lizards jumped upward, perching on the low wall of equipment. Botreg hacked the legs from one and finished it off when it pitched forward. The other landed in front of Aegir. It flexed its small forearms, and six-razor sharp claws came out. Grabbing Aegir, it tried to drag him over the stacked gear. The dwarf swung his war hammer, trying to break the beast's neck without success. As it stopped fighting. Aegir looked and saw Eldahir's arrow firmly embedded in its side.

Aegir tried to crawl back over the wall, but a maddening pain slowed him. He looked down and saw the entire left side of his chest was little more than mangled flesh. Baldo and Hority dragged him back over the wall and began trying to heal his wounds. The clicking noise sounded in force, followed by intense splashing in the shallow water and through the dried marsh grass.

Keeping Aegir behind them, Tarquin and the others turned to see hundreds of the small predators. Baldo left the healing to Hority and shouted a spell that rained fire upon them. Celedant was also active. He conjured up a huge flaming ball that rushed from his fingertips into the milling attackers. Aegir laid his head on a pack while Hority worked quickly, casting healing spells until his patient grabbed him by the front of his habit.

"Me side is healed enough."

Even though the number of dead grew ever larger, the attackers drew ever closer. Soon the small stretch of ground in front of the makeshift wall was piled high with their dead.

Knowing there was no choice, Aegir stepped forward, commanding, "Grab the gear and go. I'll hold them here for as long as possible. Me wounds are too bad to go further."

No one wanted to leave him behind, but the gray expression on Hority's face told them the dwarf was on his last leg. Grim-faced, they gathered belongings. They would not deny him this final act of bravery. The clicks began again in earnest as Aegir watched his friends hurry deeper into the swamp. Turning toward the reptiles, he called fire to rain down on them, watching as scores writhed on the blackened ground. The cleric conjured a wall to keep the creatures at bay as he cast spell after spell. He struck some with cones of force that drove the creatures backward into the swamp.

Aegir was exhausted, yet he strived to regain enough energy to call down the fire once more. It was not as strong as before. His energy faded as his body inched toward death. The cleric tried to send ice darts next, but only three appeared, where in the past, he had been able to produce twenty or more.

With little life left, the magical wall before him failed. Gripping his war hammer, he readied himself for death. He took a moment to thank Dolgar as one of the reptile's head and arm struck out. Aegir caved in its head with his weapon. He glanced toward where his friends had fled and thought himself lucky to give his life to buy them needed time for escape.

Many beasts gorged on their own dead. However, there were still a few that wanted to kill the one who had hurt them so badly. Unable to move his left arm and barely able to stand, Aegir swung his hammer with his right arm. The wall failed completely, and four of the monsters pounced. His weapon killed one before their combined weight shoved him on his back, their claws bearing him down to the watery ground.

Aegir had enough breath left to call out, "For Dolgar."

In his final act, the dwarven cleric struck down two more beasts before death overtook him.

Chapter Twenty-Seven

Taza paced back and forth in his tower room. He had already smashed his wine glass in frustration as he awaited news of the battle in the south. Then he heard the flapping of wings, and his keen hearing told him that the chimera was back, carrying a lackey that had followed the army south.

With a discreet knock on his door, one of his vampire guards announced, "The chimera is back with its burden." The door opened, and the guard threw a nondescript man across the room to land a mere foot from his master.

"What of the army?" Taza demanded.

Clearly petrified, the man stammered, "The army was destroyed and flees in all directions."

Taza was appalled at the ineptitude of the Dormin army. "Do any come in this direction?"

"Yes, my lord. The ones with families, I suspect."

Taza nodded. He understood the meaning of family, despite the fact his own had turned against him and exiled him into the void.

"The warlocks of the Council?" he asked.

The man lowered his head, awaiting death.

"They did nothing and fled when it was clear the battle was lost."

Taza fumed. What was he to do? He tossed the messenger a bag of coins and dismissed him. Fortunately, the man was so afraid that he immediately fled the city.

The vampire ruler called for his guards. Five appeared.

"It's time to act. Raise the dead and let them have the city. Turn as many humans into vampires as you can. This city will be the domain of the dead and the undead. Those you cannot turn, chase them out of the metropolis. It is the time of the undead, and this will be our citadel."

Taza stalked the halls of the citadel going to the Council Chamber. He had had enough of their tinkering and now with their display of outright cowardice, he marched to the chamber's door and threw it open. Over half the chairs were empty.

"Where are the others!" he shouted.

An old warlock motioned to the windows. "They have fled the citadel, making their way west."

Taza's anger sent electricity up and down the shaft of his staff. He slowly calmed himself and called to those waiting in the hallway.

"Come, my children," he said, gesturing for his vampire guards to enter.

A warlock tried to cast a spell, but one of the guards was there first, sinking his teeth into the luckless victim. Soon all the warlocks and sorceresses in the room had been changed.

"Go feed, my children," Taza commanded those newly turned. "Do not drain them all. We must have more vampires to defend the city."

Tarquin stared back down the path they had traveled to escape the creatures, breathing heavy and emotionally staggered from having to leave behind a mortally wounded friend in order to escape.

Eldahir stepped silently to his side, head close to their leader.

"Tarquin, you can avenge Aegir by completing this quest. All the souls that have died did so because they believed in the quest, and more importantly, in you. Now, you must see to the others. After that attack, they need reassurance, and you are their leader. Let Aegir go. Grieve later, but remember, the rest of us must get out of this cursed swamp alive."

The young man wiped tears from his face, further smearing the mud there, and called to the others. "Come, we must go. Let us do so in the name of Aegir and his brave act to save us."

The others nodded in agreement.

Lending a hand to Tarquin, Eldahir felt the slight trembling of his friend's body.

"We must hurry," Azimuth added. "The struggle in the water and the smell of blood will attract evil that dwells within for miles."

Eldahir consulted with Ralav before heading back onto the swamp trail.

As soon as the company was gone, a small, glowing orb of bright white light appeared in the middle of the islet where the battle had taken place. The orb brightened, releasing more light that frightened the creatures and sent them scurrying away. It flashed, and there in place of the orb was Dolgar, the small white-haired dwarvan god in an immaculate blue robe. The figure made his way to the torn and brutalized body of Aegir that lay partly submerged in the muddy water. Dead enemies lay around him. Dolgar projected his will, and the dwarf's body rose from the blood-churned water. Dirt and sodden leaves that littered his torn cloak slid off Aegir's body as it came to hover before the deity.

Dolgar looked sadly at the former heretic he had aided in reforming. The poor dwarf had become too fervent in his beliefs, but he had died trying to save the others. Dolgar smoothed back Aegir's hair, removing dirt and leaves. He shook his head as tears ran down his cheeks.

"Aegir, me friend, it is not yer time to pass from this world. Ye have other duties to perform in the future. I will let ye sleep safely in me temple until ye are well and needed. We will wait until this adventure is over before speaking of yer future."

He grew silent, a bright flash of light surrounded both, and they were gone.

After earlier reports he had received, Taza figured that Tarquin, Celedant, and the rest were in the swamp, driven there by Melgor's orcs. Few men ventured into the great swamp. Fewer came out alive. He was tired of everyone failing to do the job he had sent them to do that he decided to increase odds in his favor. A trip into the void to search for a swamp beast would ensure they did not escape.

Without thinking, he grasped the Staff of Adois and faced attack by the artifact. He mentally berated himself. With the staff's attacks on the rise, it was stupid to reach for it without preparing for consequences. The staff's power spread through his body, cramping muscles in an attempt to wrest control. The vampire, however, had faced worse, and he fought aggressively. The struggle was intense; straining for control almost cost Taza his life as the staff attacked his mind. If it won, it could lock away Taza's mind and take the body for its mistress Adois.

Being a seasoned vampire, Taza was not a pushover. While many would have succumbed, he fought harder until he took back control of the staff. Focusing on a pinprick of light in the far distance, he floated toward it. Once there, the light of his tower room shone brightly, beckoning him forward and back into the present. He took a moment to catch his breath. One day, he knew he would be sucked into the darkness and never return, but not today.

Regaining control of the Staff of Adois, he pointed it at a space ahead, watching as the void spread out with its beckoning darkness, and allowing it to pull him inside. He pictured a swamp and deadly hunter beasts, and the staff led him on a wild careening through the darkness. He could feel the staff whipping back and forth in its search through the void.

It paused, and Taza felt the weightlessness of the void until it told him the world he sought was near. Taza had informed the staff he needed a swamp world and the most dangerous creatures that dwelt there. The staff took off violently, dragging the vampire along. He hurtled at incredible speed toward the surface, stopping before reaching the tops of enormous forest trees.

Regaining control of the staff, Taza floated above the trees momentarily. The top of the canopy was dense, and he cast a spell to move it aside so he could float down toward the soggy ground. Although it was daylight above the canopy, the light below was diffused, casting black shadows about. As he neared the ground, Taza was relieved to discover a swampy morass that stretched as far as his eye could see.

Something huge fell toward him from above. If it had not been in the staff's interest to remain with him, the warlock would have been killed. The shadow missed him by several feet and bounded off a tree to sink razor-sharp claws into another. The creature was catlike with a slimy coat of thick, matted fur. It bunched its legs to spring up and attack again, but the vampire aimed the Staff of Adois to engulf it and the tree it was attached to in a fireball. The creature howled in pain, and the flames burned white hot. When the fire lifted, the charred bones and ashes of the beast wafted through the air settling into the swamp. A huge section of the tree that had been incinerated creaked and groaned as it leaned over and fell, splashing into the depths below.

Regaining control of the staff, Taza directed it to the most dangerous creatures nearby. He took a zigzagging course through the towering, moss-covered trees until he came to a huge mound. The Staff of Adois allowed him to hear multiple heartbeats within. Not wanting to disturb the creatures, he used the staff to raise the mound while binding the creatures. Into the air through the treetops, the huge mound rose, dripping dark greenish water and mud along the way.

Once through the canopy, Taza pictured the great southern swamp on Muiria. He sent the mound to a site that Celedant's company should be passing through, leaving an image of Tarquin and the others in the minds of the beasts. In a blink, he reached the small opening that led to his tower room and closed the split in the void.

CHAPTER TWETNTY-EIGHT

Eldahir called to Ralav, "We need to move fast and avoid being separated."

Ress joined him. "Something large is paralleling us in the swamp!"

Overhearing her, Tarquin called, "Eldahir, let's move."

They began a slow jog, careful to keep their footing on the slippery path. When the path reached deeper water, their knees were barely visible in the mud. Eldahir led them away from the ominous splashing of the unknown creature. They abandoned stealth for speed. The group needed to get as far as they could from their dead friend, the small lizard creatures, and anything else that might be attracted by the bloody water. Their passage made the water splash loudly, and the slippery path caused more than one to slip and fall.

The noise did not go unnoticed. At the nesting mound from the other world, resting on a small islet barely forty paces across, several monstrous, snake-like creatures slithered out. Born in the alien swamp, these predators had grown to prodigious proportions, over five feet wide and thirty feet long with razor-sharp bristles on their bodies. They followed the disturbance in the water to the escaping party.

As the group struggled through the slushy water, the creatures caught sight of them. The one in the lead raised its body out of the water, poised to strike. Azimuth had stopped at a deep section to help the dwarves when he saw the monster. He shoved Baldo backward. Armor dragged the frantic dwarf down as brackish water rushed to cover him.

The gigantic creature shot forward, aiming at the exact spot where Baldo had been standing. While he floundered in the water, the snake shot right over him.

"Look to the right!" Azimuth shouted. He drew his sword and slashed downward at the creature, cutting it deeply. Turning his wrist, he sliced a huge portion off the monster's back.

Before halting, the snake's sharp bristles scraped Eldahir's ribs. Blood seeped through the elf's armor. The monster did not stop. It turned in a great gush of froth and attacked.

The second beast came at them more cautiously. Ress and Morganna peppered it with arrows, but nothing seemed to bother it. Then two things happened at once: Celedant cast a spell, sending subfreezing snow and ice to assault the creature. The spell froze a five-foot section of the snake, making it thrash in the water. Yet it did not die.

Azimuth had seen enough. There was only one way to deal with serpentine creatures. He changed forms. Jumping as far out of the water as he could, he morphed into the golden dragon, and with two great flaps of his wings, gained enough altitude to make a short turn and grab the injured slithering beast as it was about to strike Morganna.

The dragon's claws clung to the slippery monster just behind the head. After several beats of his wings, he gained enough altitude to not endanger his friends. Using his mighty strength, Azimuth squeezed his claws, cutting off the air to the monster until its wiggling slowed and stopped. To ensure it was dead, Azimuth tossed the creature up into the air and with a mighty blast of fiery death, burned the body to a crisp.

Below, another creature wrapped around Tarquin's legs, its sharpened bristles penetrating his leggings. The prince cried out in pain, and the creature thundered above him to strike downward. Tarquin's quick upper body movement saved him. The creature struck, missing him and sinking its teeth into its own body. Poison bubbled out of the wounds. Tarquin struck the snake with his sword, Dragon Bolt, slicing off its head.

Azimuth swooped down to attack another assailant, snatching it up from behind the head and dragging it far enough away from the others to destroy it with his flaming breath. Tarquin's companions fought yet a fourth creature, raining blow after blow upon it until with one mighty stroke Morganna's blade severed the spinal column. The snake's head hit the water with a splash, but its body continued flopping about, knocking her into the mud-stirred water and cutting her deeply. Celedant rushed to her side, chanting a spell that brought a thin line of green from his staff, Forestae. The green ray sliced into the beast until Morganna could untangle herself from its death throes.

An unlucky creature struck at Hority, who with his holy branch and pumice stone, gouged great gaping holes in the monster's flesh until it, too, perished. The silence that suddenly surrounded them was startling. They waited for more attacks, but all was silent. After changing back to elven form, Azimuth helped a spitting Baldo out of the mud while Morganna swam back to the underwater path with a deep cut on her left bicep. By far Tarquin had taken the most grievous wounds, and Baldo knelt in the mud and cast a healing spell on his legs. The others could wait until they were safely encamped.

Out in the swamp on a hillock, a giant lizard poised, patiently waiting on its master. The lizard bent its head to drink muddy water, ignoring the battle. Its rider, however, watched with a keen eye. His shaman would want to know about these intruders. Using a whip, he swatted the lizard into a trot, its wide web feet enabling it to run across the water and deep mud back to its village.

Melgor was disappointed when he saw Cyra riding one of the Dormin horses up and down the lines of orcs, encouraging them to move forward in columns toward the city. He had prayed for her death. She was a powerful enemy. He would have preferred her to die by an enemy's hand, rather than through open battle between the two of them, but it seemed that fate had other ideas.

Slowly, like two slithering snakes, the army moved up and over the hills. As Melgor and the company of mercenaries crested the rise, they saw the beaten army fleeing north. Their shields and weapons littered the ground as the Dormin Army fled.

That night, the mercenaries welcomed Melgor to their fires and food. Although they abided Melgor's bodyguards, the orcs had to share a fire away from the main camp. After eating, Melgor showed respect by camping with Halic and his small command.

The trail had been rough going. Now it was one muddy stretch after another, with everyone sinking knee-deep into the gooey mess. With mud sucking at their boots, they had to slow down. The only one who enjoyed it was Hority.

He went barefoot, boots tied around his neck. "Wriggling yer toes in the sweet mud brings ye good luck," he told the rest. "Try it for future protection."

Although no one else wanted to take off their boots, several wiggled fingers in the mud and wiped it somewhere on their bodies. Baldo helped Tarquin along, as his legs were still wobbly.

Seeing Celedant smear mud on his cloak, Tarquin asked, "You, too?"

The wizard smiled. "Never pass up an opportunity when there's luck to be had."

"The first time we covered ourselves with mud, Aegir died," Tarquin muttered angrily.

Celedant put his hand on Tarquin's shoulder.

"Luck comes in many forms, but you often have to pay for it. We are lucky to be alive, thanks to Aegir's heroic deed."

Tarquin nodded, uncertain if he should believe Celedant. However, when no one was looking, he scooped up a palm of mud and wiped it on his chest.

The trail petered out after several miles, but Eldahir swore he had not lost it. The ground began to rise, and they found a small patch of semisolid ground. Sure enough, the trail they followed crossed the island in the swamp.

Celedant watched with keen interest as Eldahir studied the track and used his elven sight to scan the swamp. When the elf was finished, the wizard asked, "What do you think, Eldahir?"

The elf looked at Celedant with concern. "I am never at ease in the swamp. I have seen too many soldiers disappear. This islet is fortuitous, yet it has been used recently."

Tarquin looked at both Celedant and Baldo. "How far out can you set your wards?"

"If wizarding wards are like ours," Baldo said, "I can encircle the camp for about fifty feet. I can also backtrack and set wards that will be tripped further down the trail."

Celedant agreed. "I, like Baldo, have a maximum distance for encircling the camp, and I can also set upwards along the trails."

Baldo set Tarquin down so he could get a better look at his wounds. The cleric saw they had become infected. The dwarf fished around in his belt pouches for a healing draught.

When he found it, he said, "Drink this slowly. It is strong and will cure the infection." After wrapping the wounds, he went to see to the minor damages of Eldahir and Morganna.

The others set off to work their magic with Hority following along, more delighted with the mud between his toes than casting spells.

"I wish we had more elves with us," Eldahir told Celedant. "We can go for weeks without rest or sleep. However, I see in your eyes that we need to stop. It is risky, but we are a resourceful group." He squished his boot into the mossy ground. "This is as dry as we'll find. We must gather moss and dry brush. Resting on them, we should be able to stay somewhat dry. We dare not risk a fire."

Their sleep was intermittent at best on the uncomfortable bedding. That night and the others that followed became even worse. The most bothersome thing keeping them awake were the night noises and the stinging insects. Disturbances came from so close that at times they rose and drew their weapons in alarm. They soon learned to stop placing wards outside the camp because they were tripped throughout the night by wandering animals.

Chapter Twenty-Nine

Melgor had unofficially joined the mercenary band. They fought well together, and the warlock sensed an amount of safety included in their ranks. Halic and the other three orcs were happy to attend to their master, as they had started calling him. They marched to the top of the northern hill and looked down at the valley floor where the battle had played out.

It was easy to see where the bitterest fights had occurred. The dead and wounded were piled up like cords of firewood. He could also trace the battle where the charges had been made with long lines of dead men and orcs left where they had fallen.

The bowmen had inflicted the most damage to the orc host, firing down into the massed orcan army. Whole sections of orcs had been felled by arrows, and the charge up the steep hill had killed a thousand more. Fortunately for Cyra's army, the Dormin general had lacked imagination. They could have trapped the orcan army in the valley by attacking in unison. Moreover, there were no warlocks among the dead, which was puzzling.

Melgor cursed the gods that Cyra had not fallen in battle, but he could wait. She marched the orcs down the back of the hill. Those that followed across the battlefield finished off the wounded and became deft at rifling through the dead's pockets while on the march.

Tarquin and the others had been slogging through the endless swamp for the better part of the day when they reached a larger and dryer islet.

"I don't like the look of this," Ronli said, pointing to a large interlocking chain that showed signs of having been dragged across the ground. Currently, the chain was taut, but as they watched, it grew slack.

"Stand back from the chain!" Celedant warned them. "Watch the bank of the swamp. Whatever it is, it's headed straight for us."

As something slowly and cautiously approached the small islet, the water began to swirl. All watched as two wide-spaced red eyes set in an enormous dark head emerged from the water. The body was supported by three feet. As it drew closer, a foul stench rolled over them, and the dwarves knew at once that this was the mother of all croats.

"Beware the claws. They are extremely sharp. This croat makes the one we faced in the past look like a toy," Tarquin shouted.

The creature was fifty feet long, with even more unseen in the water. Its fur was so matted that the water cascaded down its body like a mini-waterfall, and when it shook its head, they were showered with filthy water. Opening its maw, the beast revealed a mouth with a triple row of gleaming sharp teeth, angling backward to draw a potential victim inward. They saw that the huge chain was attached to a gigantic iron collar around its neck, barely seen through the matted hair.

Eldahir, Ress, and Morganna knelt, drawing back their bows and letting fly their arrows, impacting the creature's chest. One arrow dangled from its neck, failing to penetrate the beast while others bounced off its nasty muck-coated back. The monster swung around, using its tail as a hammer. Striking the dry land, it made a booming sound.

Celedant stepped forward and leveled his staff at it, calling on the energies within him and melding them with the ground's magical essence. He sent a pure green bolt of energy straight at the creature, striking it on the left side as it turned to face them. The explosion caromed off the beast, leaving small fires and sparks in its dense coat. Immediately the creature's arm whipped forward, claws separating from its fingers and flying through the air. The five-foot-long nails flew straight into the area where the middle of the group stood.

Morganna spun backward as a projectile sliced through her armor, leaving five inches sticking out of her back. A second one headed toward Tarquin, who instinctively moved his head a fraction of an inch and raised his sword, slicing through the claw. The largest portion was deflected and missed him, but the severed tip gouged a thin slice of skin above his ear. A third claw hit Baldo's armor and was projected upward, flipping end over end until it impacted a tree trunk. The last, aimed at Celedant's face, stopped midair as the wizard cast a quick shield spell.

Ress jumped out in front of everyone and threw her spear with strength that transfixed the matted brute. She fell flat to the ground and rolled away from the monster as five more knife-like claws shot over her turning body.

Hority charged into the face of the creature, crying, "Foe!"

Baldo let fly his war hammer, making an audible smack as it struck the creature's right side. Tarquin looked to see if he could help Hority, but there was no need. The frenzied monk spun and danced in and out of the creature's range, his branch striking small holes through the fur but not penetrating to the skin. He became perturbed.

Hority was the target of the monster's sharp teeth. With the creature's concentration on the harassing dwarf, Tarquin moved forward, standing to the side as the tail swished past, leaving him no choice but to forward roll over it. He quickly righted himself, ready for the backswing. His sword glowed bright red as the tail approached, and he swung at its base - slicing straight through muscle and bone.

The creature howled in pain so loudly that several pairs of hands shot up to cover their ears. Tarquin used the remaining stub of the tail to vault to the animal's back, sliding on the fur until he was atop its shoulders.

There, he took a calculated risk, gauging where the heart might be, and drove his red-hot sword straight into the croat. When his hilt stopped the blade from going further, he noticed the arrow had shot upwards through the creature's throat to stick out of its skull. The sword struck true, and the massive beast fell forward, flipping Tarquin to land in a puddle on his backside in front of Eldahir and Ress.

"You could had done that with less drama," Ress commented dryly.

"Ye might have hurt yerself," Hority chimed in as he poked the monster's head to examine the sickly slime that dripped to the ground from its mouth.

Holding a blob of goo growing stiff and binding his fingers together, he called to the wizard.

"Celedant, might we bottle this? It would make an excellent glue and has a fragrant odor of fish less than a week dead."

Celedant looked at the honest face of the Clorian and reached into a pocket, tossing him a small empty bottle.

"Just a bit, Hority." From what he could see, the stuff most likely would solidify inside the bottle, making it completely useless.

The dwarf could not catch the bottle, as his hands had become solidly glued together and intertwined with his beard. Shaking his head and smiling, Celedant spoke the words of a small spell, and the goo that bound the dwarf crumbled away.

Hority jumped up. "A miracle of Clor! I am free." Using his fingers, he forced the goo into the bottle, but by the time it was full and the stopper sealed, the wizard had to free him again from the clutches of the odiferous gunk.

While Eldahir inspected the trails for a way off the islet. Celedant and the others stood around the great beast.

"Never seen a beast like this. How about you Celedant?" Azimuth commented.

"It isn't from the void," Tarquin assured him. "That thing has lived here a long time. When I was with the Borderers, we fought a smaller one once."

"No, my friend," Celedant said in reply to the dragon's question. "I have never seen a creature of that ilk. Look at the collar. The neck and fur have covered it. This creature was placed here a long time ago as a guardian. A guardian for what, we will have to wait and see."

"It is as Eldahir said," Azimuth replied. "Many things lurk in the deep swamp that have yet to be seen."

Baldo concentrated on helping Morganna. The claw was severed and then pulled through her. Because of what she had endured before meeting Tarquin and the others, she was no stranger to pain and hardly moved during the procedure. However, she pounded the muddy ground and grunted. The dwarvan cleric bandaged the wound and gave her a potion to promote healing and provide relief from the pain.

Seven trails led off the small islet, posing a dilemma for Tarquin and the others. Eldahir, Ralav, and Ronli scouted around until they found the beginning of a seldom-used trail that led west in the general direction they needed to go. An ancient rickety wall of warped wood and a gate had been built at the start of the path, causing some concern. Still, they had no choice and stepped off firmer ground onto the damp mossy path. By this time, they had spent so much time walking in muddy water that they not only disliked the path, they downright abhorred it.

"Soon it will be nightfall," Eldahir said after they had walked for some time. "I had better scout ahead for a place to camp. We need to get as far away from that dead croat as possible, as its carcass will attract other predators to feed."

Tarquin led the rest at a fast pace along the path until Eldahir finally returned just as twilight fell over the swamp.

"We must hurry," the elf told them. "I found a suitable place to camp that we can reach before full dark."

Eldahir jogged ahead, water spraying with each step. His and Morganna's elven heritages kept them upright. As the others followed, however, there was a lot of slipping and stumbling until they eventually reached firmer ground.

"This patch of dry ground is larger than the last, and you can see the approaches from the swamp," Eldahir said, his breath still even and normal. "There is a copse of cypress trees nearby. We can cut the branches and sleep reasonably dry on top of them."

Exhausted, the others followed him into the trees by the light of Forestae. While the swamp took its toll on their spirits, the battle with the giant croat had made them weary beyond measure. Even the most stouthearted struggled against the constant strain of keeping on the path and wading through murky water. Tired of Elvan form, Azimuth longed to reclaim his dragon body. Soaring through the sky was far easier and less tiring than all this walking.

The ground was soft under the cypress trees with a deep covering of dry leaves. Everyone spread out, cutting tree branches for bedding.

"I think I will return to my dragon form tomorrow," Azimuth told Celedant as he followed his friend around the camp setting wards. Flying is less tiring, and I grow tired of holding this shape."

"Now you know how your dragon spies feel in elven form. Some have maintained it for years," the wizard smiled.

"Don't rub it in," Azimuth grumbled. "Condensing my massive bulk into the puny size of an elf would be like you taking on the form of a bug."

Celedant finished the words of a spell to blow warm air over the camp and turned to his friend.

"I never thought of it like that. At least in your natural state, you will be able to scout far ahead and warn us of danger and possible traps."

When they returned to the center of camp, they found Baldo purifying several pans of swamp water magically, much to Hority's displeasure. He came close to calling Baldo a heretic, but not wishing to offend his friends, he sulked off to find a wet spot in which to sleep.

Oppressive darkness engulfed the camp quickly, with the swamp's damp fog obscuring the moon and stars as the band shared another cold meal of smoked venison and dried fruit. It wasn't long before each headed off to their own bed of branches. Since witnessing the heretical cleansing of Clor's holy water, Hority was nowhere to be found.

Possessing the same elven stamina, Morganna would have taken her turn at guard duty, giving Eldahir a break. With her injuries, though, he convinced her that sleeping would better promote healing, and once again, the tireless elf stood guard over his friends during the night.

In Dorian, the orcan army moved at a fast pace and were challenged several times by small groups of horsemen, but these skirmishes did not deter Cyra. Night had fallen when Taza's forces attacked. Several hundred zombies entered the camp and were upon the orcs quicker than their sluggish movement might suggest. As they fell onto the sleeping orcs, their lethal bites turned their victims to zombies as soon as they died.

Most orcs did not know how to handle the undead, so many suffered arrow wounds or sword blows. Cyra knew how to deal with them. She rode around the battle, calling for her soldiers to sever the heads from the wounded's shoulders. The orcs that had formed a shield wall to push the undead away readily followed her orders. In the darkness, however, this was hard to do, as it was difficult to determine friend from foe.

The battle did not subside until the sun crested the mountains. Although several hundred zombies had attacked, their numbers had grown to over a thousand as victims were changed into the undead. The remaining army was forced to advance over the battlefield, beheading every corpse they came upon.

Chapter Thirty

Celedant had placed his bedroll beside Tarquin's. Or had he? He turned his head slightly to the right to find the prince sleeping mere inches from him. Something wasn't right. The wizard realized that instead of branches, he felt a cold floor beneath him, and that wasn't all. A soft white light illuminated the room he now realized they were in, and he surmised that the floor and ceiling were made of marble. The wizard slowly sat up, his staff and the encased Staff of Adaman next to him with the voice of Adaman in his head assuring his safety and to be at peace.

A passive, serene voice echoed in the vast temple.

"Celedant, on a quest for the Staff of Adois, please wake our friend. Otherwise, he might snore through what I have to say."

Celedant nudged Tarquin and whispered, "Something's amiss."

Tarquin jumped up and was about to draw his sword, but the serene voice stopped him. "Ye willna need it here. This is an ancient temple, buried deep beneath the rubble of the destroyed region of Zeiglon."

A small, white-haired dwarf wearing an immaculate blue robe came forth from a recessed door. He introduced himself.

"Welcome, I am Dolgar. Surely our mutual friend, Aegir, has told ye about me?"

The wizard and Tarquin nodded.

"Why have we been brought to this temple?" Celedant asked.

"A just question," Dolgar replied, nodding. "Ye are here because I have taken an interest in this quest of yers, but ye knew that I helped Morganna become the wood elf she appeared to be in both mind and appearance, much to the distaste of her

Illanni kinfolk."

Dolgar saw concern on their faces. "Donna worry. I have conferred with Thierry, who is busy with many things. I have also spoken from a distance to Clor."

Both men smiled.

"Clor is a god who adheres to the tenet of his faithful Hority?" Tarquin asked.

Dolgar smiled sadly. "Yes. Clor is a forgotten god, glad to be left alone as the other gods argue and battle. He prefers to be by himself, concentrating on the greater meaning of filth. No god good or evil wanted him on his or her side. Nevertheless, a few of us occasionally check in on him. He is in quite a stir now. One of his flock has joined a quest to explore the wasteful world, as Clor calls it."

Celedant chuckled. "Yes, we have the pleasure of traveling with one of Clor's monks. Through various means, we have bathed him several times, much to his displeasure."

The white-haired god chuckled as he sat on a marble bench.

"Yes, since Hority began his travels, Clor has had to tinker with a portion of their rule. Now back to why I have summoned ye here. As ye know, Thierry cannot easily intervene, but he knows that one of his most adept clerics accompanies ye. I canna recall his name."

"Baldo," Tarquin supplied.

Dolgar snapped his fingers. "Yes, that is the name. Ye must forgive me, but since my intervention with first Morganna, and then with Ress, I canna stop me self from keeping an eye on yer quest. That's why the other dwarvan gods chose me to speak to ye. Once the prophecy was confirmed, yer world was in danger. The two of ye inherited a struggle between twin gods that has gone on since the creation of yer world."

The wizard and Tarquin exchanged glances. This was old news. The prophecy, and Celedant's subsequent visit to recruit him was the very thing that saved Tarquin from becoming the new Parthian ambassador to the high elves. Diplomacy, for him, would be dull indeed, compared to the life of a warrior.

"As ye know, many of yer friends have sacrificed their lives for the good of yer world to help you complete this quest. Do not let the deceiver, Adois, use that against ye. Soon her staff will take control of Taza. He will no longer be its master, but a slave – a vessel to be used by the staff. Ye must act soon. Time has grown short. While ye have been mired about in the mud, so to speak, the vampire has advanced his plans."

"I have never been to Dormin as it is now," Celedant told him. "I could use the Staff of Adaman to open a rift to the Citadel, but my limited knowledge of the area makes me hesitant."

Dolgar motioned him forward, placing both hands on the wizard's head. Suddenly Celedant was hovering in midair within a vast entry hall, and in his head, he heard, "Go down those steps. They lead to Taza's Tower."

The link was broken, and Celedant took an unsteady step back to gather himself. He spoke to Tarquin:

"Lord Dolgar has shown me the way to Taza's tower. We should be ready to leave in the morning."

Dolgar held up his hand. "No, ye will not need to leave as soon as that. It has to be within seven days' time. The staff will let you know. Upon yer arrival in Dormin, it will be time for the end game to play out. That is more than I should say, but I am a god and have a bit of leeway."

Suddenly the marbled temple disappeared, and the two were back in the swamp. They found Eldahir standing over the wizard, trying to wake him.

When Celedant opened his eyes, the elf spoke softly so that only the wizard and Tarquin could hear.

"Azimuth took to the sky early this morning. He tried to reach you, but for the first time in your long association, he was unable to speak to you telepathically. Alarmed, he contacted me. He said it was as though some kind of barrier had been placed around your mind."

"I can't go into it now, but Dolgar paid Tarquin and me a visit. Please keep this secret."

Eldahir thought about the overenthusiastic response this news would bring from the dwarves and nodded. "Agreed."

"What did Azimuth have to report?" the wizard asked.

"There are several large animals paralleling our path. I know not what they are exactly, but we will meet soon enough. It would be better if they crossed the path first. Come, we must eat on the trail."

Tarquin called to the others. "Azimuth reports something very large to the left and right of the path. Be vigilant. Again, my friends, our dire need to leave the swamp means we eat on the run. No noise - and keep up the pace."

Everyone accepted this as normal and went about the business of breaking camp. Eldahir was well down the path when the others, munching on biscuits and dried fruit, joined him.

The path dipped down into stagnant water and before long, they were ankle-deep and knee-deep in places. Eldahir led them, sure-footed. Not one strayed from the path, their line spreading as they went. They made headway as they pushed through the fetid water as quietly as possible. Hours later, all were soaked from plodding along the path, tired muscles protesting.

Eldahir came to a stop and held up his arm. In the distance, the sound of heavy splashing filled the air as large feet strode through the water. The mysterious animals were bracketing the path. A moment later, the creatures came to a sudden stop, surrounding them. Though Eldahir and the others could not yet see their enemy, they continued moving cautiously down the trail, now waist-deep in the murky swamp water.

From out of the fog came the sound of rushing feet, big feet bringing giant black lizards with red stripes charging at them, webbed feet perfect for swamp travel. The monsters were ten to twelve feet above the ground and twice that length, and were ridden by green-skinned Aloi, holding long spears to drive them, using the blunt end on the lizards' flank. The other end held wicked, sharp, curved blades.

Eldahir whipped out his bow, quickly dispatching several Aloi riding on the backs of the lizards. From behind him, an Aloi warrior rose from the water and dealt him a blow to the head with the handle of his sword. Eldahir fell, floating face down and unconscious. More Aloi rose from the water, surrounding them. They were outnumbered five to one.

"Sheath your weapons!" Celedant ordered. "Do not fight here, or we will all die." Mentally he said, *Azimuth, do you see what is happening?*

Yes, Celedant, the dragon replied. *Shall I intervene?*

Not yet. I have a feeling we are about to discover something important.

An Aloi picked up Eldahir, throwing the elf across its broad shoulder and striding down the path with ease. Other Aloi relieved the others of their weapons and tied their hands behind their backs. They escorted the five, each with two guards, down the path.

Soon they approached a village that appeared to rise from the water. Their captors marched them across the hard-packed ground while other Aloi of all sizes, both male and female, stood about, cheering. The younger Aloi threw rocks, hitting the prisoners as they were marched through the village that was so surrounded by trees, it made the area dusky. No direct sunbeams managed to penetrate the thickness of the foliage. Forced through the throng, they eventually stopped in front of the largest brick mud structure. Celedant had seen all the smaller ones with families milling about. These were family homes, but this larger structure probably housed their leader. It was forty feet long and thirty wide. A conical roof allowed smoke to escape.

The Aloi held them in front of the building; they watched as their weapons were placed in a smaller attached structure with a stout wooden door that was closed and secured with a crude lock. With a flourish, the animal skin that served as a door to the main building was drawn aside. The captors' grip on their arms grew tighter.

A tall, bare-chested male Illanni with a long sword attached to a fine leather belt stepped forward. He had an abundance of necklaces around his neck and bracelets at his wrists, indicating power and position within the tribe. The Illanni was heavily tattooed with geometric patterns over his body. The brash-looking Illanni paced up and down the line, eyeing each of the prisoners. He stopped in front of Celedant, giving him a quizzical look, and bared his fangs.

"You are the leader, are you not?" he asked.

"I lead this company," Celedant answered carefully. "We were going to negotiate with you for passage to the forest."

The Illanni spat in Celedant's face. "Nothing but lies. Human, dwarf, and elf, you will make a delicious meal for my children, after I feed."

He turned and disappeared into the large building, its leather door flapping closed behind him. Two guards barred the entry.

The prisoners were led to hacked-off tree trunks stained with dried blood. The Aloi tied each of them to a grizzly pole. In the center of the village, several large iron pots, pitted with rust, were brought forth and suspended over a roaring fire. Six Aloi approached, muscles straining as they hauled out a huge cutting board, which they set down near the cauldrons.

"He does not know who we are or about the staff," Celedant whispered.

"They make terrible first impressions," Botreg said aloud.

His comment got him a swift spear butt jabbed into his ribs. Ress aimed a powerful kick at the Aloi, but he hardly noticed. Botreg let his body sag against the ropes, coughing as if the blow had stunned him. All the while, his hands secretly worked to untie the rope that bound him.

The huge Aloi turned his attention to Ress.

"A female dares to touch me?" he demanded, ramming his spear into the belly of the firedrake slayer. He stalked away toward the fire, leaving two guards who seemed more interested in the beginning of the festivities than guard duty.

CHAPTER THIRTY-ONE

Azimuth wasn't the only one aware of what was happening. Tarquin had just relieved Baldo as rear guard and the worrying job of keeping Hority from wandering off. When the others were captured, the pair held back. The prince quickly estimated the number of enemies surrounding his friends. He knew that the two of them could be of little help at the moment. There were just too many Aloi. Azimuth's voice entered his mind.

Hide, my friend. Celedant wants to determine exactly what is going on here. When the time is right, the three of us can rescue them.

The dragon had no sooner finished speaking when Hority began to charge the Aloi. Tarquin slid off the trail and dragged the dwarf with him into the deeper water, his hand clamped securely over the dwarf's mouth before he could call out his war cry, "Foes!"

They dropped below the surface, and catching sight of a patch of green reeds, swam toward them. Tarquin was about to grab the dwarf and pull him along, but he held back when he realized that the Clorian could swim. He was amazed, considering that Hority had lived in the dry climate of the southern Mordolwyn Mountains all his life. Soon they felt the muddy bottom and resurfaced, hidden among the swaying reeds.

They watched as their companions were led down the submerged path, hands bound, and shoulders held by Aloi guards. Once they were out of sight, Hority prepared to swim back to the trail, but the prince grabbed him and held a muddy finger to his mouth. Moments later, five Aloi warriors came down the path in search of escapees.

After they were gone, the two comrades swam until they reached the path. Hority held onto Tarquin's shoulders as he scanned the area for more manlike lizards. He examined the mud and despite what was happening, asked, "Can I learn the differences between the path's firmer mud and thicker swamp mud?"

A frustrated Tarquin shook his head. "No. Maybe later."

Hority created a maddening disturbance with his arms and legs as he climbed onto the path. His eyes were alight with religious fervor as he said, "This is a mighty quest. We must rush to save our friends in peril."

Only a quick grab by Tarquin nabbed the dwarf's hood. "My mighty friend, we must not rush the attack. Azimuth has been in touch with me and advises caution. Let us follow and find out where they are taken. Then we can formulate a plan of rescue."

Hority nodded. "Ye offer wise advice, me friend. Clor would approve of caution."

Before they could move on, Azimuth, having reverted to his elven form, came cautiously down the path.

"I saw where the Aloi took our friends from the air and decided to join you. The village is large enough that I can change back to dragon form if necessary."

"Good idea," Tarquin agreed.

"However, I have an idea that may save the day," Azimuth said, giving him a wink.

Tarquin, Azimuth, and Hority followed the trail until they smelled smoke. The three stepped off the path, anticipating being up to their necks in water. Surprisingly, it was only knee-deep. Spotting the smoke in the distance, Tarquin took the lead and picked out an approach that led toward the fire. Cautiously, the three inched forward, using the reeds to hide their progress. Since the muddy ground now rose above the water, they had to lay flat and crawl through the muck. Using the marsh grass for cover, they edged closer to the boundary of the compound.

Tarquin took a deep breath. "It's as I thought. These are the northern cousins of the Aloi that fought beside us in Zeiglon."

Hority pointed to the center of the village. "They seem to be setting up for a party."

Azimuth gestured to a series of long, pointed tree trunks decorated with human and orc heads located on the far side of the village.

"Look over there...our friends."

Hority grunted. "It appears they may be the main course for tonight's feast."

Tarquin scanned the settlement and surrounding area with a soldier's eye.

"It looks like the village was built to protect that bridge. There are trenches for archers and sharpened stakes that would funnel attackers together, making them prime targets."

Azimuth pointed at the bridge. "That is our way out of this accursed swamp. See how the ground is higher? It leads to a forest that would not grow under the swamp's conditions. On the other side of the bridge, the track we've been following turns west. There is neither traffic nor fortifications on that side of the trail. Our exit from this swamp is through the village."

"The water must be running fast and deep to need a bridge," Tarquin added.

Hority pointed to a huge fenced area. "Look. Their mounts are stabled over there. Too bad we couldn't ride them."

Tarquin clapped Hority on the back. "No, my mighty monk, they could swallow you in one bite. I think Azimuth may have a better plan."

After explaining his plan, Azimuth, Tarquin, and Hority split up. Tarquin and Azimuth cautiously worked their way toward their bound friends. Hority joyfully crawled along the viscous mud to the giant lizard pen.

When Tarquin and Azimuth reached the original trail and stopped, their noses were pressed to the rotting smell of the swamp. They had to wait for a guard to turn away to move onward. While the Aloi paced back to his old spot, they slipped over the trail and continued their advance toward the village. As they drew closer, they saw Botreg furiously working on his bindings and Ress hanging limply with head drooped against her chest.

One of the guards turned to face the prisoners as Tarquin's dagger slid across the monster's throat. The other guard was about to call out, but Botreg, now free of his bindings, jumped him, wrapping the rope he had untied around the creature's throat. He held on tightly until the Aloi fell dead.

The two Aloi, standing guard at the entrance to the chief's hut, were facing the fire and did not notice what was occurring. Their concentration was on the festivities about to begin.

Azimuth sliced through Celedant's bindings.

Botreg, atop the Aloi, called out, "Check Ress. She is grievously wounded."

The prisoners remained where they were, pretending to be tied to the posts, while the two dead Aloi were dragged into the darkness. Baldo, slipped away, sliding to a halt beside Ress. He untied the rope binding her to the post, catching her as she fell heavily to the ground.

Baldo turned her over to assess the damage. An Aloi spear thrust had missed her heart but penetrated her lung, and blood bubbled out of her mouth. He turned her onto her side, allowing the blood to flow freely, so she could breathe. She needed healing, more than he could provide on the battlefield. She would need rest. Praying to Thierry, he placed his hand over the wound until the blood slowed and stopped.

Tarquin, handing Ress into Baldo's care, whispered, "Wait for the diversion." During the months of their journey together, the two had fallen in love. He wanted nothing more than to go to her side, but he realized the only way to get her to safety was to concentrate on escape.

"Our weapons are locked in that shed," Celedant whispered.

Botreg crept to the shed, picked the rusty lock, and returned with their weapons.

The delighted Hority, whose body was completely covered in slime, crawled up out of the swamp where he could clearly observe the captives, watching while Tarquin and Azimuth exited the water and began freeing the others.

He waited until all were released, which was the signal that he was to cast the spell. As he began to chant, an Aloi appeared, curiously looking out into the swamp. Hority had to stop the spell while he silently told the creature to move on. Once the Aloi had turned its back and returned to the center of the village, Hority was ready. He called on Clor's aid.

There was a loud "whump," and great pillars of flame rained down on the stockade facing the Aloi village. He added another spell, sending sharp darts of flame to strike the giant beasts, resulting in a classic stampede. A delighted Hority watched the confusion he had wrought. Terrified by the fire that fell from the sky, the giant lizards destroyed their pen, accidentally killing one of their kind. The behemoths began rearing and moving about the enclosure, making loud hisses and gurgling cries. The sharp darts of pain sent them running through the village and into the swamp.

The others watched in satisfaction, admiring the little Clorian monk's power.

Baldo, having cast several healing spells on Ress, asked, "If I may? I will begin casting flame strikes on yon furthest houses, dens, or shelters - whatever they may be. That will kill all within. Tis a powerful spell that drains me mightily."

Ress nodded weakly, and he rose to his feet to begin the attack.

In unison, the spellcasters released their power. Baldo felt energy pulsing within his holy figure. From the sky, huge cascades of flame fell onto four mud houses. Despite the never-ending wetness of the swamp, the huts blazed, and screams from within could be heard. Celedant sent a wall of rolling bright orange fire coursing across the village, gaining speed as it went. It struck the Aloi preparing for the feast. The creatures simply disappeared, leaving only small mounds of charred remains of what used to be Aloi. Azimuth added a lightning spell that cut through the remaining enemies.

Eldahir efficiently picked off the warriors trying to advance, while Botreg stood by the large dwelling the Illanni leader had retreated to and attacked the two guards.

It was a losing battle as they slowly pushed the assassin backward until Hority appeared out of nowhere. The skinny dwarf, with mud flying from clothes and beard, dispatched the last two with his branch. His clarion call of "Foes" rang through the night.

"To the bridge! It's our best way out," Tarquin shouted.

"I will meet you there in a moment," Celedant called back.

Chapter Thirty-Two

The wizard ran into the leader's building, his staff easily deflecting two minor spells at the entrance. Not all of the guards had rushed out, and he came face-to-face with six hugely muscled Aloi. An Illanni stood just beyond the defenders. The guards charged, and Celedant's sword struck out to pierce the chest of the first Aloi. He summoned the power of Forestae and cast a spell that slowed time, allowing him to advance unharmed. Swinging his sword, he dispatched the remaining guards. After releasing his spell, their remains fell to the packed soil of the chamber. He stopped ten feet from the Illanni leader, who stood over six feet tall and was covered in trinkets and tattoos that the Aloi viewed as gifts from their god.

Baring his fangs, he asked, "What are you doing here, warlock? Did Taza send you?"

"Not so lucky, vampire. I am a wizard, not a warlock. Taza and I are on opposite sides. Why aren't you in Illan with your ilk?" Celedant asked.

The Illanni's smile faded, "Taza's peace is a dream. It is our place to take all that we want, killing the sheep like you and your friends."

The wizard laughed. "Your friends lay dead in the village. Your avarice and dreams are smashed. Come and die!"

The Illanni was fast even for a vampire; instantly, he was beside Celedant, exerting a bone-crushing hold on the wizard's right wrist. Celedant was forced to drop his sword, fearful his wrist was broken. Using his left arm, he swung Forestae, smashing it into the vampire's face. He heard bones crush under the blow. The Illanni loosened his grip, and Celedant was able to pull free and put distance between them.

The vampire drew a gleaming sharp longsword and slashed at the retreating wizard. Celedant danced away, the weapon barely missing his mid-rift. He lowered his staff, calling forth from the ground, water, and air as a blast of wind blew the creature across the room, sending him crashing into several woven baskets against the wooden wall of the shaman's hut. As he struggled to get up, Celedant began chanting a spell.

Completing the spell, the Illanni threw his sword across the room. The sharp blade hit Celedant in the left shoulder, cutting deeply to the bone. Off balance, the wizard's spell was cast; a green bolt of energy flew across the room, striking the throne the Illanni had set up. As Celedant regained his balance, he looked at the vampire. His spell had destroyed the throne and sent sharp splinters into the right side of his enemy. Although painful, they would heal very quickly. There were only two ways to kill a vampire.

The Illanni threw a basket at the wizard. He cast a spell of his own, encircling the spot where the wizard had been with fire. Instead of catching his foe off-guard and wounded, he watched as Celedant rolled clear, searing pain lancing his shoulder and wrist. Snarling in anger, the vampire drew a dagger from each boot, both a foot long and charged.

Grasping Forestae in his left hand, the wizard struggled to keep up with the Illanni's deft use of the daggers. He blocked most of the dark one's strikes, but a few penetrated his defense, slicing into the wizard's clothes to the skin. Celedant saw an opening and struck out with Forestae, catching the shaman in the solar plexus. The Illanni went down to one knee, breathing heavily. Celedant reversed the staff and struck the dark one on the back of the head.

This staggered the vampire, but not enough. He jumped into a standing position. Forestae sent a thrust of power that threw the Illanni backward to topple over the remains of the imposter's throne. As Celedant spoke the words of another spell, the vampire untangled himself from the throne and the wicker baskets behind it.

He came out casting a spell of his own that sent fireballs flying at the wizard. Celedant, however, was faster. Crying out the final words of his spell, he sent a roaring flame from Forestae that struck the Illanni dead center in the chest, while trying to dodge the fireballs hurled at him. His wounds slowed him, and one struck mid-thigh, burning through his cloak and leggings, charring the flesh beyond and knocking him to the ground.

With the fireballs dispersed, Celedant staggered to his feet and stood over the vampire, who lay spread eagle on the floor of his shaman's ceremonial hut, slowly being consumed by fire. Assured the vampire would no longer rise, he retrieved his sword with the uninjured arm and sheathed it, leaving his hand free to hold Forestae as a crutch. It was all Celedant could do to flip aside the leather doorway and stagger after Tarquin. Seeing his lifelong friend was wounded, Azimuth hurried back to lend a hand.

With their powerful war chief now a pile of ash, the Aloi warriors left in the village attacked. Leaderless, only brief skirmishes still plagued Tarquin and his friends, ending with the Aloi either being killed or slipping away injured to lick their wounds.

The company reached the bridge and their would-be escape route. Tarquin sought out Baldo, who was carrying Ress.

"How is she?" he asked anxiously.

"She will live," Baldo replied, assuaging Tarquin's fear.

They hurried onto the bridge, but a third of the way across, they were forced to halt. At some point, the Aloi had burned the center span, leaving a void where they needed to go.

"The Aloi had no intention of letting anyone escape the swamp," Azimuth said.

The span they had burned was short enough for the heavily muscled Aloi to jump, but none of the humans, dwarves, or even the elves could project themselves that far. They stood quietly, listening to the screams and wails that came from the village. Eldahir, Botreg, and Morganna sent arrow after arrow into the few pursuing Aloi.

Supporting the wizard, who could hardly stand, Azimuth called to Tarquin.

"Might these wooden planks be of help?"

Tarquin examined them. The boards were all that remained of the missing bridge pieces.

A small mob of Aloi rushed them. Eldahir quickly shot three arrows. They were followed by cries of pain. Botreg skewered one of the attackers, and Morganna drew her sword to run off the rest.

Tarquin called above the uproar, "Hority, take care of Celedant. Azimuth, help me place the boards on what's left of the crossbeams."

Many of the boards were burned, too damaged to use. Azimuth had to find the good ones.

Tarquin was near the end when Azimuth called, "That's all there is. The rest are too badly burned."

Tarquin nodded and shouted to the others, "One at a time. When you reach this point, you'll need to jump a gap of only a few feet."

Tarquin braced his legs, making sure his feet were on solid wood, and bounded over the gap, landing solidly on the other side. Baldo, having taken care of the unconscienced Ress, lifted her and bounded across the planks, nimbly leaping the waterway, despite wearing full plate mail and carrying Ress. The others quickly jumped across, leaving Hority and Celedant. The dwarf uttered a few words, and his palms glowed brown. Laying them on Celedant's thigh, he closed his eyes. When he removed his hands, the savage burn was partially healed, leaving a vivid red scar. The two quickly jumped over the swift-flowing water and followed the others as they rushed away from the bridge and what remained of the Aloi village.

They ran a mile into the woods before stopping to catch their breath and rest from the battle and flight. Baldo saw to Celedant's shoulder and wrist, which had been broken in his fight with the Illanni.

"Not my moment of glory," the wizard admitted. "It was folly and hubris. I should not have entered the leader's hut alone."

When the healing was done to the best of their abilities, Celedant and Tarquin had an animated discussion about where to go next. It was finally decided they would follow the edge of the swamp west toward the mountains until the Staff of Adaman could lead them to a nexus point. They knew the hills were overrun with orcs from the siege, who could put a quick end to their quest. After their trek through the swamp, no one could be sure how far west they had gone.

Baldo called to Tarquin and Celedant from where he knelt next to Ress. The two came over to see a very pale Ress with a bandage wrapped around her chest and dried blood on her face and armor.

"What can be done, Baldo?" Tarquin asked worriedly.

The dwarf shook his head. "Nothing more. I have done all that I can do out here in the wilderness. She needs rest. I'm afraid that Ress canna continue on the road with us."

She smiled up at the prince. "Tarquin, I've run my race. Leave me in a hidden area. I'll heal up and make my way east to Southgard."

Dropping to his knees beside her, he took her hand. "This place is overrun with orcs between here and there," Tarquin said, his voice filled with concern. "You'll never make it."

She laughed, sending her into a fit of coughing.

"Easy does it," Baldo scolded. "Ye must crawl before ye walk."

She nodded. "Think of all the fire-drakes I killed without help from anyone. The orcs won't know what hit them."

"You're too badly injured," Tarquin said.

"You need not worry, Tarquin," Azimuth assured him as he joined the little group. "I will call one of my brethren to carry her to Southgard, where she will have access to the city's best healers." He looked down at Ress and smiled. "There you may rest and let nature take care of your injuries. Just promise you won't try to dispatch the dragon I send."

Ress bit her lip so as not to laugh. "I promise, Azimuth. As we both know, firedrakes are nothing compared to a majestic dragon. I will be honored to ride to Southgard on one of your brethren." To Tarquin, she said, "As for you, my love, I won't let you out of your commitment so easily. When this is over, we will be married."

"Tarquin, we must continue," Celedant said. "Ress will be fine. Come. We must find her a secluded spot where her wounds can begin to heal, while she awaits Azimuth's kin. Whichever dragon arrives, it will keep her safe with a spell for the duration of the trip."

Tarquin nodded but was slow to get up. "I leave her in your care, Azimuth," he said with tears in his eyes.

They stuck to just inside the tree line that day, coming across little more than a few streams that flowed into the marsh. Their first camp was by a stream. Taking turns, they washed the filth off themselves and their clothes. They hung the clothing to dry on bushes and tree limbs and huddled in blankets. It took three of them to get Hority in the stream and his habit off.

The pale skin underneath came clean quickly. Hority admitted that Clor would allow his followers only short amounts of time in clean unholy water. Celedant levitated Hority's drying habit, which still was dripping slightly brown water, high onto a tree branch.

Hority kept trying different ways to get his habit down as Celedant moved about the wet clothes, casting simple wind spells to dry them.

The wizard eventually brought the monk's habit to Hority.

"Please do not be angry, my friend. I wanted you to dry off before adorning yourself with what you deem as clothes."

Celedant secretly turned the spell on the dwarf to ensure he was dry before Hority could get dressed. Meanwhile, Baldo went around to his friends, casting small spells to cure lingering wounds or dispense a powder to alleviate any diseases the swamp might have given them.

Only their exhaustion enabled them to sleep that night. Morganna and Eldahir shared guard duty, each half the night, so the other could catch up on much-needed rest. Tarquin thought he would never drift off. He continued to worry about Ress until Azimuth received word that she was safe in Southgard.

Chapter Thirty-Three

Two days later, Tarquin and the others kept the swamp in sight while heading west. Ralav held up his hand, motioning the others forward. They had come upon a ford where the muddy ground was churned up on both sides, indicating a number of feet had trekked through it.

The old tracker pointed. "See those tracks? They're coming from the south out of the swamp."

Tarquin squatted to examine the tracks. "Aloi, and there appears to be a lot of them. Word of our attack has spread quickly among those scaly beasts."

Eldahir scanned the area on both sides of the river, distinguishing the Aloi tracks from huge booted feet. "About a day ago, some fifty Aloi met several hundred men at this crossing. What say you, Ralav?"

The old dwarf looked up. "I agree, but I think there were more than several hundred – much more. They crossed over to the other side of the stream, but they didna return this way. Those tracks are the strangest I have ever seen. The size worries me. Could they be young giants?"

Celedant pondered this. "Difficult to say, but I doubt it. The tracks are larger than those of men or elves. I suspect Taza may have recruited more warriors from the void." He looked around. Even though he saw nothing out of the ordinary, he shivered as if an icy had finger crept up his spine. "I can feel the noose tightening about our necks."

Behind them, horns sounded in the distance.

"I'll not try my luck with the swamp again," Celedant declared. "Quick. We must find shelter in the hills."

At ease in the wooded landscape, Eldahir dropped behind the company where he could watch the advancing enemy. The men had scouts, but not many. They were dressed strangely in gold-layered armor, and they carried large, unusual weapons that mystified the elf. At this distance, Eldahir estimated their height to be eight or nine feet. When he could, he picked off one of the scouts with a perfectly placed arrow to inspect him closer.

The dead scout wore a face plate, and when the elf removed it, what he saw took his breath away. Celedant was right. The creature was alien to this world, obviously brought through the void to hunt them down. The face was distorted, stretched from one side to the other, its nose located more to the right, and its eyes pulled greatly in that direction. Deep purple blood oozed from the wound where the arrow had pierced him. Eldahir heard shouting near his location.

In a clearing, the alien creatures and a contingent of Aloi were having a heated debate. It looked like a fight was imminent, which he and the others would welcome. Eldahir used his sensitive elven hearing to determine what had angered the two groups.

A red-armored creature, certainly a commander, shouted, "The warlock, Taza, sent word that our quarry would use this route. The warlock was right." He pointed up the path. "The gems we were promised are within our grasp. The enemies will soon be cornered in the hills. It is only a matter of time before they are overwhelmed."

The Aloi pointed at the sun. "We cannot be this far from water. Already two hatchlings have died without the precious liquid. My brothers suffer and will soon meet that fate."

The commander dressed in red snarled. "You swore to me that you would help in their capture. What's a few soldiers to you? It means more reward for the rest of us to share."

The Aloi leader thought before answering, "This quest does not serve my people. We would go into yonder hills and never see the swamp where we were hatched again."

The man spat in the Aloi's face. "There's your precious water."

He fired his weapon into the Aloi's midsection. Apparently, that was the sign to attack as his soldiers put the odd weapons to their shoulders and fired a volley of blue bullets that trailed fire as they struck the rear of the retreating Aloi guard, knocking many down. The golden soldiers charged. Having no choice, the Aloi drew their swords to withstand the aliens, causing a near-deafening roar as weapons met and clanged.

Watching the two-species battle allowed Eldahir to observe the way the aliens handled their weapons. It was unusual to see the Aloi fighting on dry ground instead of the swamp. The use of tails, tridents, and swords was commendable but left their rear open to attack. Without water, the Aloi's bodies slowly dehydrated, draining their energy. With their leader dead, and without a direct commander, they stumbled around in confusion. Surrounded and isolated from each other, their numbers were whittled by the strange weapons the aliens carried.

A brighter Aloi blew a loud blast on a horn, sounding retreat, but it was too late for the surviving Aloi. They were quickly brought down by the odd blue energy bullets, long before they could reach the safety of the forest. The ones that reached the trees ran straight into a corps of aliens, placed there to cut off the Aloi's escape. They were killed without mercy.

Eldahir grimly watched the slaughter. *Professional killers.*

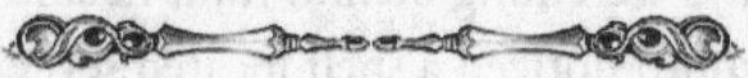

Celedant felt the Staff of Adaman exert power through him. It was neither vying for dominance nor draining his magical energy. The wizard felt compelled to head in one direction, and the others followed without question. Spread out into a single line, they alternated between running and walking. Eldahir brought up the rear, staying out of sight and keeping a close eye on their followers. Botreg stayed beside Ralav and Ronli as they ran ahead of the others. They heard more horn blasts from the direction of the creek, making everyone run harder. Before long, the trees gave way to rocky terrain.

The sound of horns was closing in behind them, but the rocky hills offered few trails and nowhere to stand and fight. Despite the tracker's vigilance, there was nothing. Every likely-looking passage ended after only a few hundred paces.

Eldahir charged past the others, pausing by Celedant and Tarquin.

"My lords, the Aloi have been slaughtered by strange men with even stranger weapons from the void. I counted over five hundred golden armored soldiers following our path. They will catch up to us in twelve hours."

Celedant grasped Tarquin's arm. "I have an image in my head of fighting them from the top of a rockslide. I believe the staff is guiding me."

Tarquin looked at him worriedly. "I can't abide running forever. Ralav, Ronli, find the area that Celedant describes. Go now."

The two dwarves ran off.

Eldahir agreed, adding, "It will be best to fight in a place of our choosing."

The others gathered around Tarquin, who looked at them all.

"Friends, you have followed a crazed wizard and a dolt of a youth for months." His words brought a smile at his joke. "I will not allow us to die in this forsaken place. We will fight in a narrow area to reduce the number that can come at us." He raised his fist and shouted. "Let a thousand enemies come and die on our swords."

The others shouted agreement. They were tired of running. A stand-up fight was needed.

At that moment, Ronli ran down a small decline.

"Sir, we found a good place just ahead. It looks like the spot that Celedant seeks."

Ralav and Ronli had discovered an ancient rockslide that sloped steeply upward to a narrow shelf. As they scrambled up the incline, it vividly reminded Tarquin of his training as a youngster on the steep slopes of Nars. In that faraway time as a young recruit, he had staggered on hands and knees up steep slopes, driven by the sergeants. The excruciating pain of bloody, gouged hands and knees was followed by more agony when ordered to descend as quickly.

Thankfully, those days were long behind him; he and the others weren't even breathing hard now. Tarquin noticed a shelf located several hundred feet from the bottom of the slope that led to a small gap in the wall.

"Ronli, did you check it out?" he called.

The dwarf nodded. "Yon trail leads to the top of this hill," she said. "It's sort of a last stand."

"Not while I'm here," Azimuth told them. "There will be no last stands!"

They answered loudly with a heartfelt "Yes" or "Aye."

While Azimuth cheered the company on, Tarquin looked to the defenses.

"Hority, take our packs to the top. Find a place to make a wall, and stack them and any rocks you find. Be ready to aid our wounded."

Hority bounced from foot to foot, hand raised.

Tarquin looked him in the eye, saying sternly, "Hority. Aegir is dead. You and Baldo are the best healers we have, but we need Baldo's weapon here. That leaves you to tend to the injured. Think how Clor will bless your helping us and still managing to get dirty. I can think of no more noble filth than the dirt and hill's pebbles, mixed with blood soaking into your habit."

The dwarf's eyes lit up. He grabbed three packs and darted up the trail.

Tarquin called to the others. "Carry or roll those rocks. We need to move as many boulders and rocks from below as possible and take them up to the shelf's edge."

Everyone got to work gathering large stones and rolling boulders from the rock face or up from the slope. Azimuth was stronger than his elven appearance suggested as he rolled even the largest boulders uphill, using draconic strength. Indentations in the rock fall offered firm footholds to push the boulders that were just below the rim. Before long, they had built a decent wall. Eldahir's bow twanged, and a scream shattered the silence in the forest as night closed in.

Chapter Thirty-Four

Eldahir made a grand gesture with his hand between firing off arrows.

"The hounds have cornered their prey!"

Tarquin could estimate several hundred brightly armored soldiers in the tree line one hundred and fifty paces from the rockslide, with more hiding in the deeper woods. The elf shot several arrows into the gathering while Tarquin and Morganna gathered arrows and readied their bows. Elven bows were stronger and more accurate, thanks to elven magic, giving Eldahir and Morganna the advantage. As the elven warrior continued his assault, the other two waited up the slope. Soon everyone but Celedant had bows or crossbows ready, waiting for the order to fire.

Eldahir called to the others. "Aim for their necks, the most exposed area. Only a solid shot will penetrate their armor."

The enemy below raised their shields. Others were secluded in the trees as more arrows cut into their ranks. As they formed a shield wall, a golden soldier carrying a silver rod given him by Taza emerged from the group and ran toward the rock slope. Tarquin shot him through the chest, and the golden man fell backward, raising a cheer from the defenders.

"Look below!" Eldahir shouted.

This time, several aliens sprinted forward. The defenders' arrows splintered against their golden mail. Many aliens were pitched to the side or fell backward as arrows and crossbow bolts took their toll. Yet there were more than Tarquin and the others could bring down. Finally, one of the men struck the stones embedded in the hill with a silver rod just before an arrow hit his neck, and the ground beneath them began to grate and move.

Out of the hillside emerged the first of several dreaded rock golems. Celedant knew that warlocks often summoned these creatures, but never having faced one before, the others did not know how to fight them. The monsters were eight feet tall, formed from the very rock that formed the slide. The closest one shook off loose soil, staring up at the shelf and the creatures his master Taza wanted eliminated. To these magically formed creatures, there was no right or wrong, no emotions at all. They were made to kill.

"Arrows can do no good here. Baldo, can your hammer harm them?" Celedant shouted.

The dwarf smiled grimly under his faceplate. "I'll give it a try."

The cleric of Thierry whispered a few words to his god, whirled the hammer above his head, and let it fly.

The magical hammer struck the first golem in the chest. A mighty boom sounded as chunks of stone exploded with enough force to make the creature stagger, loosening stone and gravel. The hammer reappeared in the dwarf's hand.

"More are coming," Celedant warned.

The other aliens were not idle. More behemoths marched up the rockslide. Celedant called out a spell that melted one of the golems into a pool of viscous substance that slid down beneath the rock fall.

Taking a running leap, Azimuth jumped off the side of the cliff; several companions watched in amazement as he morphed into his natural form – a golden dragon. He hadn't done that in their presence often, so it came as a shock when he did. Climbing upward, he turned and swooped down at the enemy, avoiding the range of blue bullets.

Emitting a mighty roar, he dove for one of the golems, raking it with magical fire until the rock monster exploded in thousands of stones and chunks of rock that rained down on the golden clad warriors below. A cheer rose up from the defenders.

"Kill the magic users before they summon more," Eldahir shouted.

He, Tarquin, and the others concentrated their arrows and bolts on the aliens, depleting the ranks of those closest. Seeing too many of their brothers die, they retreated rather than remaining exposed to the arrows. The first stone golem had reached the shelf, even while Baldo's steel hammer continued to knock off huge pieces of rock. The monster swung a massive fist, sending Tarquin flying backward to slam against the rock face. He remained on his hands and knees, shaking his head to stop the ringing and trying to steady himself.

Celedant sent a lightning bolt zinging down the slope, blasting another one apart, stones flying high into the air, while Azimuth attacked and destroyed yet another. From above, they heard a fanatic cry.

"Foes!"

Heads stared upward to see the scrawny figure of Hority. The dwarf jumped, brandishing his branch. He fell twenty feet, his habit billowing outward, displaying a view of his muddy legs along with the most disgusting loin cloth any of them had seen. He landed and rolled to a stop.

Hority's feet hit the rockslide. He ducked and dodged until he was face-to-face with one of the creatures. Hority looked harshly at the golem, who, like the others, was momentarily stunned.

Before the slow-thinking creature could attack, Hority waggled his head and thrust out his gnarled stick with the pumice rock bound to the end. There was a blinding flash, and the rock golem dissolved into pebbles.

"Keep the golden ones occupied, Celedant ordered. "They will attack when their creatures fall." He chanted a spell, using Forestae to shoot a huge fireball that turned the trees under which the soldiers were hiding into a blazing furnace.

Azimuth added his own fire to the inferno, skirting the edges to catch those escaping the main blaze. Arrows rained down as the brave little Clorian danced, skipped, and somersaulted to escape the golem attacks. One by one, the golems fell before the magic of Hority's staff until, having enough of its master's orders, the last golem turned and charged into the burning forest. Cries of distress were heard from the soldiers, for the creature was stomping straight through the gathered aliens, crushing many underfoot. After that, the forest became quiet.

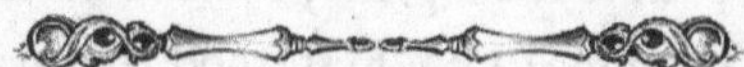

The monk of Clor hopped up to the shelf and rubbed dust and pebbles into his frock, face, and hair, drawing everyone's attention. No one spoke as he closed his eyes and offered a prayer to his god. His body was covered in bruises and bloody cuts from the rocks. Baldo winced. The dirt would surely cause infection in those open wounds.

Celedant joined Hority. "What manner of weapon do you yield, Master Clorian?"

Hority shrugged and twirled his branch midair and around his back.

"I donna rightly know. I found this branch while gathering food from the nearest dwarvan city. Did ye know that those eastern dwarves toss wagonloads of proper food out every day?"

Several listeners could imagine the so-called 'delicacies' that filled those waste pits.

"I ramble. One day while taking a holy mud bath, I submerged me head, and me fingers wrapped around this old rock. Removing the mud showed this chunk of pumice. I used some worn leather straps and tied it to the end of me branch. I prayed for an entire day that the rock would never fall off in battle."

He stared at it. "To me amazement, it turned out to be magical, dispatching most beasts with a touch, especially the undead. I canna stand those foul creatures."

Fearing Hority would talk on through the night, Baldo interrupted. "Me good Clorian, it appears this device was arranged for ye to find and carry on yer quest of spreading Clor's will."

Hority dropped to the ground in a fit of religious fervor, praying and rubbing his face into the ground, tossing dirt and whatever else he could lay his hands on into his habit and hair.

Everyone watched Hority's actions, awestruck, at his devotional, until Celedant interrupted.

"Friends, let's leave Hority for now. Baldo, would you keep your eyes on him? We have a larger problem demanding our attention."

Following Celedant's gaze, they looked at the forest where campfires had sprung up. Tarquin counted them, and after a moment he said, "I would guess a hundred fires. If you count four men per fire, we have a huge problem on our hands, and you can believe that word of our being trapped will spread among the orc tribes. Taza has a price on our heads."

Celedant agreed. "A price he is most anxious to pay after his other attempts have failed so miserably. Come, let us take counsel at the mount's summit." As he walked, he waited for feelings or warnings from the Staff of Adaman, but it remained silent.

Filing up the narrow path to the top, they came to the low wall of stones and the opening where their packs were stored. Rest, food, and water would restore their strength from the flight and fight they had just endured. Hopefully, they would find a way to escape.

Chapter Thirty-Five

A blackened kettle sat above a small fire, boiling water for tea. Several stones banked the embers out of habit. Bundles of wood, gathered after they had left the swamp, assured they would eat a warm meal, the first in many a week. Morganna was stationed below, keeping watch from the rock shelf. When the teapot whistled, everyone jumped. Baldo grabbed Hority, who thought they were under attack.

Ralav poured cups of tea and sat at his place in the circle.

The wizard began. "All of you understand what this quest entails."

The others nodded as Celedant reached around and brought forth the soft hide carrying case for the Staff of Adaman. He slowly untied its binding strings and slipped the staff out so that it lay sparkling across his knees. Many of them had never seen it before, but even those who had caught their breath at its beauty and power.

After a moment, the wizard returned the staff to its carrying case and tied it back up.

"The Staff of Adaman must not fall into the hands of Taza or his henchmen. If he unravels its mystery, all things good will be corrupted into evil visages of their former selves. Evil will rule this world, and Taza will rule as its master, for he has the twin of this staff."

"If Taza joined the two staffs, wouldn't it bring about the same geological disaster that happened in Zeiglon?" Tarquin asked.

"It would indeed. I have been told that the Staff of Adaman cannot be used for evil by evil. I don't know if Taza is aware of that," the wizard replied. "Even if he did not foolishly attempt to use Adaman's Staff, without an opposing force, the Staff of

Adois would take over the world, and there would be nothing we could do to stop it."

"I am puzzled," Azimuth said. "You mentioned a while back that the two staffs want to destroy each other. If they were both in the same vicinity, how could Taza or anyone stop them?"

"Excellent question, my friend. Unfortunately, I don't have an answer. I fear that should both staffs be controlled by one person, good or evil, the resulting destruction could be much worse than before - it could possibly tear a permanent hole in the void."

"How can one destroy the other without causing consequences?" Eldahir asked.

"If each staff is wielded separately by an equally powerful wizard or warlock, I believe the deed can be accomplished with minimal damage. Remember, with Zeiglon, one evil warlock held both staffs, resulting in complete disaster. Once the Staff of Adois is destroyed, Adaman will likely destroy his staff, too. We must accomplish this quest, no matter what it takes. Failure would be cataclysmic."

While everyone else silently contemplating the reality of what they had been charged with, Hority sadly shook his head.

"Clor would be much displeased if we fail."

The members of their group exchanged grim glances over the fire. Clor wasn't the only one who would be displeased. Many feared that it could lead to a war of the gods.

"Hority is right," Celedant said. "In that one theological statement, he has summed up the essence of this quest. The counterbalance of good and evil would not only affect this world but also send shock waves throughout the universe in the struggle between good and evil."

Tarquin and the others listened intently. They now understood that none of their comrades had fallen in vain. They had fallen for their separate gods and for the salvation of the world. They had paid the ultimate sacrifice for something more important than any individual. As Celedant spoke, some members of the quest had tears running unashamedly down their cheeks as they remembered their fallen friends. Celedant let them mourn. He believed that all were now aware of the ultimate nature of their sacrifices.

"In Southgard, I journeyed to a secret room hidden below the deepest mines. There I used my newly-acquired powers from the staff to shield this artifact from Taza's mind, and more importantly, the Staff of Adois. With both parts of the Staff of Adaman joined, we have come to the point where the end of our quest is within our grasp. We must end this evil once and for all."

He looked each person in the eye before continuing.

"Tarquin and I were visited by Adaman in our dreams. He pressed me not to use his staff until the time was right. He spoke of magical power on Muiria. Adaman called these intersections nexuses. At these points, the magical power inured into our world is closest to the surface and the most powerful. The Staff of Adaman is seeking a nexus – on this desolate hill."

He scanned the faces of his friends. "However, you must be aware of the danger involved if the staff is used. It will most certainly alert Taza to our whereabouts. I believe that when the time comes, it will open a rift in the void, and when we step through, we will appear in Dormin. Adaman has imprinted a nexus point near Dormin in my mind. Tarquin and I were warned that the staff would have to be used, but we were not told when. I must wait for it to reveal the time. I do not control the destiny of this relic. It controls ours."

Tarquin asked the pertinent question on everyone's mind.

"Can the staff teleport all of us, and will anyone be waiting at the other end?"

"The staff can take us all. It is more powerful than you can begin to imagine. We will need to clasp hands, but I think it wise to use rope to bind us together in a long line as a precaution. We will not be teleporting, as you might know it, but actually opening a rift in the fabric of the universe. I will step through the void with all of you and into a glade in Dormin. I don't know what kind of reception we will receive."

"I cannot stress enough this warning," he added. "The few ticks of the clock we are in the void can be extremely dangerous. If you become separated from the exit and each other without the rope, you will float in terror until you starve to death or are eaten by one of the leviathans that dwell in the void. We must be tethered together."

As night fell, Tarquin, Celedant, Azimuth, and Eldahir looked down the slope toward the woods where their enemies were preparing to bed down for the night.

"They will lose many soldiers crossing the fields to the bottom of the slope," Tarquin said quietly. He pointed to the south. "See that small rise? That's where they'll station archers or whatever the weapon that Eldahir described. Eldahir, you and Morganna should arm yourselves with as many arrows as you can carry, taking also those of the others. As our best archers, make every shot count."

The elves nodded and exchanged smiles with the others. Few people, other than elves, wizards, sorceresses, and dragons, knew that elves use a little magic to guide each arrow, guaranteeing a perfect shot every time.

Celedant pointed to the small rocky breastwork. "This won't hold for long, I fear. We can send it tumbling down the slope once the enemy nears the top."

"If they use their special weapons on the hill or below, it will make the defense of this shelf extremely difficult," Tarquin said worriedly.

Celedant smirked. "Oh, I have a surprise or two ready, and our cleric and monk are always willing to call the wrath of their deities down on their foes."

"And don't forget me," Azimuth added. "Few can withstand dragon fire."

Tarquin perked up. "Now that's a plan!"

Celedant remained silent as they rejoined the rest of their comrades, sorted through the equipment they would need, and donned their armor.

They spent a chilly night on the exposed hillock, bedded down wearing armor with weapons at hand. Eldahir kept watch on the enemy below. As the sun rose, Eldahir and Morganna strolled down the path carrying every useable arrow the group possessed. They took a high position, providing them with a perfect angle for the shooting platform. Next to take their places were Baldo and Hority. Celedant bent low, moving toward larger boulders that offered the best concealment.

Tarquin and Botreg sat on the trail away from the fighting where they could be signaled.

Botreg chewed on a tough piece of jerky, pointing it at the others.

"I once wished I had magic in me blood, but now, I'm grateful I don't."

It took less time than expected for the golden soldiers to get organized. Their captains arranged them in ordered ranks, hidden inside the tree line. Small groups were also placed to each side on the small rises as expected.

"They have positioned warriors to each side, Celedant," Eldahir called. "I do not like their magical weapons."

As he finished speaking the aliens charged; the lines remained in exact order as they ran through the field at the bottom of the slope. Eldahir and Morganna released arching arrows that struck the advancing line. In response, beams of blue light struck the rocks below as the creatures approached the shelf. Their projectiles chipped the stones, keeping the defenders' heads down and leaving severe burns on the stones.

Celedant stood up and calling on his wizardry, aimed Forestae at the left-most group of aliens. Huge lightning bolts struck the advancing enemy, leaving two blackened craters among the creatures on the hillock. That single spell broke up the mass of soldiers, leaving a score dead and wounded. The strange beams of light stopped for a moment, and their yielders backed off when they saw many of their troop lying dead.

Baldo stood next, calling on Thierry's aid. Huge columns of fire fell from the sky into the enemies on the other hill. There was no way to tell how many died, for the field blazed like an inferno. A blue beam struck Baldo's left shoulder after he cast the spell, causing a small explosion and knocking him off balance. Luckily, it left only a blackened dent on his shoulder plate.

Azimuth had remained at the campsite on top of the hill. As the battle began, he transformed into his dragon form. Taking several steps, he hurled himself off the hill, taking to the air. He coasted over the hills and came at the enemy troops from the west. Since he was flying low and his shadow was cast behind, the aliens charging across the field never saw him coming. Opening his massive jaws, his roar released a blast of dragon fire that flowed over the soldiers at the rear of the attack, melting their plate mail and incinerating them.

Hority also cast his spell, and a horde of small mice appeared among the rushing golden soldiers. Concentrating on the battle, they paid no attention to the hundreds of terrified mice running about their feet, except to snatch them up and eat them.

Eldahir, shooting arrow after arrow as fast as only an elf could, called out: "Hority – mice, really?"

"A Clorian mystic told me people are afraid of mice," the dwarf called back. "How was I supposed to know they would eat them?"

The soldiers reached the bottom of the rocky slope. Heeding the elf's words, Hority waved his branch toward their on-rushing enemies. Suddenly, all along the rocky slope, stones shot out from their age-old resting places. Enemy warriors stopped as their front lines collapsed from the flying rocks. Larger boulders sliced through the attackers, tossing soldiers right and left.

Hority called out innocently to the elf, his voice sounding like that of a scolded child.

"That was better, wasn't it?"

Eldahir cracked a smile as he aimed at one of the leader's red armor, amazed at what Hority had done. "Yes! More spells of that type would be helpful."

He let fly his arrow, and one of the red plate-mailed aliens flew backward, an arrow through the right eye of his faceplate. In the frenzied charge, the alien warriors didn't see their commander fall. They continued running up the slope, believing that reaching the shelf was the only way to survive.

As the soldiers started the climb, lightning bolts, fireballs, and other horrendous spells rained on them. Many were struck down by these spells, but their numbers were so great that the troops continued to gain ground. Eldahir and Morganna shot at every creature. Most, however, had run back to the safety of the forest after the magical attacks and Azimuth's appearance. The elves reached for more arrows but came up empty. More weapons and magic were needed.

A dark shadow moved across the field as Azimuth swept down once more, raining dragon fire on the enemy at the foot of the embankment. The golden soldiers were ten paces from the shelf when Tarquin and Botreg charged the stone wall.

Together, they shoved a loosened boulder down the slope. It accelerated, tearing through the advancing aliens. The others followed this example, diminishing the foes. The enemy reached the shelf and began climbing.

Bolstered by Eldahir and Morganna, swords and axes went to work, defending their position. They chopped, thrust, and kicked the aliens who gained the shelf, but there were still too many. Soon the enemy and defenders were intermingled. Baldo used his hammer to great effect, destroying the creatures attacking him.

In the field, Azimuth continually turned and flew over all areas, incinerating every enemy soldier within reach. The field troops started running for the safety of the woods.

Hority was the only defender who seemed to be enjoying the battle. He bounced, rolled, and jumped about the shelf, striking down enemies with a touch of his branch.

Celedant stood on a boulder above the attackers, using his sword and staff to great advantage. He chanted a minor spell, bringing down several golden soldiers. Meanwhile, Eldahir and Morganna stood back to back using the same strategy with swords and spells.

An alien dressed in red realized how few of his troops were left and called for a retreat. The enemy soldiers now believed they would die on this shelf of stone, so the retreat was greeted with relief. They jumped down, running and rolling to the foot of the slope as fast as possible. There, the remaining commanders pointed to the forest, and the attackers fled the battlefield.

The cost of the attack was tremendous for the golden soldiers. Bodies were strewn from the edge of the woods to the top of the sloping stones. Relieved it was over, Tarquin let the aliens run, knowing the fight had gone out of them. There were few injuries among the defenders. The worst was a deep slash to Morganna's arm. Baldo took care of it, and the battle-weary comrades made their way up to the hilltop. It was time for rest and food.

Reaching the small summit, the company sat down, breathing heavily, while Raslov set a pot of water for tea on the fire. Eldahir sat near the edge, eyes scanning the approaches for signs of danger. Azimuth reversed the direction of his wings as he came in for a landing.

When the tea was steeped, it was distributed in cups to all who accepted with a smile or word of thanks. Celedant took a sip, letting the hot liquid refresh him. The wizard thought he felt a slight tremor in the stone of the hill. He set his cup down, and the liquid the tea began to vibrate. A light was growing brighter through the Staff of Adaman's carrying case. The wizard quickly unwrapped the staff, which illuminated the hill in a bluish color.

All eyes were drawn to the staff, and Celedant said, "The Staff of Adaman has signaled us. It is time to face the final tests." Standing, he added, "Come we must prepare. Bring everything necessary."

Before they were ready to go, Hority was smearing ash over his head, and in places, small smoking fires were breaking out in his hair. Baldo's head bowed in silent prayer, and he walked over to Hority, dragging the persistent monk while dousing the mini-blazes in his clothing.

Celedant looked all of them in the eyes.

"Remember - Taza's Staff of Adois will detect my use of Adaman's Staff. It cannot pinpoint exactly where we will have appeared. However, it will pinpoint where I used it. Those soldiers that thought us easy prey will rue the day they crossed Taza by letting us escape."

Tarquin went to each friend, checking that the rope was secure and the straps were tight.

Botreg said, "I'll bring up the rear, Tarquin."

He turned to his old comrade answering, "When was the last time you volunteered for anything unless I pushed you. I'll be behind all of you. If there is an accident, I will follow you into the void."

Celedant warned them, "So, immediately when we are in Dormin, be ready for anything. Cut the rope and follow me. Look for a place to hide if needed. It will be odd enough if we appear in front of someone. Once there, we will head to the north gate, assess the situation in Dormin, and plan our next move."

The wizard took firm hold of the mythril shaft, concentrating and allowing the Staff of Adaman's energy to infuse his body. Slowly a dark hole opened before the company. Celedant strode confidently into the rift while the others approached with trepidation. Oddly, for the company, it was like no more than stepping through a doorway. The void for the dwarves looked like an endless crevice. Baldo had to grasp the ever-curious Hority. They emerged in a wasted field where crops lay unharvested and brittle to the touch. Celedant quickly sheathed the Staff of Adaman in its magical leather bag.

Cutting themselves free, Eldahir called, "Quick, there is an old farm. We can hide there."

No one argued as they sprinted to the dilapidated farmstead. The company vaulted a tumbled rock wall that once had surrounded the farm. Landing, they squatted, studying the interior landscape. No one spoke as they slowly entered the half-burned house and barn. The company spread out, searching for potential enemies.

Finding the area safe, they gathered at the house; the small barn was leaning against the low wall, threatening to fall at any time. When they were all in the house, the company spread out so they could see all the approaches to the farm while conversing.

Celedant shrugged. "This used to be a glade many years ago when Dolgar walked Muiria. Things change in the blink of a god's eye."

He pointed, "That way is north where the city lies. But this puzzles me. We can see where crops covered the hills surrounding the city, but the land seems to be long dead."

Eldahir inquired, "Could not the Staff of Adois be causing this? Is it responsible for the befouling of the land as it spreads its influence outwards from the city?"

Celedant said, "That is as plausible as any explanation. As any."

Chapter

Thirty-Six

Cyra was the first person to ride onto the plain that led to the city. She knew it would take a day to sort the army for the crossing. She wished she could ride ahead and enter the city, but she needed her army to scale the walls and bring down the gates. Still, something niggled at the back of her mind. Something wasn't right. A dark magical aura encased the whole area.

She did not understand, but Cyra knew she needed to get to the city as soon as possible. After the battle, hundreds of horses had wandered around the battlefield, and she had ordered the main units and those most trustworthy to capture the mounts. One unit was the mercenaries Melgor had attached himself to, which meant that he and his bodyguards each got a horse.

Cyra ordered her trumpeter to sound the call to bring the horsemen forward. As they arrived, she rode among them, calling, "There lies the city. We must reach it quickly."

Cheers rose from her fanatical troops, but the mercenaries remained silent.

"We must reconnoiter the city before our army approaches," Cyra called. "Move out."

She spurred her horse forward, and the trumpeter blew the signal. The horsemen rode at a fast pace with Cyra leading the column. Her foot soldiers started the long trek across the plain.

Chapter Thirty-Seven

While they remained hidden in the burned-out farmhouse, Tarquin and the others watched the refugees from the city crowd the road to the west, carrying all their possessions.

The opening of the rift had alerted Taza to his foes' presence. He smiled evilly when his enemies sprang his long-awaited trap. His mistress Adois had informed him of the nexuses before Celedant knew of them. The vampire had kept a special group of monsters for this occasion. With a word and the wave of his staff, he released them to kill the wizard and prince.

A crackling erupted from outside the farmhouse, and a vortex appeared, growing steadily larger. When the vortex was complete, five huge mastiffs leapt from the blackness, landing on all fours. They raised their heads and sniffed the air for prey. Smoke shimmered off their hides, rivulets of magma ran across their bodies like veins, and where their paws touched the ground, small fires broke out. Celedant and Azimuth exchanged a look. These creatures were hellhounds, guardians to the nine hells, and the beasts had been sent to destroy them.

Eldahir and Morganna reacted first as a beast jumped into the wrecked house to confront them. They both shot arrows at the creature's face, but the arrows burst into flame and turned to cinders before they reached the target. Tarquin struck with his sword, stabbing the fiend through the back and abdomen, to little effect. As he pulled out his sword, he felt the beast's heat through his glove as though he had placed his blade in a white-hot dwarvan forge. Red flames of hell danced along its length from the heat of the monster.

The other three beasts burst into the farmhouse. Celedant called, "Forestae – protect us!"

The weapon sent a bright green beam at one of the monsters. The beam struck it in the chest, and destructive energy engulfed the beast, injuring it. Unlike the first hellhound, it stumbled into the far wall, pawing at the energy encasing its body. When it was halfway to the floor, Hority attacked. The Clorian monk struck the wounded hellhound a severe blow on the back with his branch, and it stiffened, spread-eagled and dead.

Another hellhound spun on its hind legs, knocking Morganna over to land in the corner. One of its front paws took out Tarquin's leg, sending him tumbling toward a fourth hellhound.

Celedant again called forth his staff's power and sent a rush of cold air against the beast nearest Tarquin, encasing it in ice. This was but a respite, as the creature's heat melted the icy prison encompassing it.

"Water will hurt them most!" Eldahir shouted. He cast a spell, and rain fell from the ceiling, pelting the beasts.

The hellhounds howled in pain. Each drop sizzled when it struck their bodies. One creature bowled into Eldahir, flipping him over its back to land in the middle of what had once been the floor of the main room. The hell hound stood above Eldahir, the elf's clothes smoldering, its paw poised to strike, but at the last second the elf rolled out from under the jabbing claws.

Meanwhile, Hority turned his attention to the first creature injured by Celedant's spell. It stood on its feet, biting with blood stained teeth at the small dwarf as Hority danced in and out of striking range.

Baldo approached another hellhound, standing in the middle of the room. He rushed out, swinging his hammer and unleashing a blow to the side of the creature's neck. The beast's head spun and its mouth opened. Like a furnace blast, its fiery breath blasted the dwarf. Baldo felt torrid heat encompass him, but his mythril armor and magical facemask deflected the attack. Designed to withstand heat like the breath of a firedrake, it protected him from the hellhound's attack.

Baldo struck again, his hammer landing squarely on the hellhound's head with a loud crack. The beast recoiled, and Tarquin struck next, sliding his sword between the beast's ribs, seeking its heart. His hand and glove would have caught fire had not Celedant immediately cast another water spell that rained on the animal, soaking it. Tarquin safely withdrew his blade.

As the dying creature struggled to hurl a blast of burning breath at Tarquin, Celedant released the staff of Adaman from its case and stuffed the crystal end into the mouth of the hellhound. The force repelled the creature's fiery breath, causing the monster's head to explode in a flash of fire. Its headless body collapsed to the ground, smoldering in death.

Another hellhound dodged Hority's staff while Ralav and Ronli plied their axes expertly until it fell on its side and moved no more. The group encircled the remaining fiend. It struck out, searing claws burning through Morganna's armor. Wounded, she fell backward and quickly put out the fires that had started on her armor and clothes. The rest struck the hound with their weapons. Horribly wounded, it managed to burn the hands of several attackers yielding weapons. The hellspawn staggered and fell on its side. Tarquin stepped forward and drove Dragon Bolt into the creature's heart. It twitched twice and lay still.

What happened next would remain in their memories forever. The floor surrounding each of the hellhounds split open, forming a deep, sulfur-smelling pit with no bottom. The pits swallowed the bodies in its fiery depths, setting the house further ablaze. Then it closed.

Azimuth, who had remained at his post at Celedant's urging, watched the road. As the flames in the farmhouse began to build, people escaping Dormin had stopped to witness the battle. As the fire blazed larger, they scurried away, looking back with nervous glances. They had seen too much magic and were eager to escape its clutches. Celedant and the others fled the roaring fire that engulfed the old farmhouse. When they were clear, Baldo and Hority saw to their wounds, and they began their trek north to the city.

Wearing her damaged armor and checking her wounds, Morganna kept an eye on the opposite direction in case more hellhounds or monsters from the nine levels of hell came at them from behind. There, she thought she saw something on the far hills that flattened out to form a plain leading up to the city.

"Eldahir, what do you make of that?" she called, pointing in the direction she wanted him to look. "I may know what it is."

The elf stared into the distance several moments before saying, "It's an army on the march. They're still a goodly distance from the city – a day or two at most. But their cavalry is riding hard ahead of the foot soldiers."

"We must hurry," Celedant interjected. "I don't want to be caught between Taza and an unknown army."

"I have been watching the road opposite us," Tarquin added. "Oddly, the only traffic are refugees coming from the direction of the city gates. I haven't seen a soul heading north since we got here. I've also seen individual soldiers in various uniforms mixed with the travelers."

"That *is* odd," Celedant said. "Nevertheless, in this confusion, we can approach the gate like travelers. With the staff hidden again, once we are in Dormin's warren of streets, we should be safe. Come. The city gates lay just a mile or two beyond those trees."

He ushered them to the dusty side of the road, moving against the pedestrian tide for the gates into Dormin. As they approached, they saw there were no guards on the walls or even at the gates. Tarquin had been right about the garrison soldiers being in the crowd as it fled.

Tarquin stopped a man leaving with his possessions balanced precariously on his head.

"Good sir, we're traveling to Dormin to sell a few trinkets. Why is everyone leaving? What has occurred?"

The man suspiciously glanced back at the city. "The guards went on a killing spree, looting all the houses. We have not seen our king in weeks, and a warlock named Taza has proclaimed himself ruler. Now the dead walk at night and even the city guards have abandoned us. Worse yet, an army of orcs are marching on the city from the south."

Tarquin let the man go and looked to the others.

Eldahir pointed to the setting sun. "We need to find somewhere safe if the undead own the night's streets."

"Follow me," Celedant urged. "I know of a place if it still exists." He led them into the city of Dormin, where they ducked into a vile-smelling alley teeming with garbage and rats. Baldo snatched Hority by the arm to prevent him from running off with a righteous gleam in his eye. Suddenly, the scores of citizens fleeing the city stopped, jamming the streets. They began pushing and shoving forward an inch at a time, their increasing fear spreading like an epidemic.

"Looks like we came at a critical time," Celedant said. He led them through a maze of alleys, the last being one they had to enter sideways. Sunset fell as they heard the first screams.

"Not far now, not far," the wizard whispered.

The narrow alley ended at a courtyard with no other exit in sight.

"We're trapped," Tarquin said. "Botreg, Ralav, keep an eye on the alley."

Celedant looked around, rubbing his beard. "Patience, my friends. It has been very long time since I was last here, but it's coming back. Never fear."

"Something coming this way," Botreg warned.

He and Ralav stood on either side of the alley's entrance as a fair-headed man walked into the courtyard. Seeing he was unarmed, Botreg and Ralav relaxed as he stared blankly.

Hority was the first to notice the slack skin and expressionless eyes.

"Undead!" he yelled.

That word brought Botreg and Ralav's weapons down on the newly-turned ghoul.

As the head toppled, Celedant, who had blocked out the drama, said, "Ah, I remember."

Approaching a section of wall, he whispered a spell and used two fingers to give a slight push on two knots in the boards, and with a grating sound, the brick wall to his right opened. Everyone looked warily inside. The dark passage was the last place they wanted to go. The stale odor of wetness wafted over them, and only Hority was eager to continue.

"Further in is a secret staircase once used by the thieves' guild. At the top of the stairs is a room with windows that look on the streets below and the citadel."

The crystal on the wizard's staff suddenly blazed greenish white, lighting the path and stairs ahead. Tarquin, the last to enter, looked for a mechanism to shut the wall. Finding none, he pushed the door, and it settled into position. The stairs, still solid with little decay, hugged the wall as they ascended, and at the top, light from Celedant's staff showed an old but solid door.

The wizard turned to look back down the dark stairs. "Botreg, your skills are required here. This door needs to be checked for traps."

The slight dwarf wove his way up the crowded steps. "Not a problem. Have ye known it to be trapped before?"

"Yes," the wizard replied. "When the thieves' guild let me stay here, they sent a man to fiddle with the key and handle."

Botreg went through his series of tests, examining the handle and keyhole closely.

He glanced back at the others. "Baldo, Hority, do ye have a spell to detect traps? I want to be sure before I go about disarming this."

"Yes, but I donna know how specific it will be," Hority replied.

"My own spell can tell us if it's trapped, but not where," Baldo added.

Botreg sighed. "Wishful thinking. Go ahead and cast yer spell."

Baldo cast his spell, and his eyes opened wide.

"Botreg, whatever the trap is, me spell warns that it is a powerful one."

CHAPTER THIRTY-EIGHT

Cyra and her horsemen arrived at Dormin as the sun slipped over the western horizon. They drew to a stop at the city gate to study the battlements.

"Talchic, come forward," Cyra ordered.

Melgor drew even with her. "Your ladyship."

She motioned to the city. "What's wrong here?"

The warlock looked at the walled city. "Even in this light, I can see that no one walks the battlements, and there are no fires in the guard towers. However, there are huge fires burning within the city. Whole sections are burning."

"Harrumph," Cyra uttered. "We cannot wait for the main army. Something strange goes on here, and I need to know the situation."

Botreg sat against the wall, staring at the door and trying to get a feel for the trap, speculating how he would have set it. The room belonged to the thieves' guild, both accepted and outlawed simultaneously. There should have been no competition except for the city guard. If the rich were robbed and reported it to the king, he would have ordered the guards to crack down on the gangs. However, the king and the head of the thieves' guild had a secret understanding that prevented that.

The others watched as the former assassin sat looking at the door. A guild hideaway, a safe house to conceal important people who were on the run, or possibly a place to store treasure. Botreg ran his hands through his dark hair. None of these scenarios boded well for an easy trap.

The door would not pose a serious threat to a force of guards searching for a hidden room. How would he set the trap? In his mind, Botreg imagined two guards approaching the door. They searched for a trap but finding none, signaled their mates on the stairs. Upon opening the door, a fireball or similar spell would be activated, shooting down the steps and vaporizing the soldiers. After a day's work of cleaning the site, no one would know.

Botreg straightened. "That's it, simple and effective. All would die except one or two."

He jumped up from his sitting position, causing the others to tense. The dwarf veered from the door to the wooden portion of the wall that fronted the steps. In the near darkness, illuminated only by the magical light of Celedant's staff, Botreg could make out the deadly end of the trap.

He had missed the signs in the dark, and if Celedant had not called for his attention, most of them would be dead now. Upon closer examination, the rough wood paneling revealed a paper-thin outline of the trap's door.

He turned to Celedant. "Do ye remember if those that brought ye here did anything odd when they opened the door?"

The wizard's mind sought those memories. "The man who led me to this place tried to block my view, but because he was shorter than me, I saw something odd taking place."

"What did he do, exactly?" Botreg asked with eagerness.

The memories flooded into Celedant's mind, the smell of raw timber, the semi-darkness lit by the man's lantern. His escort had made sure his body blocked what he was doing. Nevertheless, Celedant had seen the man grasp the handle and depress the lock while running his hand across the top. Celedant opened his eyes.

"Thought ye might have fallen asleep on us," Botreg said sardonically.

The wizard shook his head. "Oh no. I was letting my memories return to the time I was last here." He described what he had seen many years ago.

Listening intently, Botreg re-examined the door, motioning for Celedant to bring the light closer. Now that he knew what he was looking for, he spotted it at once – a small raised plate where the handle met the wood - so subtle, he might have not have noticed it, and they would all be dead. He slapped his forehead before taking several deep, calming breaths.

When he was under control with his senses keen and a clear mind, Botreg faced the lock. The dwarf mentally played out everything he was about to do. He turned to the wizard.

"If ye would stay here with the light?"

Celedant nodded. "Of course."

Botreg knew how to handle this, but precautions didn't hurt. He leaned around Celedant and said, "Pass the word to Tarquin and the others to move back to the courtyard. If we live, we'll open the door. If ye hear an explosion, find somewhere to hide."

"Hold up a minute," Celedant said. "Pass this back to Tarquin." He unshouldered the Staff of Adaman and passed it down the stairs. He watched as the others filed downward to wait until the door was open and all was safe.

Botreg looked up at the wizard. "This'll be tricky. set with a fireball or other spell, it will shoot down the stairs, killing everyone waiting for the door to open."

"As clever a trap as I ever heard. Let me know when you need my magic."

Botreg flexed his fingers, practicing the movements he would be repeating. "Here we go."

The former assassin took a soft piece of cloth from his pack and ran it carefully over the handle. He paid close attention to the slide mechanism. In his mind, he imagined trying to slide it, but figured that his finger might slip because it was covered with dust. The dwarf did this for some time, just like polishing his boots as a Borderer.

When he took the cloth away from the doorknob, he studied what had been collected. There was dust a plenty, but he was more interested in the area that cleaned the slide. Botreg had been able to put more pressure with the cloth on the slide trap, knowing the chances of it tripping were low. He found that spot and examined it closely. There was dust, but he could make out a spot or two where some sort of grease or oil had been captured as well.

Fluffing out the cloth, he stuck it back into a pocket of his pack. "Well, kind sir, move up against the wall beside me. I'm givin' her a try."

Celedant put his hand on Botreg's shoulder.

"Wait." The wizard uttered a single word and said to him, "I just cast a spell that should protect the two of us if things go amiss."

The dwarf smiled. "Yer distrust in me ability is quite upsetting." Inwardly, he was relieved. Botreg squeezed the handle and slid the plate behind the raised toggle handle. Several seconds passed before they let out the breath they had been holding.

Botreg looked up at the wizard. "Sometimes I mistrust me own ability," he admitted. "This was one time. Now let's open the door and see if we get killed by another trap." He eased the door open part-way, peering all about its edges; seeing nothing, he pushed it fully open.

"See this small hook on the inside?" he asked, pointing to it. "The slide loosens it, and this small wire slips off. The wire disappears behind those boards."

"We've made it so far," Celedant said. "Let's examine the trap further."

Botreg took out another dagger, this one concealed on the outside of his pack. It was very thin, and he carefully opened the hole where the wire led. Once it was wide enough, he sheathed that knife and brought out a stronger blade from his boot.

"My friend, you are a walking arsenal."

The dwarf grinned. "Each weapon has a special purpose, but please don't mention the hidden one. I've a pot of 100 gold pieces for the one who guesses how many weapons I have."

The wizard laughed. "Your secret is safe with me."

Stooping on his haunches, the dwarf used the dagger to pry away the boards several feet to each side of the wire. The wizard's light exposed the trap.

Botreg looked closely and got to his feet.

"Magic. That, I believe, is yer department."

Celedant snorted, placing the lighted end of his staff inside one of the holes. He followed the wire to where it was attached to an ancient wand.

"If we had pulled the door without releasing the trap, the wire would have pulled the wand tight, making it pivot and strike that dowel, activating the wand." He examined the setup again. "The thief setting the trap could easily go out the window. Remove the rest of these boards. No sense in taking more risks than necessary."

The dwarf agreed and did as the wizard suggested, pulling the rest of the boards loose. With deft fingers, Celedant removed the wire and withdrew the wand.

"If the wire had been pulled far enough, the wand would have fired as the secret panel fell outward."

"Go get the others. I want to examine this wand closer." As the dwarf went to fetch the others, Celedant discovered the wand was nothing more than a foot-long piece from an ash tree. There was nothing special about it.

Chapter Thirty-Nine

Melgor, still using the name Talchic, rode next to Cyra as they searched for the main gate. They found it after rounding one of the guard towers.

"Stop. Look to the gate."

The gate ahead was wide open, a black maw enticing prey to enter. The accompanying riders, some two hundred men and orcs, drew up on their reins and stared.

Cyra called forth a company of orcs. "Enter the city and examine the gates. I want to know if they were broken in battle. Ride a few blocks into the city and report what you find."

The orc captain grunted his displeasure, which got him a stern look from the sorceress. He thought it would be better to wait until daylight, and he was right.

"I will accompany them, Lady Cyra," Melgor offered. "I have a more astute eye for differing signs."

She nodded. "Proceed, Talchic, and report back to me."

Melgor and his four bodyguards rode at the head of the company of orcs. Unless the gates had been damaged sufficiently, he did not think they would be able to tell if they had been tampered with. Nearing the gates, he saw that both had been flung wide open. He noticed blood spattered on parts of the road as well as numerous household items tossed here and there.

This wasn't a battle. The citizens were escaping the city, he thought.

Easing his horse past the gates, he called to Halic and his other three bodyguards. "Careful, my friends. This smells like a trap. Come away from the main group."

He paused to let the company of orcs ride further into the city. They were barely out of sight when loud screams split the night, and he heard orcs battling around the corner.

"Hold my horse, Halic."

Melgor dismounted and advanced up the darkened street. At the corner, he stopped and peered around to see what was happening. The orcs had ridden into a trap. Hundreds of undead swarmed them, pulling them off their horses and pinning them to the ground. There were so many undead that the orcs could not retreat. Instead, a few broke loose at the front and rode up the street with howling undead running after them.

He ran back to his horse. Still adapting to having the use of only one arm, it took him a few tries to mount. Pulling on the reins, he galloped toward the gates, bodyguards close behind. He still heard battle cries as he exited the city. Melgor rode up to Cyra, panting.

"Talchic, get it together." Little did she know he was putting on an act for her to underestimate him.

Melgor calmed himself. "There were hundreds of undead waiting for our arrival. The orcs were cut off. Only a few at the head of the column got free and rode deeper into the city."

He paused to take a drink from his waterskin, making sure she saw his hand shaking.

"The gate was opened from inside. It appears the citizens made a mass exodus."

Tarquin and the others lit torches and lanterns to see in the near pitch-black courtyard. Ronli heard a noise from where the narrow alley opened into the place where they were standing. Where the ghoul they had killed moments before lay half in, half out of the alley, they spotted another undead creature on top, devouring the remains. Ronli drew her short sword and stabbed the head of the monster, but that did not kill it. The ghoul raised up and screeched a warning call.

Azimuth swiftly moved beside her, his sword out. He severed the head from the body. All around they heard the calls of other undead closing in on their hideaway. Since they did not know how long it would take Celedant and Botreg to disarm the trap, they planned their defense of the smaller passage leading to the stairway. They had to slip sideways through the end of the passage they had taken to get there. Tarquin and Morganna squeezed through, following the alley to the opening at the street. A gathering of undead stood there.

"We'd better head back and warn the others," the prince said.

They didn't have time as the undead charged. Tarquin's sword was out, hacking and slashing as the undead slowly pushed them down the alleyway. Hearing the commotion, the others ranged themselves around the alley's exit in the courtyard.

"Tarquin, Morganna, it's time – run!" Azimuth shouted as they drew close.

He and Eldahir fired spells at their pursuers as soon as Tarquin and Morganna cleared the alley. Two lightning bolts leapt forward, lighting the darkness and searing and blowing apart the undead that jammed it. For an instant, the passage was clear of undead, but a moment later, it began to fill once more as the enemy advanced. Baldo knelt at the entrance to the alley, drew forth his holy symbol, and called upon his god, Thierry. The alleyway froze as the holy symbol radiated power, and the ghouls burst into ashes.

The howling and screeching continued as more undead attacked, trying to get them. Hunger and the need to kill kept them running toward living beings. Hority took Baldo's place and held forth his holy symbol. The first rank of the undead disintegrated. As they fell back, the fighters had time to take up positions by the exit that led to the stairway.

Soon the undead reached the courtyard. Azimuth, Eldahir, and Tarquin quickly attacked each creature as it entered the area, severing arms, legs, and heads as the undead poured into the courtyard. Suddenly, the attack stopped, and a single figure stood at the entrance to the alleyway.

Even in the darkness, Morganna instantly recognized him as an Illanni vampire. She warned the others, got down on one knee, and summoned what power she could before sending a fireball rushing down the narrow alley. The fire burned the undead and washed against the vampire who had raised a shield, but almost too late. He howled in pain and attacked, summoning his power and sending bolts of energy bouncing off the courtyard walls at them.

One caught Azimuth on the shoulder, spinning him around to fall face down on the filthy cobblestones. Another struck Baldo on the top of his helmet, but the mythril deflected the energy away, leaving him with only a loud ringing in his ears. The others dodged the energy or were lucky enough to be out of the way. Eldahir watched as the vampire slowly marched toward them, his feet disturbing the ashes that littered the ground – ashes from the undead that had preceded him. The Illanni had a sneer on his blackened face, burned from the fireball that had engulfed him. He was saturated in smoke, and several small fires burned his dark clothes. He nonchalantly patted them out before sending another spell hurtling toward them.

Morganna, who had just stood up from a kneeling position, was caught by a viscous fluid. It bound her right arm, picked her up off her feet, and traveling the length of the courtyard, slammed her into the opposite wall. The fluid formed a solid substance that held her several feet off the ground, pinned to the wall.

As the vampire stepped into the courtyard, Ronli and Ralav struck at his legs. He raised his arm and sent both flying across the courtyard to slam into the wall next to Morganna. Tarquin charged next, his sword, Dragon Bolt, glowing red. A vicious fight commenced, and he managed to drive the vampire back into the narrow alleyway, sword ringing on sword and scraping against brick. Tarquin pressed the attack. His sword danced like a feather left and right, left and right, with the vampire's rapier parrying as best he could.

With the alley behind the vampire filled with the undead, the vampire backed into them and launched himself at Tarquin. Their duel continued. Tarquin bled from several injuries, but his opponent hardly seemed to notice the sword cuts where Dragon Bolt had made contact.

Suddenly from behind Tarquin, Azimuth called out, "Back!"

The prince turned and ran as Azimuth finished his spell, sending an invisible force that rolled off his outstretched hand. It knocked the vampire into the undead, pushing the entire mass halfway down the alley into the roadway. Others cast spells that struck the vampire, draining him of the little energy that remained until he slumped to the ground at the feet of his minions.

Morganna tried to cut her way out of the viscous fluid but could not. The others spread about the courtyard, ready for the coming tide of undead. Eldahir stepped into the opening of the alley and cast another fireball that rolled down the confined space. The vampire, who had managed to get into a sitting position, was trying to stand up when he was struck by searing flames that ate his flesh hungrily. With a loud scream, he exploded into dust that scattered across the alley's grimy floor. The fireball killed several ranks of undead, but there were always more, ready to take their place.

They charged the courtyard and burst from the alley, resulting in a free-for-all. Swords, axes, and hammers severed heads, broke the bones of the skeletons, and filled the courtyard with the bodies of the undead. No relief came as more undead filed in from the alleyway. They fought relentlessly, waiting for the secret door to open, praying that Celedant and Botreg had successfully disarmed the trap.

Morganna fought one-handed, clinging to the wall. The number of bodies made it hard for anyone to move about. It was as if every undead creature in the city had come to attack them.

Finally, when it felt like the attack would never cease, the secret door at the base of the building opened, pushing dead bodies backward. Botreg stood in the doorway and looked out, shocked at first at the battle taking place. Regaining control, he saw the undead were flooding into the courtyard.

"Celedant we need your help!" He jumped into the middle of the melee.

The wizard rushed to the secret door and assessed the situation. Holding up his staff, Forestae, he summoned its power and released a devastating lightning bolt, striking the brick building above the alley. There was a vast explosion, and the building toppled, filling the alleyway and trapping the undead beneath the rubble. The way into the courtyard was blocked.

They finished off the remaining undead and followed Celedant inside after Tarquin and Eldahir freed Morganna. Leaving the devastation behind, Tarquin pulled the secret door closed. He followed Celedant and the others up the stairs and into the secret room that lay beyond.

CHAPTER

FORTY

When everyone was safely inside, Botreg went to the broken windows and looked out at Dormin's citadel. The room where they were holed up was small. Outside, it was deathly silent. Tarquin set watches and suggested they try and sleep if they could.

That night, however, no one was able to get sleep as screams and cries for help echoed throughout the town. A loud fight near the gate escalated the noise even more. The undead were on the prowl. Only people ensconced in safe hiding places escaped the reign of terror.

Toward morning, the quiet that descended was both eerie and a relief. Everyone slept a couple of hours until midmorning. Upon rising, they looked out the windows at the citadel and streets below. Only a few people scurried along what had once been a busy thoroughfare.

The citadel was lifeless. No guards walked the ramparts or stood watch on the towers. The silence that had fallen over the city was even more oppressive.

"Come," Tarquin said. "We must pack. It's time to try and enter the citadel."

Since the alleyway was blocked by tons of brick and mortar, they had to tie a rope to a crossbeam and one by one let themselves down from one of the windows. Celedant led them through a warren of alleys to the main street where they continued toward their goal.

Suddenly, from alleyway and side streets came the screeching of zombies and skeletons. A moment before, they had been advancing up a quiet road. Now they were surrounded and fighting for their lives. The skeletons wielded weapons found throughout the city. Some were true swords or spears, while others wielded table legs.

"I have had enough," Azimuth growled. "Clear the area!"

Celedant urged the others back against the corner of a nearby building, where he, Morganna, and Eldahir erected a massive magical barrier around the group. As soon as he had enough space, Azimuth's elven form swirled out of focus and expanded into his natural form. When the fog and mist around him dissipated, the enormous golden dragon stood before them.

He gave a mighty, earth-shaking roar that vibrated the buildings around him and stood in front of his friends for protection. Facing the advancing horde, he opened his mouth and spewed wide jets of flame at the undead. His long neck let him turn his head in every direction, so none of the enemy could escape. The battle lasted only a few minutes. When it was over, Azimuth bugled in triumph and resumed his elven form to the cheers and clapping of the others.

"Remind me never to make you angry at me," Celedant chuckled.

"I have to admit," Azimuth said, "being so long in the confining form of an elf has begun to take a toll. It felt great to have room to resume my natural form and fight as I was born to."

Tarquin laid a hand on his shoulder. "You were a spectacular sight, my friend. After that long night of little rest, it felt good to stand back and watch."

They continued their advance on the citadel, moving up the main street. Although the crowds had decreased from the day before, those citizens who had not been able to escape yet shouldered their possessions and left. Celedant led his group into the section set aside for nobility and influential citizens. Horses and wagons crowded the front of many white-plastered, three-story homes. This section was built up to the citadel walls, using them as part of the structures, and the remaining people filled cart after cart with precious belongings.

Fear was etched on everyone's face whenever they looked back at the citadel. Many more of the houses bore the signs of forced entry and destruction. Whole sections of the city were burning, leaving dark oily smoke and noxious clouds that stained the beauty of the blue sky like darkened wounds.

A company of human soldiers came running in order down the street. The soldier's chain mail and weapons scabbard rattled ominously. Tarquin and the others drew their weapons by habit, but the soldiers ran by them without attacking.

One called out, "You're going the wrong way, mates" before disappearing around a corner.

A city of this size with an almost total lack of people felt surreal. As they neared the main gate of the most powerful monarchy of the west, the citadel entrance stood open, just like the outer gate. No signs of life appeared on the walls and towers. Ralav sprinted to the gates and peered inside. The cobbled courtyard was empty, so he signaled the others that it was safe.

There was no one inside, no workers or guards. They were not challenged as they entered. Instinct warned that this was a trap. Eldahir and Morganna sprinted up the stairs of the gatehouse to make sure it was empty.

"We're being watched," Tarquin said in a low voice when they returned. "Form up tight and be ready for anything."

"Can I un-volunteer?" Botreg asked though he didn't mean it.

His words brought a chuckle or two, and Tarquin shot his friend an angry stare. No one dared to speak after that, but the subtle looks passed between them spoke volumes. They were sure something was going to happen. It was as though the citadel itself was sending warning signals up their spines.

As they inched toward the doors to the building, scanning in all directions, Tarquin's senses were wound so tightly, he could feel the sand and cobbles beneath his boots and smell the scent of unwashed bodies that wafted from behind the ornate doors. None could miss the smell of what awaited them. They gripped their weapons tighter, and Celedant, Azimuth, Morganna, and Eldahir each prepared a spell to send at what awaited them.

Far from the gate, the company of horsemen under Cyra's command waited uneasily until the sun crested the mountains.

She called her commanders together and pointing to two orcs said, "You two, fetch the troops and bring them here as fast as they can run. I must reach the citadel as soon as possible," Cyra added, urging her men to move with all speed. "The inhuman monster that commands these undead must be dwelt with. Come, we ride."

As she took the lead, the different companies followed, making Melgor wonder why they were so devoted to her. She was using no magic that he could tell, and all these orcs were demoralized after the battle at Southgard. He wondered what her purpose was. If she hated Taza, why? Not one among them knew of the ordeals the vampire had put her through. Then he had another thought. If she could destroy her nemesis, was she planning to take his place?

The huge doors pushed open on well-oiled hinges. As sunlight entered through the door, the band of friends saw their adversaries. An uncountable horde of undead stood to one side, a company of King Rondel's soldiers on the other. The undead must be spellbound since they did not attack the king's soldiers. No one moved. Hority broke the silence by charging, his branch waving above his head while he screamed his god's name. "Clor! Clor!"

The others had no choice but to follow the monk into the mass of enemies. Celedant released his spell down a side corridor. Azimuth, Eldahir, and Morganna did the same, but in different directions, while the rest charged after Hority. Eldahir looked the epitome of an elven warrior when he launched himself into their foes, spinning and slashing at the undead that surrounded him. Before long, undead heads and limbs flew from where he was fighting and disintegrated skeletons dissolved into ashes on the marble floor of the palace.

Tarquin had followed Hority only to find himself surrounded by the undead. Dragon Bolt gleamed with fire as he slashed the blade with deadly accuracy, decapitating as many of the skeletons and zombies as his sword could reach. Not one of them could keep Hority in sight. Celedant marveled at the little monk, who dashed about here one second and there another, leaving piles of undead ashes in his wake as he yielded his pumiced-topped branch.

The wizard hurled a fireball down the side corridor, also crowded with undead. The intense heat disintegrated the first few rows, and as it weakened, it tumbled down the hall, catching fire to other undead along the way. While Azimuth and Morganna fired off more spells, Celedant made his way through the undead, his sword plied superbly while his staff Forestae threw the undead from him as if they were little more than dead leaves in the wind.

Taza's remaining loyal troops observed what the outsiders were doing and retreated. There wasn't much fight left in the king's human guards as one, and then another slipped down a side hall. As their number diminished, shields and weapons were dropped. The guards had lost their courage and decided to save their lives rather than fight for a losing cause. The soldiers raced toward the gates of the citadel, intermingling with the fleeing citizens.

Baldo's hammer flew like lightning through the densely packed enemy, leaving a path of fallen undead in its wake. As the hammer returned to his hands, the dwarf waded into the mass of enemy, switching his weapon from hand-to-hand and using both arms, honed on the practice field of the monastery's training grounds. To him, the fighting hammer felt light as a feather, and with each swing, undead fell - never to rise again.

Azimuth and Celedant fought back-to-back with swords and staff. The wizard cleared a portion of his mind to study the entrance gallery, comparing it to his dream. He located the curved stairs going up around the side of the room with the lower chamber at the back.

"The tower stairs are down there! We must hurry. I sense undead approaching!"

Celedant pointed to a wide white marble staircase leading down to the lower levels. The undead that met them were few in number. Instead of posing a threat, they were just a hindrance. Fighting their way forward, two dwarves nearly stumbled as they reached the top step. Others fought a rearguard action against the remaining undead, their backs to the stairs.

Eldahir, Morganna, and Botreg held the remaining undead. Tarquin's boots were covered in slime left by a dying ghoul. He looked to the right when he heard the grating sound of bone on bone and saw a new wave of undead heading toward them from a darkened corridor.

Beset by enemies from all directions, Azimuth and the wizard found the arched entrance to the tower. It had no door.

Who but a fool would assault Taza?

The others guarded the tower opening while Celedant and Tarquin conferred. The decision was to fight and hold off the undead horde until they reached the top of the stairs.

"Quickly. Up to the top. We can't hold them here," Tarquin called out. At that moment, he saw Ralav down on the ground, holding Ronli's head in his lap. She had a huge slice through her abdomen and knew she was done for.

"Ralav, quickly now! We must hurry."

Holding his young niece, the old dwarf made eye contact with Tarquin and shook his head. Gently lowering her head to the floor, he stood up with both his and Ronli's axes and charged into the oncoming horde.

There were tears in Tarquin's eyes as he turned and began climbing the stairs. He wanted to order Ralav to cease and join them on the steps, but he knew it would do no good, and he understood his friend's grief. Turning, Tarquin ascended the stairs behind the others, leaving Botreg and Morganna as rear guard. Climbing past them, Botreg called out.

"Ralav? Ronli?"

Tarquin gave a short shake of his head and continued climbing. The steps ran upwards to the right, offering the advantage when swinging downward from the right with a weapon. The attackers would be fully exposed to the blades of the defenders in order to have enough room to swing their weapons. Even so, they crowded onto the stairway below.

CHAPTER FORTY-ONE

Cyra rode through the gates as the sunlight and wind cleared the smoke that clung to the doomed city. They were amazed to find citizens still escaping from the town through the gates. She slowed the column and ordered everyone to keep an eye on the side streets. When they came upon the remains of the night's battle, they discovered countless beheaded zombies and crushed skeletons as well as a number of dead orcs. Most had been torn asunder. A few struggled to rise.

These were dispatched by the horsemen, who leaned over and used their weapons to behead the creatures. The remaining undead from the night before attacked, plowing into the sides of the column. Swords and axes rose and fell as the horsemen fought the crazed undead. Melgor turned to watch as Cyra charged back to help. Using an arcane spell, she sent out fist-size energy balls that upon impact disintegrated the undead. Slowly the battle swung in favor of the horsemen, but the undead fought to the last.

Melgor turned to Halic. "This is an evil place. Go now and ride back to your homes." Halic was about to protest, but Melgor would have none of it. Handing over the last of his gold and the packet of diamonds, he smiled.

"I won't need this where I'm going. Go now, and get clear of this place."

The stairs stretched on for an eternity. The tower had to be the tallest ever built, with landings for rest at intervals along the way. On these unusually large landings, seats had been placed for a climber to rest. Celedant could tell they were nearing the top from the vibrating twin staffs as they began to counter one another.

The wizard was out of breath when he paused to take a pull from his water skin. He cleared his throat and called to the others, "We're at the top or - very near. Try and hold them here."

Tarquin and the others piled debris from the landing at the opening of the stairway. At least it provided a solid barricade. As they worked, they heard boots slapping the stairs below.

Tarquin called ahead to Celedant, "We'll slow them up. You go ahead."

Celedant barked a command that no one would dare disobey.

"I need you to come with me. Now!"

That was when the prince realized that as an integral part of the prophesy, he had to confront Taza, along with the wizard.

Baldo patted Hority on the shoulder, saying, "I guess it's up to us, me friend. We'll hold the undead back and then follow."

Botreg shrugged at Tarquin. "Ye always did volunteer me. Therefore, I will stay." He called out, "Watch out for him, wizard."

Hority, covered in ash and blood, shook and wagged his head, causing dust and soot to fall from his beard. Suddenly their enemies were upon them, tearing at the feeble wall. There was no holding them back. Hority rushed to the opening of the landing and found a giant skeleton, carrying a two-handed sword, swinging it wildly and crawling over a table. It crashed into the stone mere inches above the dwarf's head.

Hority touched it with his strange branch, and its bones disintegrated. The begrimed dwarf yelled, "Another for Clor and his favor." He and the others fought bravely as they withdrew up the stairs of the tower, giving their friends time to accomplish their mission.

Celedant motioned to Tarquin. "One last...."

Before he could finish speaking, a force exploded, sending him crashing against the prince as he turned.

Tarquin looked up to see armed vampire guards descending. He knew the others could not fight and still block the stairs. He ran into their midst, hindering the vampires. Tarquin stabbed his blade back and forth, trying to dodge and parry the vampire swords. He was so close that when one used its immense strength against him, he was merely shoved against another. With sword and dagger, the prince kept the vampires in confusion. One who had turned his back to the fight on the landing felt the deep bite of the wizard's sword as it cleaved off his head. The vampire exploded into dust.

Knowing he could not allow Tarquin to be killed, Celedant had followed him into the fray. When the last of the Illanni vampires were dispatched, the wizard paused and took up the Staff of Adaman, placing his beloved Forestae into the leather case.

The Staff of Adaman vibrated wildly as it neared its twin. Bruised and cut, Tarquin locked eyes with Celedant, who nodded. They started up the final flight of stairs together.

Below, Eldahir and the others had little difficulty defending the barricade until Botreg killed several zombies almost at once. As they collapsed, the makeshift wall slid down the steps with them. The fighting paused as each opposing force stared. The undead leapt through the debris and charged as the friends formed a line, slowly backing up to the stairs leading upward. The undead swarmed after them, envious of their life force and craving their flesh.

Swords and a war hammer were swung repeatedly while Azimuth, Morganna, and Eldahir fired off spell after spell. Soon the floor was littered with ash, bones, and zombies, but more of the deadly creatures surged. Members of the quest had roused a deadly nest of killers.

During brief reprieves, the cleric and monk used holy symbols to banish groups of undead to the hells from whence they came. Baldo called down giant columns of electricity that incinerated the undead beneath. Hority and the other magicians sent bolts of energy at the skeletons to set them ablaze.

When the group felt the first vibrations rumble through the tower, they turned and ran, taking the steps two at a time. Heading ever higher, they bounced against each other and slammed into the stone wall. Below them, the undead struggled to stay upright but still came.

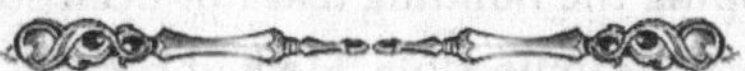

The warlock Sellis, imprisoned by Taza months ago, sat patiently in his cell, facing the door. Feeling the foundations of the citadel tremble, he stood to weather what was coming. It was the wrong move. The room tilted, sending the disgraced warlock sliding down and across the floor. The opposite wall stopped him hard. He heard the rendering of stone overhead as fine cracks formed in the cell walls. As it worsened, Sellis climbed to his feet and widened his stance like a sailor at sea. A huge chunk of ceiling crashed down, barely missing him. He looked longingly at his teleportation ring...if he could extend his hand beyond the magically inured room.

The room shifted left, and more stones caved in. Then what seemed like a miracle happened. He saw a glint of sunlight. Sellis dodged the falling debris and, moving cautiously, he slid and crawled toward the light to a crack that had opened to the outside world. The warlock climbed up the rubble toward freedom. He stuck his hand and arm into the hole as far as he could, cutting them as tremors pushed the stones further apart. Sellis wedged his shoulder into the hole and felt warm sunlight on his hand. Momentarily, he thought of his hidden house and blinked from view. Seconds later, the room was obliterated as the citadel's foundation was torn asunder.

Once his fingers had felt the morning sun, Sellis could think of no place better than his secluded retirement estate. His form blinked from existence under the tons of rock that crushed his old cell. He reappeared before the lavish estate, hidden deep in a forest with access to two city-states. As he materialized, his eyes widened in horror - his face reddened, and his body trembled. His life's dream lay devastated in a tumbled pile. The wood was blackened from what must have been a ferocious fire, and the surrounding estate had been plowed and salted.

Sellis fell to his knees as a wild scream tore from his throat. Moments later, he gathered his wits and cast a spell to locate the vault that held his treasure. His magic passed deep through the ruins without locating what he sought. He turned his attention to the barn that had also burned to the ground. They had even found the gold buried under the pigsty. Closing his eyes, he called upon all the knowledge he had amassed as a warlock to regain his self-control.

He scanned the area, exploring the grounds and locating orc tracks crisscrossing the estate. A board was nailed to a tree. All it bore was a red 'T.' Yet he knew that Taza could not be bothered to handle a mere orc raid. Maybe Melgor had been sent on the mission. Now in control of his demeanor, Sellis pondered his options. If he had been Taza or Melgor, he would have done the same. His mind focused on Dormin's treasure vault, deep beneath the citadel in bedrock.

With everything he owned destroyed, he decided to go back to the citadel and take what he needed, hoping the building had not been so devastated that stealing some of the treasure would be impossible. He had no idea what awaited him when he arrived.

Chapter Forty-Two

Cyra spurred her horse up the street, calling her troops to follow.

Melgor left the mercenaries and rode hard to catch the sorceress. *This is the end game,* he thought. Taza's citadel was near, and he suspected Celedant was already there. He could take revenge on both at the same time.

The horseshoes on their mounts struck sparks as they galloped up the cobbled street. When Cyra arrived at the main gate to the citadel, she rode into a mass of undead trying to get through the main doors. The soldiers cut their way through the mob of undead, who had their backs to the front gate. Cyra cast spell after spell and expertly used her sword as her horse mounted the steps and entered the citadel. Melgor used his staff to fend off the undead behind her.

Soon the hall became cacophonous with horses and undead. The melee was a shocking scene of creatures being trampled, and riders pulled from their horses. Melgor saw the captain of the mercenaries call for retreat, and his men cut their way out of the hall.

Melgor kept pace with Cyra as she fought her way to Taza's tower. Once there, she dismounted and calling her orcs, she started up the tower steps. Melgor followed and spied a dead dwarf laying against the wall. Knowing the dwarf was part of the group that traveled with Tarquin, he now knew for sure that the prince was here.

They found themselves on the tower steps having to fight their way upward, as the stairs were crowded with the undead. Cyra took the lead, pushing back the assailants and slicing off their heads. Her orc guards did the same. Melgor was glad to be caught in the middle of the fight as it flowed up the steps. The combatants provided plenty of protection, and only occasionally did he have to ply his staff. A zombie leapt from the steps above and landed on the orc in front of him. Whipping his staff downward, he crushed its skull. The orc looked up appreciatively.

The citadel began to rumble, causing the tower walls to crack. Several orcs lost their footing and tumbled backward down the steps, taking out several orcs with them.

Cyra turned to see the chaos and called, "The only way to live is to reach the top. Move!"

Above the pandemonium, Celedant and Tarquin burst into Taza's chamber. What was left of the vampire guards continued the attack. Having grown tired of excessive fighting, the wizard pointed the Staff of Adaman and used it in a sweeping motion, disintegrating the vampires to dust that blew away in the strong wind that swept through the tower's open arches.

Tarquin and Celedant faced the black onyx throne that Taza had recently and openly declared the throne of Dormin to his undead minions. To show his invulnerability, he had opened all the drapes in the circular stone room, and the dark red fabric flapped all around them. The undead warlock sat basking in the sunlight that should have killed him if not for the Staff of Adois. Tarquin and Celedant stared in horror at what Taza had accomplished.

Celedant called out over the wind, "Taza, is there anything left of you in your mind?"

Using a pittance of his mental power, the undead warlock slowly moved the huge throne across the marble floor, screeching and tearing it until he stopped fifty feet in front of Celedant and Tarquin. Taza stared as if they were little more than rodents that needed to be exterminated. Wild-eyed, he gripped the Staff of Adois. His few wisps of hair stood out uncontrollably as though electrified, with small sparks running along the length of the strands.

"The Vampire Lord Taza is no more," he shouted manically. "I laugh at the sun that used to be my hated enemy until the two of you came along. Now the prophecy can be destroyed. I wonder if it was ever even valid? I see you have assembled the Staff of Adaman. That is commendable. Celedant. You have proved difficult to kill. I emptied the city of humans and surrounded you with my undead allies. I knew it would be only a short time before I felt the use of your staff, and here you are."

"Taza, there is a chance to save you," Celedant offered. "The staffs can be destroyed, and you can live again, free from that power that has robbed you of any semblance of yourself."

190

The response was curt. "I lost that chance eons ago. Now, face the wrath of the Staff of Adois."

Taza stood up and stepped to the side. A mere flick of his staff sent the polished throne, weighing well over two thousand pounds, speeding off the floor toward his two adversaries. The wizard expertly waved the Staff of Adaman to block the throne and sent it sliding past Tarquin's side. It stopped, but not before bashing a great hole in the stone wall of Taza's top sanctum.

With a flick of his hand, Taza sent the font spinning and speeding at them. It caught both off guard for an instant. Tarquin raised his glowing red sword, severing the font in two. The pieces flew to either side of the humans - much to Taza's anger.

Rage grew as Celedant and Taza rushed at one another. Their staffs slammed together in an ear-splitting clash. Sparks and flames of red and blue sizzled up and down the length of the staffs as wizard and warlock fought for the upper hand. When the twin staffs touched, Celedant realized where the staffs could be destroyed, confirming Taza's similar belief.

The Dragon Tear protecting Dragon Isle was a relic not of their world. It had been created by the dragons after emerging on Muiria through a rift in the void at the dawn of time. They had created the Dragon Tear as a guardian in case their species, who had decided to make a life on this world, were to die. The dragons' deaths would leave the world unprotected from evil creatures that roamed the planes seeking dominance over all the worlds and their inhabitants. Certain dragons, tired of endlessly wandering in the void, stayed behind, using the Dragon's Tear as a beacon of purity to shine across the world and into the void for all to see.

Yet, the dragons were fully aware that good could not exist without evil. In time, they aided in the creation of Edain, the wizards' training ground. This powerful relic was the Dragon's Tear, created for goodness and intended to be the spear point to battle evil, should it infiltrate their world. If the force behind the Dragon's Tear could be destroyed, the Staff of Adois and untold evil would overwhelm the world and eventually, the universe.

That knowledge was recalled in a split-second as the staffs repeatedly clashed, causing explosions of power as they met. The wizard and warlock, focused on battle, fought as their clashes echoed throughout the tower, sending tremors down to the citadel foundations.

The Staff of Adois struck Celedant a mighty blow to his stomach, sending the wizard spinning backward. By now, Botreg and the others, by clinging to each other, had clawed their way to the top of the tower. Seeing Celedant struck down, they were horrified. The wizard, who they had thought to be invulnerable, lay gasping on the stone floor. Only a quick grab by Tarquin and Baldo saved him from sliding out of one of the tower's red-draped openings and falling hundreds of feet to the rocks below.

CHAPTER FORTY-THREE

The explosions and ominous grinding of the stones in Taza's tower and the citadel sent everyone still in the city running, many leaving their belongings in the streets. Hundreds tried to exit the gate at once, creating a massive horde. Fighting broke out, and some people were crushed to death. Many Dormin citizens tied ropes to the crenulations and attempted to climb over the crowd. Dozens fell from the ropes and died on the rocks below. That did not deter others from trying anyway. The madness that Taza had sown throughout the city was reaching its climax, and the people of Dormin were paying the price with their lives.

Taza looked condescendingly down at Celedant. The undead warlock took the Staff of Adois and struck the floor, uttering ancient words of dark power bred of pure evil. This time the tower did not just shake. It began to rise from its bedrock foundation. Mortar fell from the tower's great stones. The roof blew away, leaving everyone buffeted by the cold mountain wind.

Stone sections of the tower, including a large part of the citadel below, crumbled. Astonished, Tarquin, and the others watched the structure rise majestically from its foundations. Taza used the staff to steer the tower. Its speed increased as it flew further from its base, sailing over the mountains to the northeast.

Like Taza, Celedant knew they were heading to Dragon Isle where one thing that threatened Taza's power. The Dragon's Tear located there had to be destroyed if he were to gain complete control of the world. Celedant likewise needed to reach the ancient artifact to destroy Taza's staff that now controlled the vampire.

The edifice flew faster, passing through thin wisps of clouds at a speed that made it harder for the others to keep a grip on its stones. They had to hold on to keep from toppling to their deaths in the mountains. Flying onward, the tower began bending at the middle.

Cyra had crawled to the top of the stairs and saw what Taza had accomplished. Never in her practice of magic had she seen this. She did not have time to contemplate long as she slid across the floor toward the steps. The remainder of the tower continued disintegrating. Behind her came Melgor, handicapped by the loss of his arm. He wedged his staff between two granite blocks and held on. Cyra managed to grab hold of the staff as she slid by.

After finding his home destroyed, Sellis thought of nothing but killing Taza. His mind was filled with retaliation for Taza's vile deeds. The warlock, ring fully charged, appeared in the courtyard of the citadel at Dormin. He fell to the ground when his foot caught on something. Looking around, he saw nothing but boulders and rubble. Sitting up, he turned toward the citadel, where he saw only the foundation. Wandering around were dazed orcs and a few undead that continued attacking them.

Above, he watched in amazement as the citadel floated away, trailing the bottom of the stone edifice that continued dropping pieces on the mountains. Taza was not going to get away that easily. Holding tightly to his ring, Nashmeol, Sellis teleported, aiming for Taza's tower.

When he materialized, the wind pushed him off his feet, sending him sliding across the tower floor. Drawing himself up, Sellis was surprised to find Taza in front of him. He looked at the peaks of the mountains passing below and at his former master's enemies, all holding on for dear life, clinging to stones that had settled against the walls or pushed through the floor of the flying citadel. He stood up and pulled out his short sword, ready to attack the warlock vampire. Cutting sideways, he hoped to lop off Taza's head, but at the last second, Taza brought the Staff of Adois around and blocked the swing.

With a wave of the vampire's staff, Sellis was out the window. He plummeted past the base of the citadel, falling faster and faster, but he had Nashmeol, and suddenly, he reappeared right in front of Taza. A sudden jolt to the tower caused him to mistakenly shove the sword through the vampire's heart. He withdrew it and sliced across the creature's throat. Taza stared at him and smiled, teeth shining in the sunlight. Sellis watched in horror as the flesh that he had just cut through began to heal itself.

Taza raised the head of the Staff of Adois to strike Sellis again, but before he could, the warlock engaged his ring and disappeared, reappearing on the lawn of his burned-out estate.

I've failed, but that sanctimonious Celedant is still in play, he thought.

He had also seen the rat Melgor hanging on for dear life. Hopefully, the two would kill Taza and each other.

CHAPTER

FORTY-FOUR

Clinging to a piece of granite from the roof, Tarquin had a precarious view of the tower and the remnants of the citadel below. He stared in horror as sections of stones, and people waving their arms as if they could fly, plummeted to their death. He saw a bed of tremendous proportions slide out with several female figures clinging to the posts, while a blond giant of a man stood in the middle, hurling obscenities at Taza. The description fit King Rodel from what others had said. The King's bed spun round as it plummeted toward the snowcapped mountains.

When the tower separated from its base, Azimuth flung himself into the air and changed into a golden dragon. *Is this unfolding as I think?* he asked Celedant telepathically.

I fear you are correct, he replied, seeing the vision of Dragon Isle in the dragon's mind.

I'll fly ahead and warn them. Azimuth bugled loudly, a sound so loud that it reverberated in everyone's bones. So loud, that it reached the telepathic ears of his kindred on Dragon Isle. *Danger! Warn the masters and all on our isle to prepare. Taza comes, and he has been taken over by the Staff of Adois. Prepare to fight as death comes on swift wings!*

The quest members were climbing through the undulating doorframe to the tenuous safety of the tower floor. Morganna pulled Hority to safety after he attached himself to a crumbling stone. The rest survived by holding on. The tower buckled and shook in flight as it dropped more of its foundation.

Once the tower cleared the mountains, the ground below shrank. To Tarquin's horror, a shadow lord flew by, holding the reins of his giant draven mount with a misty hand. All about the tower flew these vile creatures, escorting their master. They acted like guards, continuously scanning the sky to make Taza secure. When the ocean appeared below, the shadow lords and their mounts spread out in a giant V-shape with the tower at its center.

Gale-like winds whipped Taza's cloak wildly from where he stood in the middle of the tower room. He was controlling the spell with the Staff of Adois, which he held aloft as dark red energy pulsed through his body.

Celedant desperately held onto a broken column and shouted, "Taza, surely there is some humanity left in you? Even a faint remnant from the past?"

Balancing the Staff of Adois to control the spell, Taza snarled, "You're wrong, wizard. I have never been human. I was born a vampire. Even so, I do not go by that trite name any longer. You may address me as Adois."

The wizard tried once more.

"Taza, you cannot let this artifact of evil control you," he pleaded. When he got no response, he turned his attention to the staff.

"Adois, you have no right to this man's body and mind."

Adois in the visage of Taza shot Celedant a disdainful look.

"A vampire with a mind...a nuisance. They feud and vie daily for power and influence on their worlds. I will bring peace to my domain. My warriors will swarm this world, and everyone will bow to me. I will advance the dominance of evil over the power of good - the legion of evil gods will rejoice!"

Tarquin added his voice. "You will die this day, abomination, unless you resist the staff and regain control of your mind."

The tower began to shake and pitch from side to side as Adois focused on the human. "Quiet, dog, or you will end up at the bottom of the sea!"

Tarquin, who had made his way closer to Celedant, slapped him on the shoulder and pointed in the distance where Dragon Isle was rapidly approaching.

"Brace yourselves - this will be a hard landing!" Celedant shouted.

Speed increased as the tower flew toward the small island. All that was left now was the top of Taza's tower and its foundations. The islands grew from tiny specks in a vast ocean to large islands in a sea. As the tower drew closer, the wards that protected the island were swept aside like a mist barrier by the Staff of Adois' power. Yet they retained part of their intended use and alerted the island of the impending attack.

With advance warning from Azimuth, the masters, wizards, sorceresses, and dragons of the island had taken up positions throughout the city as the stone monolith came hurtling toward them. On impact, the remains of the citadel base and tower touched the ocean, scooping great furrows from the water, preceded by giant breakers of white foam. The breakers rose high enough to crash against the walls of Edain, where many great wizards had learned their magic.

Those still clinging to the tower felt an enormous jolt as the masonry of the destroyed citadel struck and buried deeply in the sand that surrounded the island. The tower struck one of the walls of Edain, completely obliterating it for hundreds of paces in both directions, while shards of stones flew a quarter of a mile.

The tower disintegrated, although the top section, closest to the Staff of Adois, remained intact, while its occupants spilled over one another into one of the flowering courtyards.

Even though the wards had been brushed aside, they alerted everyone in the complex, giving the wizards time to ready their defenses. More importantly, thanks to Azimuth, the dragons throughout the isle had been alerted. The shadow lords that had survived the battle at Southgard flew silently into Edain, their magic striking down wizards in training not yet ready to face such formidable foes.

The battle wizards struck back, sending huge fire cones upward, striking the shadow lords and their mounts. Whenever the wizard fire burned through the attackers' magical barriers, it killed both riders and mounts, who dropped from the sky in a trail of smoking ash.

The dragons roared in pure rage when they saw the draven and shadow lords. They had lost kin, mates, and children in their first battle with the demonic creatures. To every dragon came the mental image of Southgard. With the call of revenge striking a primordial chord in their subconscious, the dragons emptied the aeries of all adults. They turned in the air and flew in a mass that blotted partial daylight, creating a dark shadow as they approached their enemies. With the shadow lords and wizards locked in brutal combat, no one noticed the oncoming dragons.

Death fell over many as dragons, wizards, and shadow lords were killed or wounded while falling from the sky. Taza's last spell before crashing into the city was to open a rift from which flew gigantic beasts with large scales that resembled elongated dragons. But these creatures had short necks with spike-covered heads and long legs with razor-like blades running from wrist to shoulder.

The shadow lords and dragons were destroyed by turns as both sides' spells flew back and forth in an epic melee. Dragons weren't usually killed so easily, but the magic used was so fierce that at times, even they succumbed. Many errant spells struck the city of Edain, leveling buildings and blasting craters in the island's stone and rock formations.

A problem sprang up when a shadow lord's mount survived and landed in the city. The wizards had to cast spells from a distance; otherwise, the giant draven would charge forward, its sharp claws ripping into a wizard or sorceress, wounding or often killing them. Far worse, the creatures issuing from the void partook of a killing frenzy, attacking dragons, shadow lords, wizards, and each other. The city of Edain's sky blacked out like an eclipse with each death.

The first dragons to arrive, few in number, kept watch. Then came the massed dragons, flying from many aeries, emitting thundering roars of loss before striking the shadow lords and void creatures. The three forces were so intermingled the wizards of Edain feared their magic might inadvertently attack hit the dragons, so they turned to helping the wounded. Some of the battle wizards remained on the walls, keeping watch on the sky, and a few cast spells to aid the dragons.

The combat that waged high in the sky was fiercest, as dragons were struck by disintegration blasts, which turned them to ash that spiraled down to the ground. Meanwhile, the shadow lords faced the same fate as the dragons. Fire lashed out, burning through the mounts and shadow forms alike. The new creatures' scaled bodies seemed immune to many spells. They flew toward a dragon or shadow lord and in midair, locked razor-lined legs around its prey. Moving its legs up and down, shredding their captives. The creatures released them to fall to the ground.

Desperate to defeat these monsters, a battle wizard hurled a lightning bolt at one of the creatures. The bolt exploded the thick scales on impact, searing through and bursting out the other side. The other wizards and dragons also cast spells in lieu of direct combat.

As their losses began to mount, these dangerous creatures from the void propelled themselves westward, using flipper-like feet to soar through the sky. They had not been prepared for a pitched battle when they came through the rift. Fearing defeat, they flew to safety.

Chapter Forty-Five

This was the moment that Dolgar had spoken about to Aegir. The god knew the cleric was needed for the final battle. In a blinding flash of light on a small hillock outside the city, Aegir appeared and assessed the battle. The once-unconventional cleric vaulted toward a young green dragon with a gaping hole in its side. The rider was trapped beneath. Very few dragons had time enough to gather their bond mates for the battle, but this one had.

Aegir placed his hands on the dragon's torn flesh, and it quickly healed. He pulled the rider from under the dragon and healed him, too. A shadow lord swept down to kill both, but with a wave of his hand, Aegir blew the attacker into a thousand pieces.

The cleric continued his search. Among piles of rubble, he saw several friends. Eldahir lay like a rag doll on a large stone, and he could smell poor Hority. Morganna was digging through the rubble around the armored hand of Baldo sticking out in the air. Azimuth straddled the rubble, using claws to help Morganna dig. Aegir joined them, bending over the wounded and moving huge stones off bodies. He found Hority crushed beneath a great stone. Shifting it, he knelt and placed his hand on the monk's chest. Hority gave a huge gasp, back among the living.

Frustrated by their slow progress, Morganna straightened and uttered an arcane word, and all the rubble parted from the dwarven cleric. A simple spell, she smacked her head with her hand. Aegir hunkered down beside his friend, and with a touch, Baldo crawled out of the debris.

Pointing the Staff of Adois, Taza levitated to the ground after the crash while Tarquin and the others lay sprawled and broken across the yard. As the battle raged above him, the vampire wizard hovered over to land next to Celedant's bloodied body. A great slash had opened his scalp and chest, and blood flowed over his face and robe. The Staff of Adaman lay several feet from the wizard's outstretched hand. Celedant's dirt-crusted fingers dug into the soil as he strained to reach it.

Taza bent and snatched the mythril rod of the Staff of Adaman. Standing over the stunned and bleeding wizard, he gloated.

"You see Celedant, wizard of Edain. You have failed. I, Adois triumphant! You'll be the first to see my army!" he said cruelly.

With the Staff of Adois he ripped a huge hole open to the void. An armada of ships dropped into the sea surrounding Dragon Isle. The largest ships stayed well away, while twenty smaller boats propelled by oars raced for shore.

As the shell of Taza spoke, Tarquin loomed out of nowhere and struck the warlock in the small of the back so that he tumbled onto Celedant. This feeble attack caused Taza to act prematurely. He had planned the next part of the attack for later, but the prince had accelerated his plans. Lying with his back against Tarquin, Taza lost contact with the Staff of Adaman. His loss of focus caused the jagged, gaping hole in the void to snap shut.

The vampire warlock felt an odd power coalescing all about him. Briefly overcoming this new power, Taza projected an image of wealth into the void. As he had planned, this was a last-ditch effort to attract aid from creatures that waited in the darkness. Taza, Celedant, Tarquin, and Azimuth, who had flown over to help his friends, blinked from view, but they weren't alone. Cyra rolled toward them and grabbed Tarquin's ankle.

Suddenly they were in an empty blue crystalline room. Celedant and Azimuth recognized it as the interior the Dragon's Tear. Tarquin and Taza stood up and gazed around them, amazed. Taza held both staffs protectively, pointing one forward and one backward as he eased away from Celedant and Tarquin. Cyra rolled into the back of the blue room where no one noticed her.

Taza hissed, "You will not regain the staffs with chicanery. They are mine by right."

As the last word was spoken, blue light radiated from the walls of the chamber, blinding all within the room. When their eyes cleared, the crystalline entity and caretaker of Dragon's Tear was before them, sitting in a transparent chair. Curled behind him was an ancient midnight blue Dragon. It was missing scales, and about its face, white wisps of feathers swayed when she moved. Celedant never would have guessed that there was an ancient dragon concealed on the isle, but she was no surprise to Azimuth, who moved forward in joy.

"Grandmother!"

"Azimuth, my beloved grandson. I have watched you these past two centuries, and I am proud of you."

The two dragons nuzzled each other.

When she spoke to the others, her voice was sad, and reading Celedant's mind, said for all to hear, "Yes, there is one. I helped create this sanctuary for my children, so very long ago."

Her great head nudged the crystalline man, who scratched her wrinkled neck, "Ah, I had forgotten what that felt like." She turned to Tarquin. "My kind created this crystalline watcher to balance good and evil in this world before the majority of us journeyed back to the void. This tower allows me to keep watch on my descendants while awaiting crucial times like this."

The blue crystalline man extended his hands, and despite Taza's vampiric and god-like strength, both staffs flew into the blue-hued grasp.

Taza collapsed, trying to crawl toward the crystalline figure.

"My staff - I need it."

He cast several spells at the keeper of the Dragon's Tear, but all were absorbed harmlessly.

"See, it has already taken him to use for its own devices," the keeper said. "Taza, you sought to come to this place of ancient power to destroy the one thing that could subdue you – the Staff of Adaman. Celedant and young Tarquin, however, have been successful in finding and delivering both staffs to the Dragon's Tear. Celedant knew this was his ultimate goal. For it is here that they can and will be unmade."

Taza was on his knees keening, tears running down his wretched face and thick saliva pouring from his fanged mouth.

The dragon called out, "Stand, child of evil."

Behind them stood a slim woman, and they turned to find Cyra.

"Pure evil, this sorceress is. She cannot be allowed to witness what is to come."

The blue creature raised one of its arms, but Cyra cast a spell. A red beam shot from her fingers toward the dragon. Azimuth jumped to her, but the crystalline man appeared in front of the dragons, protecting both. The beam had no effect on him.

"The tower senses your evil; you must leave," he said as his eyes burned blue.

Cyra disappeared.

Chapter Forty-Six

The ancient midnight blue dragon swiveled its head to look at the prince.

"Brave Tarquin, I am sorry this occurred while you are so young. You have dedicated your life to war and the fate of this quest. Remember, you can become far more in the world outside the Dragon's Tear. Come nearer, young Tarquin, Prince of Partha. You have an important role to play yet."

Overwhelmed by things no human had witnessed, Tarquin humbly approached.

"Draw forth your sword, young Tarquin."

Tarquin pulled Dragon Bolt from its scabbard. The dragon breathed upon the sword, and the guardian grasped the blade.

"Imbued with Dragon's Tear power - take it and smite the staffs' heads."

Tarquin took the blade from the guardian that now glowed as blue as the walls of the room. With one powerful swing, he struck the stone atop the Staff of Adois. The Staff resisted, but the power of the infused sword was too much. Small fractures formed until the crystal exploded into a thousand sparkling shards. The air seemed to rip apart as the goddess Adois screamed in angry defeat. Only the protection of the Dragon's Tear saved the inhabitants from her fury.

Taza flailed on the ground, his mind completely erased as the staff was destroyed.

Outside, the others gained a much-needed respite while helplessly watching the monstrous creatures battle in the sky.

Hoity stood up and pointed, yelling with glee, "Foes!"

Several wizards and sorceresses from Edain stood in the ruins, facing the horde of onrushing creatures. Taza's allies, the Zartarians, had reached the island in ships and charged the battered city, their plumage bright red with battle lust. The defenders gazed tiredly at these new opponents. To survive this far and face a new foe was not possible. Melgor rose from the rubble, battered and beaten, to join the defense of the isle that stood for everything he hated.

Morganna, Eldahir, and a dozen mages with longbows took cover near the Dragon's tear. Island residents had been taught since birth that the protection of the artifact was the most important purpose of their lives.

Arrows flew, and the Zartarians, who appeared to favor the atlatl or throwing spear, fought back, releasing a thousand shining white spears. The city mages cast shielding spells that splintered the spears or sent them bouncing off harmlessly. The few defenders left in the open were skewered, falling as the slender white spears tore their bodies.

Months before when Edain was attacked, the workmen had begun making trebuchets for added defense. Baldo ran to the only working ones; others had been destroyed when the tower crashed into the city, bringing down most of the walls. They had been set, ready to fire, but the militia assigned there had been killed.

Baldo's hammer struck, releasing the cogs of both machines, whose arms swung forward with a resounding crash to send huge boulders high in the air before arcing to strike the enemy, rolling through them like a scythe through wheat. Then more red-plumed birdlike enemies swept into the city through the broken stones and tumbled walls that Taza's tower had caused.

"Them birdy things don't fight fair," Hority complained. He casually ducked an overhead spear. The enemies were in the courtyard, and with a shout of glee, the eccentric monk dove into their midst, striking unending blows with his pumice-topped branch.

Morganna, Eldahir, and Baldo were ready for the attacking horde. The strange creatures fell to the arrows of the men of Edain. The Zartarians' plumage turned even deeper red and appeared to take their places for battle.

Eldahir drew his sword but was slashed across the shoulder by an odd-looking white sword. Hority was suddenly there, killing the large, armor- encased bird attacker. With a tremendous swing of his sword, the elf cleaved the legs off the creature. It collapsed, chest plate grinding against the courtyard stones and shooting sparks. A quick stab by Morganna's sword ended the creature's life.

Expelled from the Dragon's Tear, Cyra fell through the air, landing in the courtyard where the quest members and their allies battled the Zartarians. She rolled to a boulder to see where the defenders were positioned and then cast a teleportation spell, appearing beside Talchic.

"Glad to see you," he said, surprised. "We need all the help we can get."

She smiled evilly. "I'm not here to defend this barren rock. I need space to cast my spell. Quick - hold my hand."

He did, and she muttered in a language he had never heard. In an instant, they blinked away from the bloody courtyard and reappeared with blue sky above and grass under their feet.

"What just happened?" he asked.

Cyra laughed. "Have you never seen a teleportation spell before?"

"I have, but never one so powerful," he admitted.

She smiled. "Will you aid me, Talchic?"

He answered without hesitation, not wanting her to kill him right after his escape from Dragon Isle.

"Of course, milady."

When Azimuth disappeared into the Dragon's Tear, his mate kept watch on the tower. As the battle drew closer, she launched into the air and bellowed as white-hot flame spewed from her mouth. The flames rolled through the attackers, turning them into dust. As they drew closer, her tail swept aside dozens of the bird-like attackers.

The Zartarians, their plumage now a searing red, filled the courtyard, surrounding the defenders of the Dragon's Tear. The defenders realized that although extremely sharp, the attackers' weapons were weak and tended to break with solid hits.

Baldo used a staff he had found to defend himself, while he sent the hammer hurtling through the throng of Zartarians, creating a wide path of wounded and dead enemies.

Several dragons left other battles to attack the horde with great swaths of dragon fire, breathing flames that ballooned out across the enemy. They swooped around to attack again. Many Zartarians were struck by the bulk of the dragons or their tails that hurled them away in a tumbled mass of dead and wounded.

Hority was everywhere, jumping from boulder to boulder and feeling closer to his god than ever as he smote the odd monsters from high and low. These creatures were an abomination to his lord; their accursed beaks had surely been created to peck at Clor's special offerings. The monk slowed to consider how he could use one of those beaks to scoop up holy garbage in his deity's honor, but a sword strike to his chest made him duck and roll, banishing all thoughts.

Soon the attacking force had lost enough soldiers that it began to withdraw, their plumage graying in wariness. The attackers were losing the initiative. Taza's enemies were strong foes. They wielded better weapons of grey or shiny material, and they had many shamans that were perhaps stronger than their own. Further, those things that flew from the sky were unlike anything they had faced before. Their weapons broke on contact with the flying beasts.

The defenders' numbers whittled away as the Zartarians inside the city fought in the rubble that surrounded the Dragon's Tear. Many defenders formed a living barrier about the artifact they were willing to save by giving their lives in this ultimate battle. Within the artifact, something major had occurred as the ground vibrated wildly, opening small fissures all around the fighters. The staffs were being unmade.

Chapter
Forty-Seven

When the Staff of Adois crystal was destroyed, its power was suddenly and permanently severed. The remaining attackers became confused, many backing away from the fight and turning to run for safety. As often happened in battle, those with their blood lust up continued to attack, but these were few.

The destruction of the staff had released control over the creatures attacking Dragon Isle. Confused, the clan chief stood in sight of all with his tribe's memories, and mental abilities returned. He ordered them to return to the ships, realizing he and the council had been duped by the warlock Taza.

Turning southward, the depleted attackers followed their comrades away from the blood-soaked ruins that had taken so many of their warriors, their plumage deep black in mourning.

Hority called "Cowards" as they sped away.

Then he mixed dirt and blood and rubbed the concoction on his habit and hair.

Curious, Eldahir asked the question that had bothered him for some time.

"Horthy, why in the name of Clor do you do that?" He winced in sympathy pain as Baldo completed a spell to heal the elf's shoulder.

The monk looked shocked. "Ye have been with me for how long, and ye don't recognize me offerings to the almighty Clor?"

Seeing the monk's confused look, the elf added, "My dear friend, you and Clor, whom you serve so fervently, helped make it possible for us reach this point in our venture. I meant no disrespect."

"Eldahir, tonight I can speak with ye concerning the vileness of rotten flesh. It's one of me favorite subjects, as you must know."

Baldo, healing Hority's chest, interrupted the banter.

"Come friends. They need us elsewhere."

"I've returned just in time," a female voice said as a beautiful silver dragonette landed, and Ress hopped off her back.

"Ress!" Baldo cried as he ran to her and checked her over. "Yer back? Yer feelin' all right?"

"Good as new. Where's Tarquin?" Baldo nodded toward the tower that housed the Dragon's Tear. "Inside with Celedant and the staffs. It is time for them to fulfill the prophesy."

The battle was a free-for-all with dragon flames lighting the sky. The dravens added to the colorful outburst. Good and evil creatures fell from the sky as they circled over and under, and fought claw to claw. Many evil beings fell, burning red, frosted blue, or searing in pain from acid, from the sky. Some dragons were also wounded.

The wounded dragons raced to shore, knowing instinctually that a powerful healer had arrived. The wizards of the isle cast spells at the creatures, distracting them from the melee. Many dragons took advantage of this to counterattack their pursuers.

Aegir had never been so exhausted, knowing the healing power and strength given to him by Dolgar would end eventually. The mental and physical strain, both mentally and physically, would have been too much for any mortal, but he felt the reassuring hands of Dolgar firmly holding him in comfort and support.

The healed dragons thanked him before taking off to rejoin the fight. Healing was not all he did, however. The wounded dragons often warned of immediate attack, so Aegir would raise his hands, sending rainbows of color at the creatures who attacked from the sky. The island shook as the Dragon's Tear war concluded, and then the creatures flew off in different directions.

The dragons aloft set up a patrol guard, while hundreds of others landed throughout Edain. Every dragon that fought that day needed healing. Aegir visited each one, healing small wounds and dragons who were literally dying where they had landed. The blue dragon healer and her two sorceress aides were also working on their wounded kindred.

Aegir had just sat on a rock for rest when the wounded wizards from Edain began forming a line to have the miraculous dwarf's help. It was late in the afternoon before his healing was completed. Aegir's friends longed to see him, but Dolgar had encircled the dwarf in a glass substance. The dwarf lay as if in deep sleep in a flowering garden bed.

The dwarvan god, in his usual immaculate blue clothes, appeared where Eldahir and Baldo were in deep discussion with Hority. They were trying to persuade the dwarf that he needed a bath after victory. Dolgar could see the two giving way as he strolled up.

He looked to Baldo. "Ye Lord Thierry spoke highly of ye."

Baldo dropped to his knees, silently giving thanks.

"A new age appears to have emerged, and I see ye as vital in protecting the welfare of this world." He added, "I have placed Aegir in a deep sleep that will restore his old self. His actions here and to come have been noted by the gods."

He looked sternly at Hority, "Me little Clorian, what's to be done with ye? Thierry in me dreams showed ye marching and battling evil wherever ye find it. Certainly, yer abbot's missive will reach ye in time, but it allows for bathing outside of Clorian territory."

In a blink of an eye, the blue-clad dwarf disappeared.

CHAPTER FORTY-EIGHT

The dragon nodded to the Staff of Adaman.

Tarquin took another strong swing, and the beautiful Golden Amber jewel sliced neatly into two pieces that vanished into thin air.

Taza, clearly insane, clawed and rolled toward the chair of the blue crystalline watcher. Before he could befoul the sanctity of the seat, Tarquin stepped forward, driving his sword through the vampire's back and transfixing his heart to the blue flooring below.

The midnight blue dragon said, "A wise decision, young Tarquin. He suffered enough in his many lifetimes."

The guardian now commanded, "Azimuth, Tarquin, and Celedant, stand together."

They obeyed, and a glass-like shield engulfed them.

The old dragon drew in a deep breath, roaring as its magic filled the room, freezing all within. In seconds, frost and icicles formed on the protected barrier and throughout the room.

The Dragon Tear added its power as the blue crystals of the room flared blue. Suddenly the chamber was a swirling mixture of blue energy and white fire. It reminded Tarquin of dwarvan furnaces - but a thousand times worse. The shield that protected them began to bubble, letting some heat permeate their protected shell.

The fires died. Where once the guardian had held the staffs, there was nothing, not even ash or melted mythril. The blue figure waved his hand, and the heat abated; the glass protection vanished. The room was still warm, but not like earlier. The ancient midnight blue dragon had also vanished.

Celedant stepped forward, kneeling in respect. "So, it is done."

The crystalline man said, "The dragon and the Dragon's Tear have answered this evil, and it has been vanquished. While my friend the dragon sleeps protected in this domain, I will continue to watch over this world. For the saying is true that evil will never rest."

NOTE FROM THE AUTHOR

Word-of-mouth is crucial for any author to succeed. If you enjoyed the book, please leave a review online—anywhere you are able. Even if it's just a sentence or two. It would make all the difference and would be very much appreciated.

Thanks!
Steve Stephenson & K.M. Tedrick

About the Authors

Steve Stephenson an admitted bibliophile, who collects rare fantasy and science fiction memorabilia. He obtained a B.A. in history and a M.A. in library science.

K.M. Tedrick is a writer and ghostwriter in the fantasy, science fiction, and young adult genres with one book that was made into a movie, and numerous books written and published as a ghostwriter over the past twelve years.

Thank you so much for reading one of our **Fantasy** novels.

If you enjoyed this book, read where the story begins...

War of the Staffs by Steve Stephenson & K.M. Tedrick

"Offers an enjoyable romp for high fantasy fans." –*KIRKUS REVIEWS*

View other Black Rose Writing titles at
www.blackrosewriting.com/books and use promo code
PRINT to receive a **20% discount** when purchasing.